This feud between her two best friends was killing her. She had to find a way to bring them back together...

Naomi picked up the phone and dialed.

"Hello."

Wonderful, no voicemail, Becky actually answered.

"I'm so sorry, Becky. I didn't mean to make you cry."

"I know, Naomi."

"Please, tell me what's going on. Believe me, when I say this, Miriam has no idea why you're angry. If she knew what was bothering you, she could either apologize or explain herself."

"Too late for that, and no apology will ever be enough," Becky said.

"This is so absurd. I don't have words for it."

"Naomi, I don't want to talk about this. Miriam and I are no longer friends, nor is there an icicle's chance in hell, we'll ever be friends again. If there was another orthodox shul in the neighborhood, I'd go there just to avoid seeing her face every week."

Stunned was the only word to describe Naomi's reaction to the poison Becky just dropped on her. "Becky, this is horrible. You can't mean any of it."

"Yes, I do, and don't ever bring it up again. Furthermore, she's not coming to my son's wedding."

The phone went dead, but a few moments passed before Naomi removed it from her ear and set it on the kitchen countertop. She yanked open the sliding glass door, walked across the deck, and leaned against the cold wooden railing, unable to comprehend Becky's tirade.

10/27

Life-long Jewish friends Naomi, Miriam, and Becky are approaching middle-age gracefully and are content—despite a few hot flashes and mood swings—until life tosses each woman a crisis…

When Becky, the daughter of Holocaust survivors, learns of her only son's engagement to a non-Jew, she rallies against the marriage and becomes obsessed with finding him a Jewish bride.

Naomi—whose husband left her for a man, crushing her small amount of self-confidence—is stuck with a dead-end job and a big house in a neighborhood filled with couples. She hates the loneliness of weekends and the empty side of the king-size bed.

Miriam, an only child of parents who were also only children, struggles with the fact that she has no blood relatives besides her children. She recognizes that it's siblings who connect the past, the present, and the future, and the closest thing she has to sisters are Becky and Naomi.

Then a dusty discovery delivers a potentially lethal blow to their friendship. While two of the women fight to save the relationship, one desires nothing more than its complete demise.

KUDOS for *The Kiddush Ladies*

In *The Kiddush Ladies* by Susan Sofayov, Naomi, Miriam, and Becky are life-long friends until a dark secret, discovered as they approach middle age, tears that friendship apart and destroys two of the women's relationship. The other one is determined to bring her two friends back together and end this silly feud, but the one who feels betrayed is adamant, and she won't even consider any other explanation. Sofayov has crafted an intense and poignant tale of friendship, loyalty, and pride that will have you weeping and laughing, sometimes on the same page. Very well done. ~ *Taylor Jones, Reviewer*

The Kiddush Ladies by Susan Sofayov is the story of three Jewish women who have been friends since childhood, but when they're in their forties, one of them discovers what she feels is a betrayal by one of the other women. This starts a feud between the two women and tears their friendship apart, leaving the third woman caught in the middle. The story follows these women through crises in their lives, as each one struggles to cope and come to grips with her situation in her own way. Before, when something bad happened, the three women had each other to lean on, but now that solid wall of support has been shattered, and no one is quite sure what to do about it. *The Kiddush Ladies* gives us a glimpse of the life of Jewish women and how strong their faith is. It's a touching, thought-provoking text. A warm your heart one minute and will wonderful read. ~ *Regan Murphy*

ACKNOWLEDGEMENTS

Thank you to Lauri, Faith, and Jack at Black Opal Books. I'm very grateful for your time, hard work, kind words, and most of all, your patience.

Thank you to the entire crew of the Pennwriters North Hills Critique Group. Without your feedback, *THE KIDDUSH LADIES* would still be stuck in my mind and in the kitchen. Hugs and thank you to Kathy Barbati, Nonna Neft, Suzanne Mattaboni, and Elizabeth Pagel-Hogan for your plot insights and punctuation prowess.

And to my wonderful beta readers who so generously gave their time and feedback to help polish *THE KIDDUSH LADIES*: Toby Tabachnick, Tobie Nepo, Emily Sofayov, Janet McClintock, and my newest friend, Cantor Rena Shapiro. I owe you all a Shabbat dinner of brisket, matzah ball soup, and Israeli salad.

I would be remiss if I didn't include a group of very special Kiddush Ladies. To all the women who have lovingly worked to prepare the kiddush luncheon at the Chabad of South Hills, you taught me the meaning of community. Each of you holds a special place in my heart.

To Ben and Eli, this is book two. Don't you think it's time to read book one? Finally, to my business partner, best friend, and husband, Pinchas, in spite of your coe-ued lack of support for my writing hobby, I lov-yond words.

The Kiddush Ladies

Susan Sofayov

A Black Opal Books Publication

Black Opal Books

BECAUSE SOME STORIES JUST HAVE TO BE TOLD

THE KIDDUSH LADIES
Copyright © 2016 by Susan Sofayov
Cover Design by Susan Sofayov
All cover art copyright © 2016
All Rights Reserved
Print ISBN: 978-1-626945-76-0

First Publication: DECEMBER 2016

Published by Black Opal Books **http://www.blackopalbooks.com**

Dedicated with love to my mother, Cecelia Dobransky.

Chapter 1

Naomi

If the soul of their small *shul*, *B'nai Israel*, rested in the sanctuary, its heartbeat emanated from the kitchen. Naomi always said that the service brought them to the synagogue, but the food and the lunchtime fellowship made them a community.

As she passed through the doorway into the stainless steel mecca, the tension in her neck and shoulders eased, just a bit. A brief respite from the loneliness and stress, which began each Saturday evening and peaked every Friday afternoon when she opened her wallet, praying her bank account held enough money to pay for groceries. Inside the synagogue kitchen, surrounded by her friends, life became more bearable. She didn't feel alone.

Two of the four women who bore the bulk of the kitchen duties stood along the big steel worktable. In a rhythm honed over years, they chopped, diced, and sliced, preparing the kiddush luncheon for the congregation sitting inside the sanctuary.

Naomi washed her hands in the commercial-grade stainless-steel sink. The tepid water running over her dry skin reminded her of the empty tube of hand cream sitting at the bottom of her purse, and a quick glance at her chipped finger nail polish highlighted her inability to afford a manicure. While drying her hands on a paper towel, she made a mental note to buy nail polish remover.

She pulled her favorite knife from the drawer and moved to her post on the north side of the table. She opened a bag containing two dozen bagels, pulled out the first one, and began slicing, listening as her friends, Esther and Laurie, discussed a new type of quinoa salad.

The morning sunshine shone through the huge windows of the eastern wall. It reflected off the stainless surfaces, giving Naomi the sense that the kitchen was smiling. Across the room, lanky Miriam leaned against the countertop, sipping coffee and appearing bored with the subject. She joined them in the kitchen each Saturday. She didn't help, just talked, which was completely okay with Naomi. Miriam never learned to cook anything more complicated than boiling noodles and opening a jar of tomato sauce. Her excuse, a long story told with the flourish of a stage actress, involved a traumatic childhood incident with a frying pan and a burn.

Naomi never believed her story. Miriam's mother was a neat freak who didn't allow Miriam to touch anything in her kitchen. A frying pan in Miriam's hands guaranteed a grease-splattered stove top. In fact, her mother refused to allow Miriam to put ketchup on her own sandwiches until eighth grade, claiming ketchup would stain the countertops red.

Naomi laid the last sesame bagel into the napkin lined basket. As she turned to place it on the serving cart, she breathed in the warmth of the atmosphere.

"*Somebody* has to fish it out," Laurie, the newest member of the group, said, gesturing with her head toward a giant jar of pickled herring sitting in the center of the table. "And it's not going to be me. I did it last week. I'll plate the lox after I finish this salad."

Laurie's voice pulled Naomi from her reverie. "I did it the week before. I think."

"That's not true, Naomi." Esther lobbed a handful of egg shells into the trash can. "I got stuck doing it two weeks in a row."

"Please, Esther," Naomi said. "You know that stuff makes me gag. The smell..."

"Hey, Miriam, why don't you plate the herring? You're the only person who actually eats the stuff," Esther asked.

"Really?" Laurie asked, plugging her nose. "How do you swallow that slime?"

Miriam shrugged.

At that moment, Becky strolled into the kitchen. She lifted an apron from a hook on the back of the door, pulled it over her head, and smoothed it over the front of her cream-colored Michael Kors suit. Then she placed her designer black hat on the shelf. "What's going on in here?"

"The weekly herring fight. We're trying to convince Miriam to plate it, since she actually eats it," Laurie said.

Becky snorted. "That'll be the day. She'd drag Joe out of the sanctuary and make him do it. I'll plate the herring."

Only Becky laughed at the zing. Laurie shifted her gaze from Becky's face to the package of lox she held. Esther turned and opened the refrigerator doors. Miriam sipped her coffee. Naomi noticed the deepened furrows above her brow, the only sign indicating she felt the sting of Becky's cooking statement. Naomi understood why Miriam put up with it, but she still didn't like it. Miriam remained silent, as she had the last six million times that Becky threw barbs at her. Becky exploded, Miriam imploded, and Naomi negotiated the peace treaties between her two childhood best friends.

"Every week, it's the same." Laurie rolled her eyes and shook her head. "My husband does too many *l'chaims* with the Crown Royal and eats that disgusting fish. The minute we get home from the synagogue, he starts with the '*Shabbat mitzvah*' talk. Ugh, I hate the car ride home because of his horrible fish breath. There's no way in hell I'm crawling between the sheets with him."

Naomi listened and struggled to fight off the pang of jealousy that swept through her. Fish smell or no fish smell, she wished she had someone willing to crawl between her sheets. She hated the empty side of her king-size bed, which her ex-husband, Jake, was kind enough to leave behind the day he hauled half their furniture down the steps and into a U-Haul.

The fish discussion ended. The women began updating each other on their plans for the upcoming week. Rosh Hashanah loomed only three days away. Esther grumbled while she doused Italian salad dressing into a bowl of romaine lettuce because none of her kids could make it home. Laurie tried to convince them to enroll in the new Pilates class at the Jewish Community Center, insisting it would burn off the extra holiday calories in no time. Naomi listened, unable to add anything to the conversation. Her life was as exciting as tying shoelaces.

Becky cleared her throat. "Did I mention Noah is bringing home a friend, who is a girl, for Rosh Hashanah?" The work halted as all attention moved from the stainless steel table to Becky's face.

"You didn't tell us he had a girlfriend! What's she like?" Laurie asked.

"My *bubbeleh* with a girlfriend!" Miriam squealed, twiddling her fingers together in front of her chest, joy lighting her face.

"This is thrilling news," Naomi said. "He never brought a girlfriend home before."

Becky's body stiffened as her gaze moved from one woman to the next. "Don't get excited. She's not a real girlfriend."

Naomi recognized the stance—straightened spine, shoulders back and taut facial muscles combined with a lifted chin—as Becky's I'm-really-pissed-off posture.

"What do you mean?" Esther asked, her words tinged with a Hebrew accent.

"Her name is Maria. She's Catholic." Becky harpooned a long knife into the herring jar. "I have nothing against having fun in college, but this is his third year of law school. Fun time is over. He needs to find a job and start hunting for a girl with wife qualifications. Besides, I'm not spending tens of thousands of dollars for him to be distracted by a shiksa, even if she is just a friend."

Awkwardness polluted the space between them as the women continued working in silence. Naomi pulled a bag of potato chips from a tall metal cabinet and emptied the contents into a napkin lined basket. While placing it on the metal serving cart, she met Becky's gaze. The look in her friend's eyes confirmed her fears. This girl wasn't just a friend. Naomi ached to slice through the tension in the air, but couldn't find the words. Instead, she moved to Becky's side.

She placed her hand on her friend's shoulder. "Noah's smart, and he's a *mensch*. He'll do the right thing."

Becky reached up and patted Naomi's hand. "You're right."

✡ ✡ ✡

The Jewish social service agency where Naomi worked relied on community donations to achieve its mission. Each year the agency did a major fundraising push during the High Holidays. Her job description didn't require her to engage in what she referred to as professional begging, but the completed pledge forms piled up on her desk. She shifted her gaze from the computer screen to the five-inch heap of forms. A feeling of disgust washed over her. Each moment of this job contained a handful of dirt tossed on the grave of her writing career, which died the day she accepted the position over twenty years ago. With each task she completed, the memory of her former dreams faded.

Now, she could barely recall writing anything more than an email or an office memo. The journalism degree, lying at the bottom of the cedar chest, that once belonged to her grandmother, was as much an antique as the chest.

The only word to describe her job was dull—assistant to the president, a glorified beck-and-call girl. She reached for the next pledge form on the stack, exhaled, and typed the name into the first line on the screen. The next hour consisted of pulling pledges from the stack and entering the information—pull, type, file, repeat.

The professional staff, including her boss, ditched out at noon, leaving the office empty and silent. Her boss wished her *L'Shanah Tova*, sweet new year, as he passed her desk on his way to the elevator. She hoped he would give her permission to leave early, but no such luck.

But, now the clock read four o'clock. She shut down the computer and grabbed her bag. At last, the work day was over, and the holiday would begin in a few hours.

Naomi smiled to herself, grateful it was starting on a Wednesday evening—four days off. She walked down the corridor, checking the office doors to make sure everyone remembered to lock them. She checked her boss's door last. Of course, it was open. Why would he bother locking it—trivial matters were her job. Before locking the door, she stood in the threshold of the office and remembered...

✡ ✡ ✡

Pages of Help-Wanted ads spread across Naomi's tiny kitchen table and reading them frustrated the hell out of her. There were no new listings from the ones she read last week. In fact, only two new ads appeared in the last six weeks.

She mailed resumes to every newspaper, magazine, and TV station in Pittsburgh—no reply. Journalism jobs were nonexistent, causing her to spend too much energy daydreaming about moving to a more exciting place like Los Angeles or New York.

After she closed the paper, she stared at Jake's bare back, watching his muscles ripple as he washed the breakfast dishes. Most of the time she complained about their postage stamp sized kitchen, but there were moments when it wasn't so bad. She inhaled the musky scent of his cologne while running her finger down the length of his spine. Instead of the motion giving *him* chills, it made *her* shiver.

Jake turned, wiped his hands on the towel, and opened his arms. Naomi rose from the chair and let him engulf her. No place on Earth was better than being in Jake's arms.

"Naomi, maybe you could take a temporary position until a reporter job opens. And if you don't have a job in journalism when I finish medical school, we can move anywhere you want."

They desperately needed the money. He spent every waking hour in class or studying. She knew that keeping a roof over their heads and food on the table depended on her. Student loans only went so far, and neither of them wanted to move in with her parents.

"Okay, Jake. I'll find something to hold us over. But promise me, it won't be forever."

✡ ✡ ✡

The phone on her boss's desk rang, pulling her from memory lane. *No.* She shook her head, pushed the lock button in the center of the knob, and pulled the door shut, letting the phone continue ringing.

The bus came late, and by the time she reached home, her son, Ezra, had finished showering. "Hurry up, Mom. We're gonna be late."

They were spending the first night of Rosh Hashanah with Miriam and Joe. Kitchen phobic Miriam always hired a chef and a waitress to oversee special events. Naomi never said it out loud, but eating holiday meals at Miriam's house made her feel like she was living the life of the rich and famous.

She stared into the closet, deciding what to wear.

"Speed it up, Mom," Ezra yelled from the bottom of the steps.

She smiled while reaching for a navy silk blouse and a camel colored skirt. When her older son, Josh, lived at home, he would rush through his shower to be the first person dressed. He loved to complain about his slow-moving parents. Now, Ezra continued the tradition and grabbed every opportunity to repeat the admonishments she dished out to him on school mornings when he over slept his alarm.

She missed Josh. Since the holiday started on a Wednesday evening, he couldn't come home. It would be too hard to make up two days of missed classes. He stayed at Penn State and planned to celebrate the holiday with his cute girlfriend. They met at the Hillel Jewish Center on campus freshman year and had been together ever since.

✡ ✡ ✡

Miriam greeted Naomi and Ezra with outstretched arms. *"L'Shana Tovah!"* she said, before slapping a pink lipsticked kiss on Ezra's cheek. Naomi closed the ornate oak and lead-glass front door behind them.

Miriam led them to her huge cherry-paneled dining room. "Hurry, everyone is having cocktails in the dining room. Joe wants to start in a few minutes."

Naomi breathed in the scent of apple strudel and brisket that permeated the house.

A lanky teenage boy dressed in black pants and white shirt extended the tray of miniature sushi rolls balanced on his palm as they entered the room. Naomi reached for one and popped it into her mouth. Ezra plucked two rolls from the tray and struck up a conversation with the waiter. From what she could overhear, the discussion revolved around a "completely stupid English assignment."

She nudged Ezra, who was still chewing and engrossed in the waiter's opinion. "Talk to him later. Let's go." She pulled him by the hand toward the far side of the table.

A couple of the guests already sat in their assigned seats, but most lingered around the perimeter of the room, finishing their cocktails and munching on hors d'oevures. She knew from experience that Joe's family took up eight of the twelve chairs. Miriam suffered the misfortune of being the only child of two people who were also only children. She didn't even have a cousin, which was the reason Naomi never turned down her holiday invitations. Tonight, she and Ezra played the role of the family Miriam lacked.

"It's time to start," Joe announced, and the guests moved to their spots.

He gestured for Ezra to sit on his left and indicated that she should sit on his right, between Miriam and his older brother, Simon.

Simon had a great smile and a permanent impish twinkle in his eyes. For a brief moment, until his wife gave her a slight wave from across the table, she found herself wishing he was single.

Joe rose from his captain's seat, at the head of the table, and everyone followed. He lifted the silver *kiddush* cup. It reflected the soft light from the crystal chandelier hanging high above their heads. In a clear voice, he chanted the blessing over the wine. Rather than passing the cup around the table for each person to sip, he pointed to the pre-filled tiny silver kiddush cups sitting at each guest's place setting.

Joe passed his cup to Miriam, watched her take a sip, and then kissed her cheek. "*L'shanah tovah*, sweetheart," he said.

Miriam leaned over and kissed his cheek. "Happy New Year, my love."

Naomi smiled in admiration of their relationship, *bashert*—a true match made in heaven.

"Time to wash." Joe led the group to the kitchen, filled the two handled ritual washing cup, and recited the Hebrew blessing while pouring water over his hands. One by one, all twelve of the guests repeated this act.

When they returned to the dining room, the blessings continued. First over the challah they dipped into honey and then the apples. She loved listening to his deep baritone chant the ancient words. But she was even happier when the waiter finally served the first course—gefilte fish with a dill sauce, Israeli salad, hummus and cucumber salad, a mix of Ashkenazi and Sephardic traditions. She flipped open the burgundy linen napkin and set it across her lap, excited to begin the feast.

As they ate, Simon and Joe launched into stories from their childhood. It didn't take long for her and everyone else at the table to become absorbed in the hysterical images their words conjured. She couldn't stop laughing when Simon told a story about getting caught stealing doughnuts from the back of a delivery truck. He stood, waving his arms to imitate the driver, screaming in Yiddish, as he chased him and Joe down Murray Avenue.

"Don't even think of doing something like that," she mouthed to Ezra who rolled his eyes in response.

Joe could barely contain his own laughter while telling a story about a poker game gone bad. On a hot July night, he, Simon, and a few other friends were playing poker and drinking beer behind the high school. When they saw flashing lights approaching, they all started running. Joe thought he made a clean get away, until he tripped over the curb and heard his ankle crack. The police found him, with his beer can still in his hand, and called for an ambulance. His parents met him and an underage drinking citation at the hospital.

The crowd laughed through the first course and continued until the matzo ball soup bowls were removed from the table.

The more wine they drank the louder the laughter grew, until the main course was served. The crowd went silent while eating the melt-in-your-mouth brisket and an overabundance of side dishes. As much as she hated doing it, Naomi stopped eating before all the food on her plate was gone.

She turned to Miriam. "This is the point in the meal where the entire group should either run around the block or do a group nap."

"Run now and nap after dessert."

As if orchestrated, the moment Miriam finished saying the word dessert, the waiter pushed a cart of apple strudel into the dining room. The waitress trailed behind, carrying an artfully arranged fruit plate. She leaned in between Naomi and Miriam and set it on a trivet in the center of the mahogany table. Once it was perfectly situated, the waitress walked to the buffet and picked up two silver pots of steaming coffee.

"It's lovely!" Simon's wife said, stabbing the silver serving fork into an out-of-season piece of honeydew.

The lanky waiter slipped a slice of the powdered sugar covered strudel in front of Naomi.

"Regular or decaf?" the waitress asked from a point behind Naomi's shoulder.

"Decaf," Naomi replied, inhaling the rich scent. It tasted even better than Starbucks. "Miriam, what kind of coffee is this?"

"Jamaican Blue Mountain."

Naomi nodded, appreciating Miriam's love of luxury, and her ability to afford it.

"I hope everything went okay at Becky's house to-night," Miriam whispered into Naomi's ear halfway through dessert.

Naomi shrugged. She wanted to be optimistic and be-lieve the girl really was just a friend. Unfortunately, Becky's expression and Naomi's intuition said otherwise.

"I'm going to call her after everyone leaves," Miriam whispered.

Naomi shook her head. "Don't—you'll see her tomor-row."

Miriam reluctantly agreed to contain her curiosity un-til morning.

The evening ended with hugs and well wishes for a sweet new year. Naomi and Ezra were the last to leave. Miriam escorted them to the door. Ezra gave his "Aunt Miriam" a big hug before lumbering to the car. Naomi kissed Miriam's cheek and whispered, "I love you and thank you."

The joy of the evening must have overwhelmed Miri-am. As Naomi stepped back from the kiss, she glimpsed tears escaping from Miriam's eyes. Naomi hugged her friend again.

The next morning, Naomi woke early, a bit hung over from the wine and massive amount of food. Streams of sunlight, shining through the sliding glass door to her deck, greeted her when she entered the kitchen. The beauty of the day should have made her smile, but instead it emphasized the fact that her windows desperately needed washing. She opened the door and walked onto the deck. The sun's rays burned hot, like a July afternoon, not a September morning. She sniffed the air. The wind didn't even hint of fall yet. A perfect morning for walking to the synagogue. She took a few sips of her coffee and watched two rabbits nibble clover in the backyard...

Naomi gingerly lifted the omelet from the pan whispering to herself, "Please don't burn, please don't burn." She flipped it and exhaled when it didn't break. This was a special Shabbat breakfast, not their usual bowl of cereal and coffee.

She loved Saturday mornings with Jake.

He stood behind her, nuzzling her neck. "Wow, that looks awesome."

She turned and smiled. Then their lips met briefly.

"What's the occasion? Omelets don't usually make the menu."

"Do you want coffee?"

He stepped toward the cabinet. "Of course."

Quickly, she reached over and playfully pushed him toward the kitchen table. "Sit. I'll get it for you."

Jake followed her instructions and sat down, smiling. She opened the cabinet, pulled out a mug that read *World's Greatest Dad* and set it in front of him. She waited—no reaction from Jake. Her pulse quickened as she dumped the omelet from the pan to the plate. "How's the coffee?"

"Good. Really hot."

Naomi placed the plate in front of him and retrieved a mug from the cabinet for herself.

He held the mug at eye level. "Hey, where did you get this mug? A garage sale?"

The look on his face said it all—clueless. Time to be direct.

"Read the words," she said, excitement pounding through her.

They had been trying for a baby for months.

He woke up. His eyes widened. The smile on his face and in his eyes said everything. He whipped his long, lean form out of the chair and swung her around. "Really?"

She nodded.

"Baby Feldman! When?"

"April."

He kissed her hard, picked her up, and headed toward the living room. Two hours later, the omelet ended up in the trash, and the clock said it was too late to go to the synagogue.

✡ ✡ ✡

The two rabbits lost interest in the clover patch and hopped away. She went into the house. The clock above the stove read eight-thirty. Synagogue services began at ten.

Time to wake Ezra. She climbed the steps, walked a

few feet down the hallway, and banged on his bedroom door. "Get up, get up."

She kept pounding until her disheveled, lanky, son opened the door.

"I'm up," he croaked. "Now, I'm going back to bed." He turned and closed the door.

Naomi pushed open the door. "No, you're not. Get dressed. If we don't get there early, I'll lose my spot."

He smashed the pillow over his head. "You'll live."

"Fine, I'm walking without you. But don't complain when you get stuck sitting in a folding chair against the back wall."

He tossed the pillow to the ground. "Fine, I'm up."

She smiled. Ezra always sat next to Becky's son Noah. Like her, Ezra hated when someone took his spot.

The one-mile walk to the synagogue was the best time of the week to talk to him, a distraction-free twenty-minutes—no phone, no computer, or homework. Surprisingly, for a teenager, he still seemed to enjoy talking to her. Today, he babbled excitedly about his senior year in high school and college applications. Then the subject changed. "Do you think Sarah will go to the prom with me?"

"I don't know, and you won't know until you ask her." She tried to hide her smile. The idea of him taking Laurie's daughter to the prom sounded like a great idea.

"What if she says 'no'?"

Naomi bumped her shoulder against his. "Ask, that's all you can do. If she says no, I'm sure it will be the end of life as we all know it."

Ezra shook his head. "Fine, I'll ask, but not until April."

They walked across the parking lot, looking at the strange cars belonging to people who attended services twice a year—Rosh Hashanah and Yom Kippur. They entered the vestibule. Naomi stopped, but Ezra continued walking. He opened the heavy glass doors to the sanctuary, stepped inside, and pulled the special Rosh Hashanah Siddur from the bookshelf.

As Naomi adjusted her cloche black hat, the fingers of a hot flash crept up her neck. "Damn," she mumbled under her breath. Why did she even bother with the makeup? One hot flash sent it rolling down her cheeks with the sweat. She turned away from the sanctuary and headed to the ladies' room.

As she wiped the sweat from her upper lip, sadness washed over her—menopause. Between it and the gray hair, she felt old. Why didn't that son of a bitch, Jake, walk out when she was thirty-five? Then it might have been possible to find someone else. In a year, Ezra would go to college, leaving her with a dead-end job and an empty house, in a suburb populated by couples. She scrunched the tissue in her fist and slammed it into the flapping lid of the trash can.

When she finally entered the small sanctuary, her mood lifted a bit when she saw that her seat was still empty. She settled into her chair and shuffled through the pages of the siddur until she located the prayer the rabbi was reading.

When the door opened, she twisted to see who arrived. Esther, wearing the new hat her mother sent from Israel, kissed the *mezuzah* attached to the door frame before entering sanctuary. She grabbed a prayer book from the shelf then headed to her regular seat. A few minutes later, the door opened again. This time Naomi looked back, did a slight wave, and pointed Laurie to the seat beside her.

Laurie slid into the seat and smoothed her plaid jumper. She taught third grade at the local elementary school and occasionally wore her "school clothes" to *shul*. Naomi leaned over, held out her siddur, and pointed to the page number. Laurie glanced at it and nodded before quickly flipping through the pages of hers. Within seconds, her friend's clear voice joined in the prayer, chanting along with the rabbi.

Fifteen minutes later, Miriam waltzed into the room, greeting Naomi and Laurie with air kisses before taking the seat next to Esther.

Naomi continued glancing back at the door every few seconds.

A half hour passed—no sign of Becky. *Odd.* Becky always arrived first during the High Holidays, often beating the rabbi. She staked out their spots and shot vicious looks at anyone who tried to sit in them.

Naomi elbowed Laurie and gestured with her head toward the double doors at the back of the room. The two women walked out of the sanctuary into the vestibule. Once the glass doors closed behind them, they turned toward each other.

"Where is she?" Laurie asked.

"I don't know," Naomi replied, shrugging. "Ezra and I went to Miriam's for the first night. I didn't call Becky this morning because I just assumed I'd see her here."

They began hypothesizing reasons for Becky's absence. Tired? Sick? Just running late? Naomi looked into the sanctuary and noticed Esther holding her index finger in front of her mouth. Naomi mouth the word "sorry."

"Come on." Naomi pushed open the windowless wooden door of the kitchen and stepped inside, immediately spotting Becky, standing in the back corner, staring out the window, crying.

Naomi rushed to her side. "What's wrong?"

Becky fell forward, pressing her head against the plate-glass window, and began sobbing—body-racking sobs.

"Sh, sh." Naomi patted Becky's back the same way

she consoled her sons when they were toddlers, but her friend's tears didn't stop.

"He brought her home to meet us because he's marrying her." Becky spoke the words, but they were barely audible. "She already has a ring on her finger."

Laurie shook her head, staring at the floor. "It can't be."

Naomi didn't know what to say, so she reached around Becky's waist and tried to pull her close. Becky pushed her arm away, rushed to the sink, and clenched the rim of the stainless steel bowl. For a moment, she rocked back on her spiked heels. Then, with a shudder, she let go of the sink dashed to the refrigerator and yanked open the double doors. After one loud exhale, she slammed them shut.

Naomi feared the look of madness glazing her friend's eyes.

"Yes, it can be." Becky moved back to the sink and pounded the stainless steel draining board with her fist. "He's marrying her." This time her words came out as a shriek.

"Oh, my gosh," Laurie said. But it sounded more like a loud exhale than formed words.

The door swung open. Miriam glided into the room. Her eyes flitted from face to face. "What's going on in here? A meeting and I'm not invited?" She continued walking unaffected to the coffee pot.

Naomi couldn't move or speak. Laurie stood next to Naomi, shaking her head and biting her bottom lip.

Miriam, Styrofoam cup in hand, finally turned to face her friends. Her smile faded as she became aware of their stunned expressions.

"Noah is marrying a *shiksa*." Tears rolled down Becky's cheeks as she spoke the words.

Miriam rushed to her, wrapping her long arms around

Becky. Within moments, Miriam sobbed in tandem with her lifelong friend.

Naomi couldn't look at either woman, meeting their eyes would trigger her own tears. She stared at her shoes, remembering...

The nurse removed the blood pressure cuff from Becky's right arm and strode out the door. Naomi sat on an old metal chair, holding Becky's left hand, as a monitor beeped over their heads.

"Why, Naomi? How many more times can I go through this?" Becky asked, between sniffles. She hadn't stopped crying since Naomi arrived at the hospital three hours earlier.

Miriam dozed in the high-backed chair against the wall. She'd spent the night. Naomi searched for words to console Becky. But how could she say things like next time, or you can try again, after four miscarriages? If only David would agree to adopt—such a hard head. Who cares about the genes, just get a baby. Naomi stroked her friend's hand. Becky looked away.

The sound of Becky's voice wrenched Naomi's mind from the memory. "I have to stop him," Becky said. "My son will not marry a shiksa. I'll find him a good Jewish wife."

A week later, Becky strolled into the sanctuary with a girl. A single Jewish girl who just happened to be of prime marrying age. The young woman wore a dress that was a bit too slinky for a synagogue service. It was obvious to Naomi that the young lady spent a lot of time applying what the magazines called "smokey eyes." Her lips were precisely outlined with a dark mauve lip liner and filled in with a lighter mauve lipstick. Naomi watched as the young woman tried to peek between the cracks in the mehitza—the great divide that separated the men's side from the women's—to get a look at Noah.

When the setup for lunch began, Becky dragged the girl over to Noah and pointed to the seat across from him. The girl sat down, leaned forward, and began chatting with a young man who obviously found the lox and bagels more interesting than her words.

"Look at that poor girl," Naomi said to Miriam. "I bet Becky failed to mention that Noah was engaged."

"Do you think he's figured out what his mother is doing?" Miriam asked.

Naomi shrugged and continued watching the young woman employ all her wiles to get Noah's attention.

It was a struggle to focus on the conversation between her friends. Her eyes continued to float down the table toward Noah and the girl. A half-hour later, she watched as Noah finished the food on his plate, swiped the napkin across his mouth, and stood up.

"Nice to meet you," he said.

The young lady wilted like a flower when Noah turned and walked out the door. No request for her phone number or email address.

She was the first in the parade of young women, Becky dragged to *shul* under false pretenses. Naomi hated listening to Becky describe tapping into all of her email contacts and Facebook friends. Rock bottom occurred when Becky began contemplating the idea of creating a page for Noah on JDate. The insane hunt went on for months.

"Enough, Becky," Naomi snapped while dishing out hummus. "The wedding is scheduled. They're getting married in the spring. Stop bringing these girls. Do you hear me? That young lady sitting all alone out there is the last one. No more. Noah loves Maria. Can't you get it? And these poor girls, you drag them here like they're baby dolls for Show-N-Tell. It's cruel—just plain old mean and selfish. They get all dressed-up and made-up, believing Noah wants to meet them. When they get here…Hell, it's worse than going to a single's bar and having no one hit on you. You're probably crushing their egos!"

Silence bounced off the stainless steel appliances. She looked around the table at the rest of the women, waiting for someone to speak—to back her up. Ironically Laurie, the only convert in the group, broke the silence, but not with the words Naomi hoped to hear. "I'd kill Sarah if she brought home a non-Jew. I want Jewish grandchildren."

"Let it go, Becky." Naomi shook her head in disgust. "He's going to marry her."

Chapter 2

The divan Naomi reclined on faced an enormous stone fireplace that stretched from the floor to the ceiling. Out of her periphery, she could see the moon and the bare trees, which appeared to have been strategically placed to enhance the ambiance of the room. Because of the way Miriam's family room protruded from the rest of the house, the three glass walls presented a panorama of her well-manicured backyard. Some people traveled to mountain cabins to wallow in the atmosphere Miriam created in her family room each winter.

Outside the floor to ceiling window, huge fluffy snowflakes fell, glistening from the light of the moon and streetlights. Naomi loved Miriam's house. It was elegant but comfortable. Jake always said walking into Miriam's house was like walking into a hug.

Miriam lounged on the oversized beige sofa. Her black corkscrew curls looked stark against the back of the sofa, but her beige cashmere sweater integrated itself into the landscape, essentially making Miriam part of the sofa.

Beside her, Becky's jewel-toned blue, silk blouse screamed against the background of a taupe winged back chair. Everything about Becky contrasted with the serenity of the room. Her razor cut bob and blood red fingernails stated that she had no desire to blend in with the en-

vironment. Naomi smiled because these differences were
what she loved most about them. They were never boring.

She watched her friends sip tea, taking note that even
the way they held their mugs confirmed their opposite
personalities.

Miriam embraced her mug with two hands—a hug.

Becky held the handle of a china tea cup between her
index finger and thumb. Her other hand carefully balanc-
ing a saucer underneath. Naomi controlled her desire to
laugh, remembering when Becky started holding cups
this way. During her sophomore year of high school, she
did a report on English tea times and traditions. After
gathering this new knowledge, she complained that
Americans were uncultured, and she refused to hold her
cup like a "peasant."

"Hanukah is a lovely holiday, except for the cold and
the four-thirty sunsets. I could learn to like winter if it
could just stay light until six o'clock," Miriam said.

Naomi nodded and set her mug on the marble coaster
that protected the rich cherry-wood end table. "I'm in my
pajamas by seven-thirty every night."

"Buy one of those sun lamps," Becky said. "Did you
repaint this room recently?"

Miriam shook her head.

"Something looks different in here." Becky scanned
the room. "There's more beige than usual. All this beige
kind of puts you to sleep."

A quick walk through their respective homes show-
cased their natures. Becky designed her home to impress,
furnished it with museum quality furniture, and kept it
spotlessly clean. The warmest room in her house was the
laundry room when the dryer was running. Naomi snug-
gled deeper into the lounge chair. Nothing in Becky's
house offered the comfort and tranquility of Miriam's

family room. As the women sipped herbal tea, the heat from the fireplace filled the air with warmth and a lovely scent.

Tonight was a tradition started eighteen years ago when all three women found themselves living in Mt. Lebanon, within walking distance of each other. The first night of Hanukkah became a huge event. All three families gathered at Miriam and Joe's house to light the first candle. In the early years, children ran through the huge rooms, playing hide and seek. They only calmed down when Joe announced "candle time." Their husbands co-operated by singing holiday songs and eating latkes before retiring to the kitchen to drink scotch and talk sports. Now, the children were away, busy living their own lives. Becky's husband, David, and Miriam's husband, Joe, lost interest in the holiday after the children were gone. Naomi's husband was just gone.

Tonight consisted of three childhood best friends celebrating the miracle of Hanukkah by lighting the first candle together. Naomi missed the old days, but recast this night as a celebration of their friendship. One evening that belonged to them and only them.

"If I remember correctly," Becky said, looking directly at Naomi. "After candle lighting at last year's soiree, you promised to start writing again."

Naomi stared at the fire, avoiding Becky's gaze. The first two years without children and husbands were spent reminiscing about their own childhood. Last year, the conversation moved in a different direction. The first night fell only a month after Becky's father had passed away.

Their drink of choice that evening was wine, not tea. They all became a bit maudlin. The discussion turned into a confession of broken dreams, goals for the upcoming year, and bucket lists.

"She's right, Naomi." Miriam placed her cup on an antique coaster. "Did you start a novel?"

"Just look at her face," Becky responded before Naomi could form words.

"No." Fear crippled Naomi when she thought about writing anything more complicated than an email to her mother.

"Did you even try to start one?" Becky asked.

Naomi shook her head. "You promised to clean out your father's house and put it on the market. Did you finish that project?"

Becky rolled her heavily made-up eyes.

"Aha." Naomi shook her index finger at Becky. "So shush about my novel. It was the wishful thinking of a slightly buzzed middle-aged never-got-to-be writer."

"It's not too late." Miriam's facial expression dripped with sincerity. "Write a few short stories or magazine articles. Once you start writing it will all come back to you."

She's so naïve. Naomi knew that any skill or talent she ever had died a long time ago.

"Well, I plan on having my dad's house cleaned out before this damn wedding. You need to write something before the house is sold."

"I'll write the names on the wedding invitations," Naomi replied.

"That's not funny." Becky sipped her tea and turned toward Miriam. "Do you have any cookies?" Before Miriam could answer, Becky rolled her eyes. "Stupid question, you don't bake, just dial in your order."

Miriam's face reddened.

Naomi gave Becky a disapproving head shake. The "just dial in your order" was yet another stab based on a battle that occurred over a year ago. Becky needed to stop lobbing insults at Miriam.

"Speaking of invitations," Naomi interjected to move the conversation back into neutral ground. "When will they be going out?"

"End of February and there's still time for Noah to come to his senses and stop this madness."

"She's not that bad." Miriam spoke the words and quickly turned away from Becky.

"Yes, she is," Becky shot back. "Unless she converts with an orthodox rabbi within the next four months, she will always be 'that bad.'"

Naomi looked at her friends. Typical—optimistic Miriam trying to convince Becky, Miss Control-And-Dominate, into altering her life view.

Chapter 3

Becky

A few weeks after the Hanukkah evening, Becky placed the key into the tarnished front door lock of her parents' house and turned it. The bolt clicked open. She closed her eyes, inhaled deeply, and mumbled to herself, "Here goes."

Stacks of flattened boxes leaned against her leg. She reached down, grabbing them by the string that held them together, and dragged them through the front door into the living room. The flowered fabric of the sofa appeared dull under a layer of dust. The once-fashionable custom curtains now drooped. She scanned the room. Boxes weren't enough. It was time to order a dumpster.

The kitchen looked the same as it did when she was a child. The orange, brown, and green flowered wallpaper screamed nineteen seventy-two, but the ancient avocado-colored appliances still worked. At least, they did on the day her father died.

The sight of the kitchen made her heart ache. It was her mother's domain, as much a part of her as her arms and legs. Becky still missed her every hour of every day, but being in this kitchen…

It was more than grief. It caused physical pain. There

was no way to separate the woman from the kitchen. Becky always equated this room with the most meaningful moments of her life. She smiled, remembering the first time she'd brought David home. She pulled him through the living room, ignoring her father, and straight into the kitchen. Her mother pinched his cheek saying "You're so cute."

The memory warmed Becky. She'd inherited her mother's looks, but her personality lacked the softness and warmth of her mother's. She was her father's daughter, tough and outspoken. The oak cabinet next to the sink held her mother's coffee mug collection. A choke rose to Becky's throat when she lifted the pink mug that read *I ♥ Mom*. It was the first Hanukkah gift she bought for her mother with her own money. Becky, Miriam, and Naomi had gone shopping on Murray Avenue. Becky spotted it on the shelf and stood on her tiptoes to reach it. The words fit. Her mother loved and nurtured her and her two best friends. Becky decided to keep the mug. She walked over to the ancient kitchen table and pulled out one of the green-vinyl-and-metal chairs. The room was so small compared to her own kitchen in Mt. Lebanon, but many of her best memories were made sitting at the small Formica table, talking to her mom. Becky stroked her hand over the cool table top and drifted back in time…

Becky arrived home from her first-grade Hanukkah party and sat down at the kitchen table for her afternoon snack—milk, a cookie, and orange slices neatly arranged on her special pink plate. She popped a slice into her mouth. "Why don't I have grandparents like Miriam and Naomi? They get presents for Hanukkah and their birthdays."

She stared at her mother, waiting for an answer. Finally, her mother turned off the tap on the kitchen sink, wiped her hands on a towel, and walked over to the table.

As her mother sat in the seat next to her, Becky noticed the tears streaming down her mother's cheek.

"At one time, Daddy and I both had parents, but we were born during a horrible time. There was an awful war, where an evil man named Hitler wanted to kill all the Jews. He hated people just because of their religion. My parents knew our city, Warsaw, was a very dangerous place to live, so they sent me to my aunt's house. She lived far away. I don't remember how I got to her house. I was only two years old. But my aunt took care of me, like a mother. Eventually, she escaped from Poland, with me, to another country called England."

"What was her name?" Becky asked.

"Her name was Aunt Sarah."

"Weren't your parents upset when she moved you to England?"

Her mother didn't answer right away, swiping at her cheek with the back of her hand. "While Aunt Sarah was taking care of me, my parents were sent to a concentration camp called Auschwitz. It was an evil place where they killed Jews. Like millions of other Jewish people, my parents died," she said, reaching out, and clasping Becky's hands. "Your father's parents also died at Auschwitz, but before they were sent there, they put your father and your Aunt Gitte on a train to England. For a long time, he and Aunt Gitte lived in a school building before a family took them into their home."

Becky looked at her mother's face. Her eyes were filled with tears.

"Your grandparents loved me and your father so much, they made sure we were safe. Because of them, we didn't die in the war."

"Do you have a picture of your parents?"

Her mother shook her head. "No, sweetheart. I don't have a picture of them. I don't know what they looked like."

Becky blinked hard and shook her head. She wasn't there to indulge in sentimental memories. The plastic trash can still sat next to the back door, the very spot where her mother kept it. Her dad left everything exactly as her mother left it. Becky walked over and picked it up. *Damn*, why couldn't her brother take a few days off work to help with this? He lived in Los Angeles, far from this old house in Squirrel Hill. On the last morning of the shiva period, he told her that he needed to get back to work and couldn't stay to help clean out the house, nor did he know how long it would be before he could return to Pittsburgh. It became apparent that emptying the house and disposing of the contents would be her job. The only things he wanted, if she agreed, were their father's watch and his *tallit*. Becky tried to convince him to take a few pieces of their mother's jewelry for his daughter, but he refused them, believing their mother's rings and necklaces should stay with her. He told her to give them to Noah's future daughter.

Becky contemplated the irony. His daughter would get all of it, after all. There was no way in hell the daughter of a shiksa would ever wear her mother's precious engagement ring or her diamond necklace.

Becky ripped black trash bags from the roll and marched up the stairs to the second floor. As she climbed, she wished she'd packed the can of Fabreeze sitting in the cabinet under her kitchen stink. The housed smelled musty and old. When she reached the landing, the door direct-

ly in front of her was closed—the bathroom. She shuddered as nausea rocked her stomach—*No, don't think
about it.* She shook her head, turned, and walked down
the short hallway, stopping briefly outside her parents'
bedroom—a private sanctuary she rarely was allowed to
enter.

Her mind flip-flopped as she continued toward her old
room, but avoidance wasn't her style. She turned and
walked back to her parents' room.

The brass knob turned easily, but the door stuck a bit.
When she pushed her shoulder against it, it creaked open.
The first glimpse of the room caused her heart to lurch,
and walking into it felt like a violation of her parents'
privacy. It was easy to imagine her father's powerful
voice, chastising her for entering. As an eight-year-old,
she didn't dare to even knock on the solid oak door.

For a moment, a childish sense of wonder froze her in
the doorway. Instinctively, she kissed her fingers, reached
out, and touched the mezuzah. This *mezuzah* belonged to
her mother. It held special family significance because
her Aunt Sarah carried it in her dress pocket from Europe
to the United States.

Inside the small wooden case, with the Star of David
carved into the front, rested a miniature hand-scribed
scroll, containing the most important prayer in Judaism—
The Shema. Every few years, her father would take down
all the *mezuzahs* in the house, including this one. She and
her brother would walk along with him, door frame to
door frame, gazing on as he removed the small tacks that
fastened each one, on a slight angle, to the oak door-
frames. As he worked, he lectured on the importance of
reciting The Shema Prayer every night before bed and
every morning. The prayer announced to the world that
Jews believe in only one God.

She and her brother silently watched as he lifted the

delicate scrolls from the cases and placed them into a plastic sandwich bag, ready to take to the rabbi. He described how the rabbi carefully inspected each Hebrew letter to make sure they hadn't faded or the parchment hadn't deteriorated. If this happened, the scroll wouldn't be kosher.

Becky shook off the memory and crossed over the threshold into the bedroom. It remained exactly as it was the day her father passed away, except for the heavy coating of dust now covering everything. The scene—with the beige chenille bedspread crisply creased under the pillows and cascading backward, covering two rather deflated-looking pillows; the Ethan Allen furniture her mother Pledged once a week; and the framed high school graduation portraits of her and her brother—overwhelmed her with nostalgia.

Her father had the habit of always leaving the closet door half open. A week after the paramedics removed his body from the bed, Becky came back, changed the sheets, and made the bed, exactly as her mother always did. She deliberately left the closet open—for her father.

Becky's gaze focused on the bar inside the closet. She could only see the left side. Even though her mother passed away years before her father, her clothes still hung beside his. Every time someone suggested to her father that it was time to throw away or donate her clothes, he would come up with a new excuse to put it off. "Like father, like daughter," Becky mumbled as she walked to the closet and dropped her supplies. "The house should have been emptied a year ago."

The closet wasn't very large by today's standards. On the right side hung her father's five dark suits, one for each day of the work week. Their buttons all faced the same direction. Behind the suits hung his white shirts. He retired years before, but still wore the same suits to the synagogue and holiday dinners. The few casual shirts he wore on weekends hung next to the white ones. She ran the palm of her hand across the dusty shoulders. Time had faded the lines down the shoulder seams where the hangers had creased them.

Her mother's side remained untouched since the day she died. Unlike her father's side, her mother's was a mess. Becky always found it weird that her mom—a clean fanatic, who waged all-out war against dust, spots, and smears—couldn't care less that her side of the closet resembled the jumbled mess of a teenager's bedroom. Dresses hung crooked on hangers that hooked onto the bar in every direction except straight. The clothes lacked any order, synagogue dresses mixed with day dresses. Her mother insisted on wearing dresses or skirts every day until she died. One year for her birthday, Becky bought her a pair of blue jeans. She smiled gratefully, when she lifted them from the box, but never wore them. Becky expected to find them, complete with tags, in one of the drawers.

What she really wanted to see was sitting on the shelf above the clothes. She stretched, reaching her hand out, until she clasped one of her mother's synagogue hats. One by one she pulled them down and blew off the dust the best she could. They smelled a bit musty, but each triggered a memory. A camel-colored one with a wide brim started a movie running in her mind's eye...

Becky scooted into the pew next Miriam and Naomi.

"Is it true?" Miriam whispered into her ear.

Naomi sat next Miriam. Becky could see Naomi craning her neck forward to see around Miriam, her eyes wide with anticipation.

Becky smiled at her friends and nodded. "It's true."

Before she could continue speaking, her mother slid into the pew in front of them, turned to face them, and put her index finger in front of her pink lipsticked lips, shushing them. Not a mean reprimand shush, but a smiling, twinkle-in-the-eye shush.

Her mother looked beautiful in her camel coat with the matching camel hat. She even wore matching high-heeled shoes with tiny gold buckles across the front. She looked like a movie star. "My mom said the baby will be born in June." Becky announced this news to her seven- and six-year-old companions as if it was more important than a man walking on the moon.

Becky placed the hat on the floor and began putting together one of the boxes she brought from home. Before setting the hat inside the box, she ran her fingers along the rim. Her throat tightened a bit, remembering another moment with her mother. "Some things aren't meant to be," her mother said a month later—after she miscarried for the second time.

She placed the hat into the box and picked up another. This one triggered a smile—a blue pillbox with dotted mesh overlay that draped over her mother's eyes. Each Friday afternoon, during the walk home from school, Miriam and Naomi tried to guess which hat her mother would wear to Saturday morning service. The pillbox was Naomi's favorite.

Becky pulled the camel hat from the box and held it up with her left hand—perfect for Miriam's black curls and blue eyes. On her right hand perched the pillbox. Naomi would finally get her wish and own it. Even though it looked a bit old fashioned, it would emphasize her wide-set hazel eyes and her elegant jawline. Her mother would approve of giving the hats to her other daughters.

Becky gathered the rest and tossed them into a box destined for the Jewish Community Center's pre-school dress-up corner. Then she sealed and labeled the box.

To make sure she didn't miss anything, she stepped onto a small stool retrieved from the bathroom and ran her arm along the shelf. It hit something—an old shoe box.

Becky carried it to the bed and sat down, holding the box on her lap. Inside were pictures, a handkerchief, a few old ticket stubs, and stack of yellowed letters bound together with a pink ribbon. She stared at them for a moment. Something about them seemed odd. Then it dawned on her that there was no address or stamp on the front, just her mother's first name.

The ribbon and letters weren't as dusty as the rest of the articles in the box. Based on the worn condition of the envelopes, they had been opened—a lot. She loosened the knot and an envelope slipped, landing on the floor beside her. She pulled out the thin piece of stationary and unfolded it.

My Dearest Mildred,

Becky quickly read the sentimental words of love. When she reached the bottom of the page, she dropped the letter to the floor, ran to the bathroom, and violently threw up.

Chapter 4

Naomi

Naomi read the ornate calligraphy scrawled across the creamy envelope: Ms. Naomi Feldman & Family, before pulling out a gold embossed invitation from the double-lined envelope. A small piece of gold tissue paper floated gracefully to the floor. She quickly scanned the ornate print until reaching the words she prayed wouldn't be there, *Black Tie.*

Damn, of course, it was going to be a black tie wedding, but seeing it printed on the invitation made it financially impossible to ignore. She began a mental inventory of her pathetic wardrobe, knowing full well that not one hanger held anything that fit.

Black tie presented no problem for Miriam and Esther. They owned racks of stunning clothes. And if they didn't want to wear a repeat, their very high VISA card limits solved that problem.

Naomi scrutinized her plain black skirt—a practical style for both office and synagogue. Actually, the website where she bought it said, *practical for office, church, and easily adapted for evening wear.*

Practical sucked. She tossed the invitation onto the kitchen table and opened the door to the basement. "Ezra, time to get dressed." She didn't wait for him. Instead, she walked to the sink, filled the coffee pot with water, and scooped good old-fashioned Maxwell House into the white filter. As she scooped, her mind drifted back to the wedding, calculating the cost of a shower gift, wedding gift, and a new black suit for Ezra. She shook her head, not even enough left over to buy a pair of pantyhose.

"Mom, is it too late for scrambled eggs?" Ezra emerged from the basement. "It will only take me a few minutes to make them."

"Go get dressed, I'll make the eggs."

She cracked four eggs into the bowl. Of course, her older son, Josh, would be a groomsman, which would entail renting a tuxedo. She dumped the eggs into the hot pan and watched them sizzle. Maybe, if she dug deep into the back of the closet, there would be one leftover dress needing minimal alterations. She could have it dry cleaned, taken in, and made presentable.

Ezra needed a new suit for graduation. She would just have to hit Jake up for the money a few months earlier than planned.

She tried to avoid thinking about Jake, but every time a money issue arose, it was impossible not to. Ever since he walked out, the money fountain dripped dust. The cheap son of a bitch preferred spending their life savings on the new man in his life. The SOB actually had the chutzpah to tell her to be grateful he gave her the house.

"Grateful," she shouted at the empty kitchen. How could she be grateful? After twenty-three years of marriage and busting her ass to put him through medical school, he announced his sexual preference for men. Naomi squeezed her temples—*Ughhhhhh.*

"Hey, Mom," Ezra yelled from his bedroom on the second floor.

She hated when he did that. Why couldn't he walk

down the steps and talk like a normal human being? She dumped the eggs onto a plate.

"Mom, my suit's too small. Can I wear khakis and a sweater to the synagogue?"

She shook her head while walking up the steps. When would he stop growing? His present rate of growth would send them into bankruptcy in less than a year.

She obeyed the new sign taped to his bedroom door that read "knock before entering." Ezra was a great kid. Even after Jake left, he continued to do well in school and showed no signs of drinking or drugs. *Baruch Ha Shem.*

When he opened the door, it only took a glance to realize he wasn't just trying to avoid wearing a suit. "Fine, wear the khakis, but I swear that suit fit last week," she said.

"Not really," he said, yanking at the waistline of his pants. "I just pulled them down below my hips. The same way I do with my jeans."

"Hurry up, change, and eat your eggs. Synagogue starts in a half-hour and, for once, I'd like to be on time."

"Why," he asked. "No one else comes on time. Who's sponsoring the kiddush this week?"

"The Rosens. Noah is bringing his fiancée to *shul*. The wedding's getting close. It's time to introduce her to everyone."

"I heard she isn't Jewish." He offered this information as if it was a flash news bulletin.

Everyone who stepped into the synagogue during the last six months knew Maria wasn't Jewish. For goodness sake, her name was Maria. No self-respecting Jewish mother would name her daughter Maria.

"Ezra, we all know she's not Jewish." She looked at his face, so handsome. Just like his father, wavy black hair and an adorable cleft chin, but the hazel eyes were hers. Everyone said he would be a good catch someday.

But no one knew this to be truer than Naomi. "Get dressed, sweetheart," she said. "I'm leaving in fifteen minutes, with or without you."

She walked into the bedroom she used to share with Jake and ignored the feeling that the king-sized bed was sneering at her.

The face in the bathroom mirror looked tired. Jake moved out over three years ago, and the loss still reverberated through the house. Reaching into the top drawer, she pulled out a tube of concealer. It didn't cover the dark circles she cried into existence the day he informed her that their marriage was a sham he couldn't take any longer. His heart, he claimed, belonged to a guy named Brian, who worked as a nurse at the hospital.

Her fist pounded the granite vanity top. Brian—and he said there were others over the years. Naomi picked up her lipstick and fought to control the desire to smash it against the mirror.

She raked the brush through her hair and captured it in a ponytail at the base of her neck. The brown dye covered the gray and the three years of living with stress kept her thin, but who would want a forty-nine-year-old woman whose husband ditched her for a man?

That's why the support she received from the kiddush ladies was so important. They staved off some of her loneliness, but as much as she loved them all, they couldn't fill the empty side of the bed or the void that caused a permanent hollow sensation in her chest.

Not even bothering to put her makeup back into the bag, she left the bathroom and walked to the closet. It held the same boring clothes as it did yesterday.

Before Jake left there were shopping sprees when she spent hundreds of dollars at Kaufman's, Sak's, and Lord & Taylor. Those department stores closed their doors in Pittsburgh around the same time Jake pulled the credit cards from her wallet. He'd always let her buy anything she wanted. S*tupid, naïve me*—bribery to make up for all his late hours at the "hospital."

She pulled a beige cardigan off of the hanger and slipped her arms into the sleeves. It looked respectable over her black turtleneck. The black hat Esther bought her in Israel pulled the ensemble together and covered the gray roots springing from her part.

She twisted the backs on the decent-sized diamond studs Jake presented to her on their tenth wedding anniversary. Of course, she still wore them. Why punish perfectly good diamonds because the purchaser was an asshole? "Ezra," she called, "two-minute warning."

The storm that blew through in the early hours of the morning put the kibosh on walking. Snow and ice coated the sidewalk.

It would be another hour before the neighbors began digging out.

Ezra walked into the kitchen. She grabbed her keys from the hook near the phone and tossed them to him. "You drive."

As he eased into the snow-covered lot, she twinged with guilt. Even though they weren't orthodox, she still believed driving to the synagogue was wrong. They attended the orthodox synagogue because she grew up in one. The conservative *shul* never felt right. It lacked the great divide—the *mechitza,* which separated the women from the men.

They entered the sanctuary through the double glass doors. Once inside, Naomi and Ezra parted, but not before she located his hand and gave it a quick squeeze. He shambled, as only a teenager could, over to the men's side of the *mechitza.*

✡ ✡ ✡

More women than usual sat on the women's side, but her chair remained empty, waiting for her. Many women didn't enjoy attending orthodox services because of the great divide. She preferred it, loving to close her eyes and let the ancient chants soothe her soul. She didn't understand the Hebrew words, but according to the rabbi, her soul did. By Shabbat morning, her soul craved the words. Naomi grabbed a Siddur from the bookshelf and sat down.

Within seconds, Laurie slithered from her spot at the end of the row into the vacant chair next to Naomi.

"Did you get the invitation?" Laurie asked.

"Yeah, it came this morning. Expensive paper," Naomi replied, hoping the rabbi couldn't hear them.

"Of course, you expected anything less?" Laurie said.

Both took three steps back and three steps forward before beginning the Amidah prayer. The timing of the prayer was perfect. Naomi didn't want to talk about the wedding. She lost herself in the English translation of the prayer on the left side of the book.

As soon as the repetition ended, they sat down.

"She didn't invite Miriam," Laurie whispered.

"That's impossible," Naomi replied.

Laurie shook her head, eyes wide. "She didn't invite her."

The absurdity of the gossip that often took root in their small synagogue never ceased to amaze Naomi. "Of course she invited Miriam. They're closer than sisters. How could she not invite her? The whole idea is incomprehensible."

"Well, start comprehending," Laurie said. "Because Miriam just asked me if I received an invitation and, when I said 'yes,' she replied, 'I didn't.'"

Naomi shot Laurie a sideways glance. "It will be delivered today."

"I told her the same thing. Let's just hope it is."

Naomi didn't like hearing Laurie jump to this conclusion, but everyone had noticed Becky snapping at Miriam more than usual. Stress always brought out a nasty streak in Becky. She never directed it at Naomi. Miriam was always her chosen target.

"Last week, Becky told me she wasn't inviting Miriam. I didn't believe her. Now, I'm worried that she meant it." Laurie shifted her gaze from Naomi's face to the Siddur in her lap and flipped through the pages, trying to catch up to the rabbi.

The rabbi finished the Shir Shel Yom prayer, and the congregation closed their books. Rabbi Morty began every sermon with a joke, and just as he hit the punch line, Naomi turned to smile at Becky. She caught Miriam's eyes first and saw they were filled with sadness. A pang pierced Naomi's heart. She winked at Miriam, hoping it would be received with the warmth she intended.

In the last seat of the last row, Becky bent over, tugging at a real or imaginary twist in her pantyhose. She never could focus when she was nervous, and with Maria sitting next to her—adult onset Attention Deficit Disorder. When Becky straightened, Naomi caught her attention and smiled. The corners of Becky's mouth appeared to be on strike, refusing to lift into a smile.

The three of them, Naomi, Miriam, and Becky, spent almost every moment of their childhoods together. Every morning, they walked to elementary school together and back home in the afternoon. Their summer vacations were spent at the local pool, first learning to swim and then to dive. When puberty hit, their interest switched from doing front flips off the low diving board to watching the boys.

Their families shared Shabbat dinners, backyard barbeques, and a few trips to the Jersey Shore.

Rabbi Morty's tone elevated and drew Naomi's mind back to where it was supposed to be, focused on him. She wasn't a mind reader, but even with her back to Becky, she could guess what Becky was thinking *Oh Morty, please, shut up. Do you have to drone on and on today, of all days?*

After a few seconds, when Morty floated to the men's side of the divide, Naomi peeked over her shoulder again. This time she looked at Maria. The poor girl sat with her head down. Imagine the pain of sitting next to a future mother-in-law, whose only goal in life was to stop your marriage, while listening to an entire service chanted in a language that sounded like someone was choking on every word. Maria must have sensed Naomi's eyes because she looked up. Quickly, Naomi smiled and did a discreet little wave, hoping it would be interpreted as a welcome sign.

Too bad no one told Maria about last Friday night. After drinking three Shiraz's and more than one sip of the syrupy, concord grape kiddush wine, Becky confessed to Naomi and Esther that Maria was a nice young lady, exactly what she prayed Noah would find, but the Jewish version. Maybe knowing Becky's behavior wasn't a personal assault would be a bit of a consolation for the girl.

The sermon ended, and everyone stood up. A few prayers were chanted before Noah hoisted the Torah over his shoulder and began a slow parade around the sanctuary. Naomi stretched over a chair and touched the Torah as it passed. She smiled—such a handsome young man.

Noah radiated happiness, but Naomi couldn't help but think that the situation with his mother must be eating him alive. Mother or wife? *I wouldn't want to be him.*

Once the Torah was returned to the men's side of the sanctuary, Naomi headed straight for the kitchen. Inside, Miriam beat her to the faucet.

So Naomi turned and walked toward the hot-water
urn.

Leaning backward against the countertop, sipping the
instant sludge that passed as coffee on Shabbat, she
watched the rest of the crew move into their respective
positions around the work table.

Becky trudged through the door, decked out in a forest
green suit and a black hat. Her spiked heels belonged on
the feet of a twenty-five-year-old fashion model, not a
middle-aged Jewish mother. The tension in her face could
not be ignored. The wrinkles fanning out from the corners
of her eyes appeared deeper and what Naomi saw when
Becky removed her hat stunned her—gray hair sprouted
from the part in Becky's hair. Becky never, ever, left the
house if there was even a possibility of a gray hair being
spotted. If she couldn't get an emergency appointment at
the hairdresser, she plucked each one out. David made
jokes about it, telling everyone that she made him hunt
gray hairs on her head like elementary school nurses
searched out lice.

Maria trailed in behind Becky, appearing small and
timid in a plain blue suit, a look of fear frozen on her
face. The flamboyant look of the mother clashed with the
humble demeanor of the future wife. *Poor girl.* Naomi
shook her head. *Becky will eat her alive.*

Miriam finally moved from the sink, freeing up space
for Naomi to wash her hands before beginning to cut bagels. As she wiped her wet hands, Esther and Laurie
trailed in last, absorbed in their own conversation.

The kitchen accommodated four women, five if one
was as skinny as Miriam. Six border lined on fire hazard.
The room congestion didn't stop Miriam from plowing
between Laurie and Becky, maneuvering her body until
she stood face-to-face with Maria. The pretty young lady
reached out to shake Miriam's extended hand, but Miri-

am changed her mind and clamped the girl in a hug instead.

Maria's face paled, fortunately the embrace ended as quickly as it began. Miriam loved to hug, but if given the opportunity, she preferred talking. Grateful to have a fresh audience, she launched into graphic detail of her recent shopping trip to New York City. Miriam, as kind-hearted and generous as could be, more often than not caused everyone to wonder how her husband, Joe Weiss, the most humble and richest guy in Pittsburgh, married the biggest Jewish princess west of Brooklyn.

Naomi sliced into a pumpernickel bagel. Her attention split between the knife and observing Maria's interactions with the kiddush ladies—grace under pressure. Naomi dropped the last bagel into the napkin-lined wicker basket, set it on the cart, and walked to the refrigerator, opening the stainless double doors. A blast of cold air struck her face, causing a shiver to rush through her.

On the top shelf sat an outdated carton of milk. She knew it was outdated because she remembered checking the expiration date the day she bought it. Two Friday's ago, she and Becky did a Costco run to stock up on supplies for the kitchen. On the way home, they stopped at the kosher supermarket to buy cream cheese, a case of tuna fish, and that carton of milk. Becky had been on edge all afternoon. In hindsight, Naomi regretted what she did. But, as they hauled the groceries into the synagogue, she asked about the wedding plans. Naomi shuddered, recalling the simple question that ignited a hailstorm of words and emotions…

"How are the wedding plans coming along?"

"What do I care about this damn wedding?" Becky

said, heaving a bag of groceries from the trunk of the car.
"Maria's mother is gloating over the damn event. Let her
organize it. I have better things to do and think about."

"He's still your son."

Becky stopped halfway between the car and the front
door of the *shul*. "This is my worst nightmare come true,
and no one will ever be able to understand."

Then Naomi noticed Becky's face becoming blotchy
and tears forming in her eyes. Not a reaction she expected
from Becky.

"Naomi," Becky said, shifting from hip to hip under
the weight of the paper grocery bag. "My grandparents
died at Auschwitz and my entire family, except a great
aunt on each side, didn't survive the holocaust. It's only
by my grandparents' foresight that my parents lived, and
I'm alive today." Mascara-tinted tears began streaming
down her cheeks. "The only connection I have with a
family history is my Judaism. Noah's marriage breaks the
link I hold dear."

Words of comfort didn't flow from Naomi's mouth.
What words existed? Noah was an only child—Becky's
sole hope for grandchildren. But after a lifetime of friendship, Naomi knew the underlying truth. It had nothing to
do with grandchildren breaking the chain and everything
to do with potentially losing her only child to Christianity.

As Becky stood helpless in the middle of the parking
lot, Naomi could see the pain in her friend's eyes and imagined that the ache originated from the stories Becky
heard growing up. Tales of the suffering endured by generations of persecuted Jews in Poland. Noble people who
never, through torturous pogroms and genocide, let go of
their precious Judaism.

"He'll never convert to Christianity," Naomi said,
reaching her hand toward her friend.

"Doesn't matter, Naomi. Don't you understand? The minute he says, 'I do' to a shiksa, the connection breaks."

Naomi wrapped her arms around her friend and prayed for some help.

✡ ✡ ✡

"Excuse me, Naomi. I need the mayo," Esther said.

Naomi pulled her focus out of the memory, stepped aside for Esther, and navigated around the table, stopping beside Becky, who pretended to be engrossed in the task of preparing the perfect cup of instant sludge. Naomi grabbed a couple of bags of potato chips off the shelf and pulled two bowls out of the cabinet.

"Here," she said, thrusting a bag of barbecue chips at Becky. "Pretend to look busy." Naomi reached in the cabinet, pulled out a package of tasteless kosher cookies, and began arranging them on a plate. "Becky, you have to relax. The red face clashes with the green suit. Just breathe."

Becky pulled in a deep breath through her nose.

"That's it, yoga breathe," Naomi said.

After forty plus years of friendship, you noticed the nuances of behavior that others couldn't see and watching Becky's heartbreak caused physical tightness in Naomi's chest. "Maria is very sweet and seems to be very in love with Noah." Even as she said the words, the triteness of the statement made her want to stuff a sock in her own mouth.

"Stop it. Maria is everything—smart, pretty, sweet, and freakin' perfect."

"Lower your voice. She'll hear you." Naomi peeped over her shoulder and saw Maria engrossed in scooping hummus and talking to Esther.

"Fine, I'll lower my voice, but what I really want to do

is throw something or scream." Becky dumped the chips into the bowl and scrunched the bag into the palm of her right hand. "I conceded defeat—you got the invitation. And what really sucks is her parents are pretty decent too. They agreed to hire a kosher caterer if we paid the difference. At least now, we'll be able to eat at the wedding."

"Becky, I hate to ask, but who's going to marry them? A priest?"

"Hell no! Noah knows that would kill me. A judge from downtown, agreed to do it. He's a friend of Maria's father. I know him through work. Ironically, he's Jewish. He'll do the ceremony at the William Penn. I'm trying to convince Noah to break a glass and stand under a chupah. Since the judge is Jewish, maybe it will count for something."

"That would be nice." Naomi spoke the words, without really understanding what Becky meant by "maybe it will count for something," but she wasn't about to ask for an explanation. If a wedding canopy and glass reduced Becky's stress level a bit, that would be reason enough— what a small consolation prize.

"I don't want to talk about the wedding." Becky turned to face the rest of the women, who were almost finished with the lunch preparations. Miriam was gone, probably already sitting inside the sanctuary waiting for Musaf to begin. Maria was also gone. Naomi watched as Laurie filled the last water pitcher, and Esther returned the mayo to the refrigerator before walking back to the sanctuary.

The minute the room emptied, Naomi turned to Becky. "I need to ask you a question before we go inside."

Becky leaned back on her heels, crossed her arms in front of her chest, but didn't say anything.

"You didn't invite Miriam did you?"

"Hell no, I told you I wasn't inviting the old gossip

monger. That tongue—she'll probably put the *ayin hera* on the marriage."

"The evil eye! Are you crazy? Why would you suddenly decide to exclude your oldest, closest friend?"

"She's not my friend."

"Stop it, Becky. Why in the hell are you saying this? We're talking about Miriam. Remember her? The friend standing beside you, during birth, funerals, and other assorted major life events." Naomi didn't bother trying to control her incredulity. Becky was out of line—way out.

"She's been a great actress for all of these years. Don't let her lovey-dovey happy talk fool you. She's a conniving bitch."

Becky's words stung Naomi. Sure, Miriam and Becky squabbled countless times over the years, but never did Becky call her such a horrible name. "You're ridiculous. Miriam loves you and Noah. As the nurse wheeled you into the delivery room, she refused to let go of the bed railing!"

Becky rolled her eyes. This infuriated Naomi.

"She held Noah before your mother did," Naomi shot back, hoping her disapproval would be the smack in the face Becky needed to end this temper tantrum.

"Yeah, she probably put the evil eye on him the day he was born, and that's why he's marrying a shiksa!" Becky turned sharply and walked away.

As Naomi stared at her back, Becky hissed like a snake. "I don't expect you to understand."

"Of course, I don't understand. Nothing you're saying makes a damn bit of sense."

Becky smacked open the wooden kitchen door.

"There's nothing logical to understand. This conversation isn't over, Becky," Naomi yelled at her back as she stomped out the kitchen door. The wooden door closed in Naomi's face, further pissing her off.

She returned to the sanctuary as Rabbi Morty finished reading a chapter of Tehilim—the Book of Psalms. She tried listening as he made a few short announcements regarding the Hebrew school and the Thursday night adult education class. Her focus remained in the kitchen, with anger still controlling her breathing. Becky could be impossible to deal with sometimes, such a bulldog. Naomi inhaled through her nose, counted to three, and exhaled slowly.

When the rabbi finished speaking, the men began the process of setting up lunch tables. Since they were a small congregation, the sanctuary doubled as a community room.

After years of practice, the regulars switched the room from prayers to food in minutes.

Sarah and Ezra unfurled the white plastic tablecloth from its roll. Once the table was covered, they dashed to their favorite spots at the very end of the table.

Esther rolled the serving cart from the kitchen. Two of the younger children began placing paper plates and plastic cutlery in front of the metal folding chairs.

All the women and a few of the men helped unload the cart. Laurie's husband, Dan, emerged from the kitchen, toting the *l'chaim*—a bottle of Crown Royal and a stack of plastic shot cups. He set the bottle in front of the rabbi.

Once the set up was completed, Esther and Laurie sat down, side by side, saving Naomi the seat directly across the table. She sat down, reached for the salad, and immediately caught the gist of the conversation.

"I'm telling the truth—Becky didn't invite Miriam to the wedding," Laurie informed an obviously-out-of-the-loop Esther.

Before Esther responded, Rabbi Morty silenced everyone by standing and raising his small shot glass.

"I'd like to make a *l'chaim t*o the Rosen family for

sponsoring this lovely kiddush in honor of a guest today, Noah's friend, Maria."

"*L'chaim*," they all responded in unison.

Naomi leaned into Esther. "I think, under the circumstances, he did a pretty good job with that toast. Don't you?"

"Not bad, considering," Esther replied. "Did you know he's been meeting privately with Noah?"

Naomi lobbed a scoop of hummus onto her plate. This information kicked up her heart rate a few notches. "Really, Esther, how do you know this?"

"Well, I've been volunteering a few nights a week, helping with the accounting system. Noah comes every Wednesday at seven o'clock. They talk for about an hour and then Noah leaves," Esther replied. Her pronunciation of Noah's name sounded more like No-ach in her Hebrew accented English. "Don't tell Becky."

"I promise," Naomi replied, wondering how to gather more information on this subject without talking to Becky.

When Becky and Maria joined their little group, the conversation switched from the wedding to the regular topics: kids, recipes, and the kiddush sponsor schedule. No one mentioned the upcoming nuptials. When Naomi checked her watch, it was already 1:45. She motioned to Laurie and Esther. They began clearing the table.

Ezra snuck up behind his mother and whispered into her ear. "Mom, would it be okay if I asked Sarah to come over and hang out for a while?"

His eyes were wide with anticipation, but Naomi wasn't sure if was for her answer or Sarah's. Naomi nodded. "It's okay, invite her, Ezra. Do you want to ride home with me or hike in the snow?"

He spun on his heel. "I'll let you know in a minute."

"He's really handsome, Naomi," Esther said, while

dumping used Styrofoam cups into the industrial-sized trashcan. "You and Laurie should start planning the wedding. Too many non-Jewish girls will be chasing him at college."

"That would make Ezra very happy, but I'm not sure what Sarah's response would be if she heard you." Naomi stared across the room at Ezra. Since his last growth spurt, the facial softness of childhood morphed into the sculpted features of his father, and if nothing else, that louse could turn heads.

"Naomi, are you going to bring a date to No-ach's wedding?" Esther asked.

Naomi stopped moving—disorientation flitted through her brain. *A date? Where in the hell would I get a date?* "Ezra, of course, who else would I bring?"

In Naomi's experience, Israelis could be pretty blunt. Esther's heart pumped the blood of Jerusalem. "No, Naomi—you need a real date. Jake's been gone for over three years. It's time for you to find someone new."

Naomi laughed.

Esther gave her the stern eyebrow lift. "This is not funny."

"Sure, Esther," Naomi said and walked away from the conversation. *What a joke—me and a date.* But she wondered why it didn't feel as funny as it sounded.

"Get back here, Naomi. I mean it. I'm going to find you a date."

Naomi glanced back over her shoulder to see Esther's hand jammed against her hip. Her expression left no room for misinterpretation. Esther had taken up the challenge.

"Thanks, Esther, but let the idea go. I don't think there are any eligible Jewish men who want to date an almost fifty-year-old, menopausal woman with two kids."

"Sure there are, and I'm going to find you one." She

clasped the handle of the food cart and pushed it toward the kitchen.

Naomi continued gathering the remains of lunch, thinking about a date. What a concept. Technically, she hadn't been on a date since she married Jake. They never went out on many dates. He proposed after two months. She was so deliriously in love, she said "yes" without hesitation. Naomi shuddered a bit before walking over to Ezra and Sarah. "Well, what's the story? Walking or riding?"

"Sarah wants to ride because of her shoes," Ezra replied.

"Okay, grab your coats and meet me at the car. Give me a minute to say Shabbat Shalom to Becky before we leave."

Ezra rolled his eyes. "No twenty-minute Jewish good byes."

Naomi raised her finger and pointed at him. "Just for that comment, I'll take twenty-five minutes."

Chapter 5

Becky

Becky yanked the now-tattered tablecloth, scrunching it into her hand. "Please, please," she begged under her breath for David to get out of his chair and give her the time-to-go signal. Today of all days, she wished she hadn't married a first-to-come-last-to-go type. The rabbi didn't help matters—nothing like a willing participant in a Jewish law argument.

She scrunched the ripped chunks of the plastic protruding between her fingers. What right did Naomi have to tell her who to invite to her son's wedding? If Naomi knew what Miriam did, she'd agree. There was no way in freakin' hell Miriam would ever, ever see—

A tap on the shoulder caused her muscles to tense. She whipped around to see who did the tapping—Naomi.

"Whoa," Naomi said. "You need to relax. I haven't seen you this wound up since your mom's funeral.

"Stop sneaking up on me."

"I just wanted to say Shabbat Shalom and tell you I'm leaving."

"Good bye." Becky hoped her clipped tone adequately conveyed the message she intended—leave me the hell alone. She turned and walked away, swearing that if Naomi mentioned the word invitation or Miriam one more time, she would scream. And she didn't give a damn if she was in a synagogue.

The trouble with knowing a person for forever was they believed they had the inalienable right to get into your business. No one could ever know about this business. She dumped the tablecloth into the trashcan and walked toward David, passing a few empty chairs, and—like a little kid—she smacked her palm against each of them. Opening that box in her mother's closet destroyed her past and killed the last ounce of faith she had in people. This business was something she couldn't even share with David.

Noah and Maria ditched out at 1:30. Now it was Becky's turn to leave. If David didn't want to lift his ass from the chair, he could hike home in this shitty snow—alone. "Come on, David. It's time to go home." She stood behind his chair, interrupting his conversation with the rabbi.

"Give me a minute, Beck."

She squeezed his shoulder and glared at the rabbi. Torah, Talmud, Laws...too much talking. "No, we're leaving right now."

Rabbi Morty shrugged in defeat. She didn't care if David was embarrassed. She needed to go home, peel off her Spanx, and suffer in silence. "Now," she barked, giving the back of his chair a tug.

She didn't wait for his reply. Instead, she pulled off her hat and headed for the double doors. Before walking outside, she tucked it under her coat. It cost too damn much money to risk snow melting on it. Of course, the parking lot wasn't plowed. She grumbled a few choice words under her breath and slipped, almost landing on her backside. Damn spiked heels. They begged for the snow to creep down the sides. Her feet were frozen by the time she reached their big white Mercedes, climbed into the passenger seat, and buckled the seat belt. With her arms crossed in front of her chest, she stared out the driver's side window until she finally spotted David heading toward the car.

Normally, they chatted or gossiped during the drive home. Today, Becky stared out the window at the frozen wasteland of Mt. Lebanon. Some people considered snow-covered trees and bushes beautiful. She never could see the beauty. To her, it just emphasized that the lawns and trees were dead. *No wonder people move south.*

The salt truck must have passed their house more than once. The road was clean, but at least four inches of plowed-aside snow blocked their driveway. David reached up, pushing the button on the garage door opener attached to the sun visor. The door slowly lifted. "I guess it's time to shovel before someone falls on our sidewalk and sues us," he said.

"Whatever." Becky opened the car door, climbed out, and stomped the snow off her shoes while walking across the double car garage into the basement. Before closing the door, she glimpsed David leaning against the snow shovel, shaking his head.

Once inside, she filled the coffee pot with water but only enough for one cup. She popped in the small K-cup and closed the lid. Because David made her wait so long, he could make his own damn coffee. As it brewed, she checked her cell phone—two missed calls. The coffee smelled good, much better than synagogue instant crap. She carried the cup down the hallway and walked into her home office, slamming the door behind her.

Her home office looked exactly like she believed an office should look, rich cherry wood, a large desk, and built in shelves lined with leather-bound books. A few years ago, she bought the books in bulk at an estate sale.

She didn't even glance at the titles, just hauled them home in three big boxes. It didn't bother her that not one facet of the room was functionally useful. It looked impressive and that made her happy. She could do her real work in her office on the fortieth floor of a downtown skyscraper—a modern office, ugly but highly functional.

Becky swiveled in her chair, reached for a fat book wedged between Dickens and Shakespeare, and opened it. Its contents caused her stomach to lurch, but she pulled out the thin stack of yellowed envelopes anyway.

Miriam

Miriam got out of the car and walked straight to the mailbox, not caring that the snow reached above her ankles and ignoring the cold. She pulled out the envelopes and whisked through them, reading only the return address. None contained anything remotely close to an invitation. She trudged back up the driveway and into the house.

Inside, Joe stretched out on the sofa, watching the recording of last night's news. She knew she had about ten minutes before the Crown Royal shots escorted him to the land of loud snoring.

"It's not here." The tightness in her throat made it difficult to utter the words.

"Relax. Monday—you'll get it on Monday. The mailman probably didn't want to carry a heavy load through the snow.

"That's a dumb statement. You know the mailman has to deliver everything that comes into the post office each day."

He switched his gaze from the pretty news anchor to

her. "And now you're an expert on mail delivery?"

She nodded, knowing that talking would trigger tears. Why did she have to cry so easily?

Joe sat up and patted the spot beside him. She curled against his side, wrapping him in a hug and inhaling the musky scent of his cologne mixed with the whiskey on his breath.

"This is craziness. The three musketeers can't function without speaking to each other for more than a few days. Must I remind you that Becky called every day while we were in Rio last year?" He kissed her forehead. "The only way you will not get an invitation to that wedding is if there is no wedding. So drop the whole issue."

She kissed his cheek and gave him a squeeze. Joe never failed to comfort her when she needed it the most. He was the human equivalent of a security blanket. "Fine, I'll wait until Monday." She planted one more kiss on his cheek before rising from the sofa. "Enjoy the nap and try to keep the noise level down."

They both smiled. He stretched out and she walked up stairs to the bedroom, glancing at the family pictures that lined the wall.

The sun shone through the bedroom window, making the streaks left by the rain and snow obvious. No point in the cleaning lady washing them. There would be a lot more snow before spring.

She balled her suit up and stuffed it into the dry-cleaning bag laying on the floor of her closet. Joe was right, of course. The mere idea of not being invited was outlandish. She pulled an ancient pair of blue jeans from the closet. The softness of the washed-out denim triggered tears. The jeans were nothing special. Becky bought them for her on an impromptu shopping expedition after Miriam's last pregnancy. Becky hated maternity clothes. At the store, she made Miriam put on the new jeans and dump the pregnancy pants into the trashcan in the food court. Miriam followed her instructions simply because, as far back as third-grade, Becky acted as the fashion expert. Miriam and Naomi always followed her advice...

Miriam walked out of the dressing room and stood on the raised platform in front of the mirror. The salesgirl scuttled behind, straightening the train of the wedding gown.

"Wow," Naomi said, reclining in a soft lounge chair positioned to the left of the pseudo-stage. "That dress looks perfect on you."

Becky walked slowly around her, stopping behind her and pulling on the dress. "It fits."

"That's all you have to say?" The look of disgust on Naomi's face matched her voice.

Becky turned to face Naomi. "Yes, that is all I have to say. I'm the maid-of-honor in this wedding, and I'm going to make sure that the day is perfect—and that includes the bride's dress. Yes, this dress looks nice, but Miriam has a tiny waist and this dress isn't showing it off. She needs a dress that makes her boobs look bigger."

Naomi threw up her hands. "Fine, Ms. Chanel, I concede to you. This dress is not perfect."

"Stick to giving advice on shoes. That's your department."

Miriam turned, faced the mirror, and smiled, acknowledging her luck at having two friends who wanted her wedding to be as wonderful as she did.

Today, it seemed like the jeans were staring at her, as

if they wanted to speak words of comfort. She continued sliding her hand back and forth—hypnotically. There was something special about these jeans. She hung onto them, even though Nathan, her youngest son, was now a college senior.

"Miriam," Joe spoke softly as he came up behind her, pulling her from her reverie. "You're crying."

She nodded and, with the back of her hand, swiped at a rolling tear. When his strong arms engulfed her, she buried her face into his shoulder.

"You're jumping the gun. It'll arrive on Monday, but if it's upsetting you so much, you should have talked to her at *shul*."

Miriam shook her head. "I tried, but she walked away."

"She's just being Becky. Whatever her problem is, she'll get over it in a few days. Just, watch, by Monday, the phone will ring. She'll be in the middle of another catastrophic event and need your help."

Usually, Joe could predict the end of Becky's tantrums within a day, but today, Miriam couldn't shake the feeling that he was wrong.

But she nodded in agreement anyway when he released her from the hug.

He stood, watching as she lifted her foot from the floor, ready to put on the jeans. Before she could do it, he clasped her hand, kissed her cheek, and escorted her to the bed.

Chapter 7

Naomi

Naomi drove home from *shul* oblivious to the conversation flowing between Ezra and Sarah. Her mind remained fixated on the wedding invitations. She eased the old minivan into the garage and, before the key was out of the ignition, Ezra and Sarah bolted out of the car. In the basement, she found them already arranged in front of Ezra's computer, laughing at a YouTube video.

On a regular Shabbat, she would have stopped and asked them what they were watching or suggested they do something that didn't involve using electricity. Today, it was enough that there were no naked bodies on the screen. She didn't bother to say anything before heading upstairs to ditch her pantyhose.

As much as she loved spending Saturday mornings with her friends, she hated the rest of the day. Weekdays flew by quickly with work, cleaning, and cooking. Sundays were designated to laundry and visiting her sister. Saturdays dragged, forcing her to acknowledge the emptiness of her life.

Once in a while, Ezra would take pity on her and rent a movie they could watch together. But no seventeen-year-old kid wanted to spend Saturday night with his mother.

She peeled off the control top, sag-proof stockings and hung her skirt in the closet, relieved to feel the circulation return to her ankles. She pulled on a pair of semi-clean jeans and a sweatshirt before walking into the bathroom. The hot water rinsing away the makeup also removed the remaining chill from her skin. She slathered on some anti-wrinkle moisturizer before walking over to her nightstand and grabbing her novel of the week. The wingback chair next to the bay window in the living room was her Shabbat reading spot. The living room was her favorite room in the house. Her refuge.

Jake hated the living room, which he referred to as "a giant waste of space." When Ezra and Josh were little, he suggested ditching the furniture and putting up a tent so the boys could pretend to camp. She recommended he take them real camping and leave the furniture alone. He never took them camping nor did he remove her comfy chair and flowery sofa.

Today the novel failed to sweep her away. Her eyes kept shifting from the page to the gorgeous, signed, Chagall print hanging over the sofa. Miriam gave it to her on her fortieth birthday. Naomi didn't even want to think about the price, but it did remind her of the Becky/Miriam situation. How could friends get caught up in such bullshit? Naomi mentally rehearsed a "*value of friendship*" speech to give to Becky, but ended up dozing off with the novel upside down on her lap. It tumbled onto the floor when the ringing doorbell startled her awake.

"Ezra, answer the door," she yelled, but the bell continued sounding, and he didn't come. "Fine," she grumbled while pulling on her slippers. She didn't tell anyone, but after Jake left, she developed a fear of ringing doorbells. She didn't know why. She didn't expect him to be standing on the front porch, but just the tone of the bell caused her stomach to clench. She peeked through the window relieved to see Laurie, standing on the other side.

Laurie stomped snow from her boots. "Naomi, can you believe Becky? As if the shock of Noah marrying a non-Jew wasn't enough, now this Miriam bullshit. Where are Sarah and Ezra?"

Naomi elbowed Laurie in the side and chuckled. "An hour ago, they were in the basement, watching YouTube videos. Who knows now? Maybe they're making out on the sofa."

"Ha, ha, Naomi. That's the last thing you and I need right now—grandchildren." She yanked off her heavy-duty snow boots, set them on the small entrance rug, and padded to the kitchen. "Do you have any coffee made or should I start a fresh pot?"

"The stuff in the pot is left over from this morning."

Naomi tiptoed down the basement steps as Laurie began filling the pot with water. Just as Naomi suspected, the kids were engrossed in a movie and, based upon the seating arrangement, no kissing. Poor Ezra, Sarah treated him like a cousin.

"Hey, you two, Sarah's mom is here. We're going to have a cup of coffee. Let us know when the movie is over."

Ezra grumbled an acknowledgment.

"You better tell me my daughter is still a virgin," Laurie quipped as she pulled mugs out of the cabinet. "Do you have any soy milk?"

The brewing coffee smelled comforting. "No, on the soy and you have to ask her, not me." Naomi sat down in her chair. Jake always sat at the head of the table. She still couldn't sit in his seat. It wasn't a respect thing. More like something Josh used to say when he was little—cooties.

"So, Naomi, have you figured out how we're going to fix this wedding issue?"

Naomi cocked her head. "Excuse me? We're going to fix this 'wedding issue'?"

"Of course," Laurie said. "Someone has to fix it because Becky is bullheaded, and I can't stand watching her break Miriam's heart. Can you explain why she doesn't want her at Noah's wedding?"

Naomi glanced out the sliding glass door at the white carpeted deck. The snow covered the fact that it desperately needed to be re-stained. That was Jake's job. She didn't have the money to pay someone to do it. Maybe Josh could give it a try over summer break.

"Are you ignoring my question?" Laurie's words pulled Naomi's thoughts away from repairs and back to Miriam.

"No, I'm not—just thinking and nothing comes to mind." Naomi fiddled with her napkin. "They were fine a month ago."

Lauri shrugged.

Naomi didn't know what to think. Their last big blow up happened over a year and a half ago. She twirled her spoon against the sides of the coffee cup. "The only reason I can think of occurred well over a year ago, just before you and Dan started coming to the synagogue. There was an incident. Well, not exactly an incident, more like a battle. The rabbi's wife had just given birth to son number four. We decided to cater the Brit Milah celebration ourselves. But you know how Miriam hates to cook—she refused to help. This pissed-off Becky, who insisted Miriam could at least stand in the kitchen and wash lettuce. Rather than give in and help, Miriam offered to pay for a caterer. Becky declared it a cold and lazy gesture—"

"That's a stupid story," Laurie interrupted.

"You didn't ask if there was an intelligent reason. You

asked why Miriam wasn't invited. So let me finish. Becky climbed onto her high horse and called Joe at work. Poor guy, he didn't know what to say. I guess he went home and got into a huge argument with Miriam. In the end, we all cooked, baked, setup, and tore down, and did dishes. Except Miriam, who was so pissed, she didn't even show her face. Instead, she ordered a special Shabbat dinner for the rabbi's family and had it delivered it to their house. She even hired a non-Jewish waitress to serve and cleanup. Ever since, the relationship has felt a bit chilly."

Laurie looked as if she was still waiting for the punch line.

"Until that fight, they were conjoined at the hip," Naomi continued. "I thought they made amends when Becky's father passed away. Miriam arranged the shiva and coordinated all the meals for the family. After the funeral, everything seemed to be back to normal between them, and the occasional snide remarks about cooking were nothing new. Now, I have no idea what's going on in Becky's head."

"Well, we can't stand by watching good friends let something as stupid as a catered meal destroy their relationship," Laurie said.

"Right." Naomi nodded and tried to ignore the uncomfortable lurching in her stomach. "Do you want some more coffee?"

"I really do need to go. We're meeting Dan's parents for dinner in Squirrel Hill. Next week, you, Esther, and I must organize a plan. We have such a good group of people at *shul*. We can't let these two pig-headed women screw up our peace—*shalom bayit*.

Laurie rose from the seat and walked to the basement door. She whipped it open, but didn't bother walking down the steps. "Come on, Sarah. We have to go."

Naomi and Ezra stood shivering in the doorway, watching as Laurie and Sarah shuffled down the icy walkway. From behind, they looked more like sisters than mother and daughter. It would be nice if Ezra and Sarah ended up together. The good thing about converts was the fresh DNA they brought to the Jewish gene pool. Once Laurie pulled out of the driveway, Naomi closed the door and put her arm over Ezra's shoulder. "Please go shovel the sidewalk."

Becky

Becky stared at the clothes hanging in her closet. Seeing all the designer labels gave her no joy. What to wear was a question she couldn't care less about today. David showered, shaved, and dressed, told her to hurry up as he walked out of the bedroom. Now, she suspected he was downstairs, clock watching. *Better pour yourself a drink, David.* She turned away from the closet. The bed looked so welcoming. As she walked toward it, she sniffed the air. A hint of lavender scented the room. Instead of being calmed by the aroma, it made her more upset. The pretty reed diffuser was the last gift her mother bought her before dying. Becky regularly refilled it with the same lavender oil. Time for the diffuser to meet the attic. She sat on the edge of the bed and stared at the rich colors and patterns of the Oriental rug.

Moments later, thinking she heard David calling, she looked up and caught her reflection in the dresser mirror. She turned her head to the left and then to the right. Tears moistened her eyes—Jewish. Her face reflected her soul and the genes of her ancestors. She didn't want her son to marry a non-Jew. And she didn't want to have dinner with the girl's parents. Sure, under different circumstances, she would probably like them, but she didn't want them to be family.

"Becky," David shouted up the steps. "Hurry up, the reservation is for seven-thirty."

"I'm sick. Go without me."

His feet pounded the stairs, and his breathing was heavy when he walked into their bedroom. "What the hell do you mean 'go without me'? Get dressed. We agreed to meet with them. And this conversation will decide whose checkbook is going to bear the brunt of this damn wedding."

"I don't care what it's about." Actually, she didn't care about anything. She didn't want to talk about it and really wished David would just leave her alone. "Agree to anything they want. I don't give a shit. In fact, I may not go to the wedding."

David, the normally calm half of the couple, stomped to the closet, grabbed a dress, and thrust it into Becky's face. "This is getting old. We're beyond it. You've got ten minutes—max. Get dressed and put on some lipstick."

She followed his instructions and got dressed. She really hated fighting with him. Before leaving the bedroom, she reached out to switch off the bedroom light, but instead extended her arm a few inches past the switch plate to the picture hanging next to it. She stroked the glass—the three of them at the beach. Noah was about seven. The thrill in his eyes didn't come close to the joy she and David experienced watching him build his sand castle. In the background, her mother sat on a blanket wearing a flowered, one-piece grandma-style swimsuit. The camera caught her as she was about to clap her hands together. It was one of the few vacations they had with her mother. Becky hit the switch.

Chapter 8

Naomi

The rest of Naomi's weekend crept by slowly, just like every other weekend since Jake left the house. He packed their weekends with events and parties. A lazy weekend without plans frustrated him. An unbooked Saturday evening sent him googling for something to do. She always believed his extroverted nature kept his engine running in overdrive. Now, she realized their hyperactive social life was his way of avoiding spending time alone with her.

More snow fell on Sunday night. On Monday morning, Naomi decided to leave the car in the garage and took the bus into work—so did the rest of the people in her neighborhood. Even with the crowd, she pulled off a window seat. The view beyond the scratched bus window made her shiver—snow and more snow. The driver cranked up the heat, but each time the door opened another arctic blast whipped through the bus. But when they passed Becky's street, Naomi forgot about the weather and returned to the wedding fiasco. The date hovered seven weeks away, plenty of time to get Becky to drop the grudge. Naomi unzipped her bag, reached in, and groped around until she located her antique cell phone.

"Becky, hey, it's me, Naomi. Call me when you get this message." Relief loosened the lump stuck in her throat as she hit the end-call button. *Thank heaven for voicemail.* She had no idea what she would have said if Becky answered the phone. How could she bring her two friends to their senses?

✡ ✡ ✡

On Thursday morning, before the sun rose and before her first cup of coffee, the phone rang. Her stomach fell. *Who died?*

"Hello,"

"Becky really didn't invite me. I can't believe her. Can you believe her? She sent an invitation addressed to Joe and the kids—the nerve. This is unbelievable. It's No-ah—I love him like a son. I'm going to call and let her have it." Miriam's voice squealed at a pitch much higher than her normal squeaky tone.

"Calm down. I'm sure it's a mistake. Maybe someone from Maria's family addressed the envelopes and made the error."

"Nonsense, you know she did this on purpose. For goodness sake, I'm the one who snuck her out of the hos-pital for a cigarette after the epidural wore off. She could barely stand and refused to ride in a wheel chair. I practi-cally carried her out of that hospital. And who caught her when she fainted at Noah's brit? Me, that's who. I don't know why she's trying to hurt me, but I'm going to get to the bottom of this, and I am going to get an invitation to that wedding—whether she likes it or not!"

Even in her barely awake state, Naomi pictured Miri-am rolling her eyes and flipping her black corkscrew curls. "Please, Miriam, relax. We'll get this mess straightened out. You will see Noah get married."

"That's right. Either she sends me one or I'm calling Noah."

"Listen, I'm still in bed." Naomi squinted to see the numbers on her alarm clock. "I have to get moving. We'll continue this conversation this evening. Do not do anything stupid like call her." Naomi put the phone down on the dresser and pushed her index fingers against her temples. *Ughhhh.*

This whole situation echoed of middle school girls bickering over bat mitzvah invitations. *People don't grow up. They just get taller.*

That evening Naomi couldn't bring herself to call Miriam back. Instead, she breezed through some house work, plopped onto the couch, and watched sitcoms with Ezra. Both were in bed by 10:30. When she woke on Friday morning, it dawned on her that Becky neglected to return the message Naomi left for her on Monday. The big chicken was hiding from her. Naomi vowed to find a solution before candle lighting time. That gave her ten hours.

✡ ✡ ✡

Miriam

Miriam hung up the phone and then picked it back up. There was no way on Earth, she was going to let Becky get away with this.

"Hello," Becky answered.

"Why are you doing this? It makes no sense. Listen to me—stop it. I don't want to him to marry a shiksa either, but don't take it out on me," Miriam said.

"If that's what you think this is about, you're stupid," Becky shot back, letting the venom flow.

The phone went dead in Miriam's ear. A few heartbeats later, tears started rolling down her cheeks. She wiped her nose with the same napkin she used to wipe up the coffee she spilled while dialing Naomi. It was time to get ready for her volunteer job at the hospital. Instead, she sat down on the hard wooden chair of her kitchen table, so different from the soft backed nursing chair she sat in years ago...

✡ ✡ ✡

Becky slept in the metal hospital bed. Her hair still mussed and flattened from the delivery. Miriam sat in the high-backed nursing chair, cradling the newborn infant in her arms. Becky and David's beautiful blessing come true—a baby boy. Miriam didn't bother wiping away the tears rolling down her cheek. This baby was her blessing too.

He stirred in her arms and opened his eyes—bright and beautiful. The little thing had no idea that he was a dream that was almost given up. Even the doctor told Becky to give up after the last miscarriage. But David insisted on one more time. *Baruch Hashem*, he was right.

Becky celebrated the birth of each of Miriam's children. Miriam knew she wouldn't have survived the twins' first year without her friend. Becky was their favorite "aunt." Now, Miriam would get to be an "aunt."

✡ ✡ ✡

The heck with her. Miriam pounded her fist on the tabletop. *I'm going without an invitation. Aunts don't need invitations.*

She rose from the chair and walked up the steps toward the bedroom. The pictures, lining the staircase, documented the wonderful life she and Joe shared together.

The children's portraits hung alongside her wedding photo. The next one provided the family with a lot of laughs. She and Becky, complete with 1980s big hair, dressed in the puffy pink bridesmaid's gowns they wore for Naomi's wedding. She paused in front of an old black-and-white photo of her parents, kissed her fingertip, and swiped it across the glass. Even after all the years, her heart still winced when she looked at their photos. She adored this visual history, but today, it was the last picture that froze her in her spot. She gently lifted it from the small nail, her honeymoon picture. The two of them, looking very young and excited, standing in the open square in front of the Wailing Wall. The most amazing trip of her life—the homeland. She replaced the picture on the nail, finally knowing the solution to the problem. There was a way to make Becky happy again.

Naomi

It was 5:06 p.m. Fifteen minutes until candle lighting time and not one idea to salvage the invitation train wreck. Naomi inserted the plain white candles into the silver candelabra her mother-in-law gave her before the wedding. It was beautiful, but Naomi hated cleaning it.

She and Ezra were due at Esther's house for dinner at six-thirty. They both loved spending Shabbat at her house. Ezra claimed to dream about her moussaka and brisket.

Naomi could follow a recipe, but she wasn't very creative in the kitchen. Her mother never taught either of her daughters to cook. This was probably good, considering she raised them on a heart clogging diet, which included gefilte fish, kugal, chopped liver, and anything she could fry in schmaltz. The same foods all of her synagogue friends grew up eating—Ashkenazi food, Eastern European shtetl food—except Esther.

Esther's family originated in Persia and immigrated to Israel. Her Sephardic recipes dealt out a kick. Forget the gefilte fish and broccoli kugal, Esther served spicy salmon and cilantro rice.

After lighting the candles and murmuring the blessing, Naomi walked down to the basement into the mini workshop Ezra set up for repairing computers. "Ezra, take a shower. Mrs. Raz expects us to be there by six-thirty."

It didn't even bother her that she said the words to the back of his head.

"Do you think she made moussaka?" he asked, without shifting his eyes from a complicated-looking computer part.

"Get dressed. The sooner we get there, the sooner you'll know. Hurry and leave some hot water for me." She headed toward the stairs.

"Hey, Mom, wait a minute." He pushed his chair away from the old card table and slumped forward—elbows to knees.

Something odd resonated from the tone of his voice. She leaned against the banister of the staircase. "What's up?"

He dropped his head as if ashamed. "Dad called me today."

What have I done? My son looks like he committed a crime for speaking with his father. She forced her facial muscles to cooperate and put a semi smile on her face. "That's great, Ezra. Did he call just to talk or did he have another reason?"

She faked a cheerful tone to mask her paranoia regarding anything to do with Jake. Sometimes it was hard to remember he divorced her, not the boys. She had to give

him credit. He gave Josh and Ezra the space to process
the changes in the family situation but still made an effort
to be part of their lives. But, lately, Ezra refused his invitations for dinner or a weekend at his swank, new condo.
"He wants to take me and Josh to Florida for Passover
to see grandma's new apartment. He said she really misses us." An air of hesitancy clung to him. He didn't meet
her eyes or stop fidgeting with the small screwdriver in
his hand.

"Would you like to go?"

"I—I don't know," he stammered. "I don't want to upset you. And I don't want you to be stuck home alone for
a week."

"Don't pass up a trip to Florida because of me. I know
your grandma misses you. Go see her and enjoy some
time with your dad." As the words passed her lips, her
mind flipped to Brian. Jake wouldn't dare to take Brian
on a trip to visit his mother. Or would he? No way. His
mother would stomp her little size-five feet all over that
idea. Naomi imagined her ex-mother-in-law's voice. "Ja-
cob Feldman you can be gay in your house, but you will
not be in mine. Leave that man back in Pittsburgh."

Ezra continued fiddling with the screwdriver.

"Passover is a long way off," she said. "I'm sure your
father doesn't expect an answer right away. Think about
it, but don't worry about me. You know I spend the week
before Passover helping your aunt scrub down her house
while her kids walk around behind us eating pretzels. By
the time the first seder ends, I'm ready to take a week
long nap."

He looked at her and smiled. "Yeah, Aunt Marsha
does need you."

"Hurry up and get dressed so we can go pig-out on Esther's food."

Marsha, Naomi's orthodox sister, lived in a perpetual

state of either pregnancy or post-partum. After Jake left, Naomi spent many hours crying in her kitchen. Marsha listened, as long as Naomi whined and vented while spoon feeding or diapering her twins. Marsha tried to be supportive, but the idea of living in a penis-free environment sounded pretty good to her on most days.

Ezra set the screwdriver on the desk and covered the extremely complicated part he had been working on with an old dish rag. "I really, really hope she made moussaka." As he said it, he grabbed Naomi in a hug. "Love you, Mom."

The hug made her smile. Some days she looked at him and saw a young man. On other days, he resembled a clumsy, oversized toddler. Naomi followed behind him, watching his long legs take the basement steps two at a time.

Ezra continued to the second floor. Naomi stopped in the kitchen, rinsed out a few cups, and set them on the top rack of the dishwasher. She wished to reach a day when hearing Jake's name didn't cause her stomach to wince.

✡ ✡ ✡

The Raz family lived a half mile away. In the summer, she and Ezra walked to their house. Today, the weather sucked. Ezra drove.

Esther answered the door, wearing an apron with a giant chicken screen-printed down the front. Something red was splotched down the middle of it, making it look like a giant, bloody chicken. "Ezra!" She stretched up on her toes and engulfed the now red-faced boy in a hug, still clasping her wooden spoon in her right hand.

Naomi stepped inside the vestibule, pulled off her boots, and inhaled the aroma of cilantro and cumin emanating from the kitchen. A serious indication that Esther cooked her favorite dish, a chicken recipe with an impossible to pronounce name. For simplicity purposes, she and Ezra dubbed it green rice and spicy chicken.

"Hurry, Naomi. There's so much to talk about."

Naomi loved the way Esther pronounced her name, giving it an exotic flare.

Esther's large extended family still lived in Tel Aviv. After her son moved to Israel to study at Hebrew University and her daughter joined the Israeli army, Esther waged a constant revolt against empty-nest life. She packed her Shabbat table with willing friends and neighbors. Occasionally, she would pick up a Jewish stranger at places like the supermarket, gas station, or Macy's ladies' room. This infuriated her husband, Lewis, who on many occasions said, "Some people feed stray cats. My wife feeds stray Jews."

Tonight the house was oddly quiet. Naomi and Ezra were the only guests. Esther refused to allow Naomi to refer to herself as a guest. "You're family!" Esther loved to exclaim every time the word guest slipped off Naomi's tongue.

"Becky and Miriam," Esther said. "Must sit down at the same table and talk this through." Esther stretched her tiny arm over the huge dining room table and set two heavenly smelling loaves of challah on the bread board. Then, with a flick of her wrist, she spread the embroidered challah cover over the still steaming loaves. "I'll bake rugelach and invite them to come for coffee. Then you and Laurie will walk in, and we'll force them to talk. Honestly, this whole situation is strange. Friends, not friends, what does it matter? We're part of a community. We must take care of each other."

As Esther spoke, her hands flew in gestures that correlated with the rising and lowering of her voice. When she hit the part about community, she threw her arms into a

giant letter Y above her head. Naomi nodded in agreement about the community part, but doubted the part
about the two women at the same table. "Becky would
see right through that invitation. Believe me, I wish it was
that simple. I've known these two women for most of my
life. And, I'm baffled over how this small incident grew
into nuclear warfare."

"We must try to protect Becky from her own stubbornness," Esther said.

For a waif of a woman, Esther held giant opinions—a
huge personality stuffed into a barely one-hundred-
pound, five-foot-one-inch frame.

"Lewis, Ezra, time to start," Esther shouted in the direction of the family room.

The two men ambled into the dining room. Lewis took
his place at the head of the table, and Ezra folded into the
seat on his left. Lewis opened the Siddur and began singing Shalom Aleichem. When they finished singing, Lewis
lifted the kiddush cup and chanted the blessing over the
wine.

Baruch atah, Adonai
Eloheinu, Melech Haolam,
borei p'ri hagafen.
(Blessed are You God, King of the Universe,
Creator of the fruit of the vine.)

He took the first sip from the silver cup and passed it
to Esther. She handed it off to Naomi and then Ezra. After each took a sip of the syrupy sweet wine, Lewis rose
from the chair and walked to the kitchen sink. There he
filled the ritual, two-handled cup and poured the water
first over his right hand and then his left. As he dried
them, he recited the blessing for handwashing. Ezra, Naomi, and Esther lined up behind him and waited for their

turn to complete the ritual hand washing and recite the blessing.

"I'll call Becky tomorrow and see if there is a chance of getting them together," Esther said, right before dumping the water on her right hand. She dried her hands on the special tea towel embroidered with the image of Shabbat candles and the daintily stitched words *Shabbat Shalom*—Sabbath peace.

When they returned to the dining room, Lewis lifted the two *challahs* and recited *hamotzi*, the blessing of the bread. Naomi listened to his deep voice chant the ancient words, acknowledging to herself how much she loved the weekly rituals of the Sabbath—a security blanket she wrapped herself in every Friday night.

Lewis passed chunks of the bread to each of them. Naomi dipped it into the bit of salt she sprinkled onto a plate before heading into the kitchen to help Esther serve the first course—fish and salads.

They lingered over the fish course longer than usual, engrossed in the conversation. Lewis told Naomi about the University of Pittsburgh's search for a new dean of the English Department.

"Time for soup." Esther jumped from the chair and indicated for Naomi to follow.

"Hold that thought, Lewis," Naomi said.

Esther ladled matzah ball soup into the first bowl. "Here take this one to Ezra."

Before Naomi returned to the kitchen, Esther called her name. "Hurry up," she said, thrusting another hot bowl into Naomi's hands.

"What's the rush?" Naomi asked.

"*Zuz.*" Esther flicked her wrists using the Hebrew word for move.

"Naomi," Lewis said. "I think…"

"Shush," Esther said, wielding a butter knife in her

right hand. "That's enough work talk. Why don't you tell Ezra about the new CD that came in the mail this week?"

Lewis and Ezra shared a love of The History Channel and Lewis's collection of military documentaries. Especially, the documentaries about the Israeli army their son, Ofir, sent to his father.

Ezra lifted his gaze from his bowl. His eyes wide with anticipation over the words Israeli Army. "Really, a new one?"

"Yeah, this one is about Moshe Dayan. I didn't even open the case yet. I wanted to wait for you."

Naomi smiled. Lewis had always been a kind, thoughtful man, but since Jake left, he made it a point to spend time with Ezra after Shabbat dinner.

Her soup bowl still held half a matzah ball when Esther began clearing the soup bowls. Naomi clutched hers between her palms. "Don't take it. I'm not finished yet."

"You eat too slow, speed it up."

Esther served the main course, sat down, and chattered about the weather. It seemed to Naomi that Esther was purposely trying to keep Lewis from talking.

The two women cleared the table. Esther carried a double layer chocolate cake into the dining room, stopping next to Lewis. "Why don't you and Ezra eat your dessert in the family room? You can watch that documentary."

Naomi's eyes widened and a look of surprise registered on Lewis's face.

"Since when do you allow food in the family room?" Lewis asked.

"Today." She handed each of them a giant slice of chocolate cake and shooed them out of the dining room. "Sit down Naomi, there's something we need to talk about." She poured more wine into her friend's glass.

"Lewis met someone at the university. This man knows you."

This piqued Naomi's attention.

"He is one of the candidates for the dean position. He grew up in Squirrel Hill and wants to move back to Pittsburgh. He's single!" Esther's face glowed. "I didn't want Lewis to ruin the surprise at dinner. That's why I made him stop talking. I wanted to tell you."

Who did she grow up with that would be applying for a position at Pitt? Then her brain kicked in and reacted to Esther's words "He's single."

Naomi looked at Esther not wanting to hear more. "That's nice. A lot of people move back."

"You're not listening. He knows you and he's single. You need a date. Lew suggested JDate, but I poo-pooed that idea," she said, making her signature flicking motion with her wrists. "You need a *shidduch*, and I'll be the matchmaker."

Esther's facial expression combined excitement and resolve. It took all Naomi's self-control not to laugh in her face.

"Lewis invited him to *shul* tomorrow, and he agreed to come. So, you wear something sexy," Esther said. "Well, as sexy as possible for the synagogue. At least, ditch the comfortable shoes and put on a pair of heels. You look so...so...so...I don't know the word in English." Esther leaned over to inspect Naomi, flipping up the tablecloth to expose her legs. "I got it. You look like an old *safta* since Jake left. You're not a grandmother, flash some leg. You have good ankles."

No, no. "I don't need a *shidduch*. I've been married. That part my life is over. Please, don't do this."

"Don't you even want to know his name?"

Naomi leaned into the soft back of her chair, crossed her arms in front of her chest, and let out a loud huff. She really didn't want to be fixed up. Not that she enjoyed being lonely or having an empty side of the bed, but seriously, single men in her age group wanted twenty-five-year-old trophy wives. For her to qualify as a trophy wife, he would have to be at least eighty-six years-old. No thank you. Across the table, a mischievous smirk lingered on Esther's face.

"Fine, what's his name?" Naomi asked.

"Aaron Brenner. Do you remember him?"

Her body reacted faster than her brain—blood surged to her face and her heart pounded, but the worst part was the sweat that suddenly formed on her upper lip and the back of her neck. *Aaron Brenner.*

Chapter 9

Naomi

Naomi, I'm asking you again, do you remember him?" A tone of impatience tinged Esther's accent. She wanted an answer, but Naomi couldn't speak.

Naomi managed to pull in a deep breath and nod. But the silence inside the room grew heavier with each heartbeat. What to tell Esther? The simple answer? *Yes, I remember him.* When the real answer sounded more like *How could I forget Aaron? Some people lodge themselves in your brain and never leave. Aaron took up residence in mine on September 13, 1981.*

"Naomi," Esther said. "Are you ignoring me?"

Naomi shook her head. Her throat constricted— too parched to let out the words. *Aaron Brenner.* Years ago, she read a quote in a magazine. It read something like, a woman always remembers the man she could have had, while a man remembers the woman he couldn't have.

The words could be interpreted many ways. Maybe men related it to sex. For Naomi, the message always represented the path in life she chose. Her life was the way it was, good and bad, because she chose Jake. But, for a few years, her path merged with Aaron's. She spent many lonely nights wondering what it would have been like to wake up with him on the other side of the bed.

"Naomi, you have to say something. I don't understand your spastic head shakes. Yes or no?"

After taking a huge gulp of wine, Naomi found the words. "Yes, I remember him. I'm actually surprised he remembers me."

A big smile spread across Esther's face. "This is good, very good. You can sit next to him during kiddush tomorrow. Then you can invite him to be your date for Noah's wedding."

Esther's words, spoken in the present, didn't register because Naomi's mind floated back to a warm May night long ago, remembering kisses and gentle caresses.

"This is so exciting," Esther gathered up their desert dishes and headed toward the kitchen.

Naomi struggled to push the memories away and keep her brain on the present.

When she opened her eyes on Saturday morning, the previous evening, especially Esther's words, seemed like a dream that she couldn't wrap her mind around. But she said it. "Aaron Brenner." She rolled over, closed her eyes, and pulled the pillow to her chest...

✡ ✡ ✡

"Aaron, please, we can't do this," she said, as her hands continued roaming his naked back.

"Why not, Naomi? You know I'm crazy about you."

His lips continued kissing her neck as his hands fumbled with her bra strap. His breath, warm against her skin, sent tingles down her spine.

"Cars, Aaron. Cars will drive by. Someone will see us." The exact moment she finished choking out the words, the strap across her back sprung open.

"We're alone. No one ever drives on this road."

He tasted so delicious and smelled like heaven. She wrapped her fingers through his curls. His hands glided over her breasts and down her stomach leaving a wake of warmth. They hesitated briefly at the top button of her blue jeans.

"I never did this before," Naomi whispered into his ear.

"Me either."

✡ ✡ ✡

She opened her eyes and, for a few moments, stared at the ceiling, wallowing in the pleasure of the memory. Finally, she glanced at the clock—nine fifteen. Time to get out of bed. She pulled her robe off the hook on the back of the bathroom door and slipped it on, knotting it tightly around her waist before heading to the kitchen. Coffee. She needed coffee.

Just the idea of her and Aaron Brenner sitting in the same sanctuary, listening to Rabbi Morty's sermon, and eating at the same lunch table seemed preposterous. He was famous and successful. He didn't belong in a small synagogue in a suburb of Pittsburgh.

As the coffee brewed, the dam holding back all memories of Aaron broke. She tried pushing them back, but her mind's eye remained focused on a close up image of his face.

What would she say to him? After rehearsing a few lines, which all sounded staunch and formal or too familiar, she filled her cup and slogged back up to her room. The walk-in closet held a lot of old clothes, dresses that fit beautifully fifteen pounds ago. She pulled two dresses from the bar and held them up. Ah, the good old days when Jake's black Amex card held a special spot in her wallet. She slipped the red one over her head. It bagged across the bust and under the arms. She contorted her body to get a view of her backside. At one time, she could ask Jake the dreaded question. "Does this dress make my butt look big?" He would always give an honest answer.

She twisted to inspect the other side and thought about Ezra. *No.* She shook her head. Walking into her son's room and asking that question would be weird. She pulled the slinky material over her head and tossed it onto the bed before pulling on a simple black shift with three quarter length sleeves. It looked better. Well…maybe not better, but a lot safer.

Naomi dug in her jewelry box chastising herself for being so concerned about her appearance. On an average day, she was happy if her stockings lacked runs. On weekends, she didn't even care if her socks matched. Ezra made fun of her inside out sweatshirts, a habit she picked up in the 80s and never outgrew.

She wiggled her feet into her last surviving pair of spiked-heeled black pumps and looked at her ankles. Esther was right, not so bad.

She gazed into the mirror above the dresser. At eighteen, Aaron was the most handsome boy in the school. They started dating at the beginning of her junior year of high school. It was his senior year. Studious and very ambitious, he earned a full scholarship to Columbia. One year later, she was rejected by Columbia and ended up at the University of Pittsburgh, a mere one point three miles from her house. They wrote pages and pages of letters and sucked every minute out of Christmas breaks, spring breaks, and summers.

"Mom, are you almost ready?" Ezra hollered up the stairs.

"I'm coming, just give me one more minute." She

walked to the closet, and pulled out both of her black hats. The wide brim of the first one looked too fancy to go with the simple style of the dress, so she put it back on the shelf. The style of the second hat matched with the dress, but it took a minute to situate it properly on her head. Standing in front of the mirror she realized black dress, black hat, black shoes—a funeral. Over the last few years, it was hard to remember a day that didn't feel like a funeral. Nothing like the excitement she felt on the day she first considered breaking up with Aaron. A simple college elective in her junior year, an anthropology class, altered the trajectory of her life...

✡ ✡ ✡

She dug around inside the front section of her backpack, searching for a pink marker. Her doodles—*I love Aaron* and *Mrs. Aaron Brenner* would look much better outlined in pink ink. The black ink was boring. There wasn't a notebook in her backpack or dormitory room that wasn't a testament of her love for Aaron. She wiggled, trying to get comfortable in the stupid wooden desk designed for right-handed people.

Naomi glanced at her watch. Her patience thinned. Was there an unwritten rule that professors must be late on the first day of class? This was her third late professor in two days.

"Is this Anthropology 101?" asked a deep voice.

She looked up and her heartbeat kicked into overdrive. The boy standing in front of the room was beautiful— black hair, high cheek bones, full lips, and a Star of David hanging around his neck. His smile sent blood rushing to her face. She dropped her head, hoping her face wasn't as red as it felt.

After her pounding heart returned to normal, she dared

to look up. He hadn't moved from the front of the room, just stood there, scanning the empty desks. The moment their eyes met, he stepped forward. Within an instant, he plopped into the desk to her right, dropped his backpack to the floor, and smiled.

In a lame attempt to distract herself from staring at him, she doodled squiggly lines on the blank page in the middle of her notebook, until a hand smacked down on the desktop. She examined the arm attached to it—tan, just enough hair to be sexy, but not furry. And the biceps...

Then she shifted her gaze to his eyes. Gray—his eyes were an unusual shade of gray, backlit by a golden light.

"The professor better get this show on the road, because when we get out of here, I'm buying you lunch," said the beautiful mouth belonging to Jake.

He took her to Hemmingway's for lunch. Afterward, they walked to the Cathedral of Learning and sat down on the lawn, enjoying the last of the summer sun. The conversation flowed for hours. She listened as he described his dream of going to medical school and someday practicing in Pittsburgh. His voice cast a hypnotic spell over her. She wanted to listen to him talk forever.

When the sun began to set, he walked her back to the dorm. The next morning, when she left for class, he was sitting on the bench outside her door. She broke up with Aaron a week later.

"Mom," Ezra yelled, again. "Hurry up!"

She grabbed a multi-colored scarf and slung it over her shoulders. "I'm coming."

Everything appeared exactly as it should at the *shul.* The men were well hidden behind the mehitza and the women sat in their usual spots. Naomi took her seat, next to the wall, and mentally chastised her stomach for behaving so badly.

Esther slithered from her spot behind Naomi into the seat next to her. "He's here. You didn't tell me he was handsome."

"He used to be. I don't know what he looks like now. I haven't seen him in person since 1980-something. But a few years ago, when one of his books was made into a movie, I saw him interviewed on a morning talk show. He looked good on TV," Naomi replied.

Before Esther could respond, Miriam stuck her head between their shoulders. "I've made-up my mind. I'm going to the wedding without an invitation. After all, I helped raise the boy and let him stay at my house for a month during his junior year of high school. Don't you remember, Naomi? After he and Becky had that huge fight?"

"How could I forget?" The adult part of Naomi's brain was happy to move the topic away from Aaron, but the other less grown-up part wanted to ask Esther a million questions.

"And," Miriam continued. "I know how to make Becky happy and make her forgive me for whatever I did."

At that very instant, Rabbi Morty flashed a look that would have cooled a hot flash. "Shhh, Miriam," Naomi said. "We'll talk about this later."

A huge bleached white smile spread across Miriam's face. She nodded and opened the Siddur, pretending to know what page Morty was on.

Naomi and Esther followed her lead. Both opened their books and began following along as the rabbi read the Hebrew script. Naomi quickly turned around and showed Miriam the correct page.

✡ ✡ ✡

Becky

Becky sat alone in the last row staring at the back of Miriam's head.

Damn woman. Clueless. She pretends to have no idea what this is about. Sure, Naomi doesn't get it. She and her family were innocent bystanders. But Miriam knew. All those evenings she complained about being stuck home alone, claiming to have no idea where he went. Bullshit, she knew exactly where he was going. She may be a princess, but she's not stupid. Some friend. She's deceived me for the last thirty years. All those dinners and trips with the three families...

Nauseating.

Becky wanted nothing more than to throw her siddur at the back of Miriam's head and walk out the door. Instead, she had to sit and suffer, watching the damn woman whisper to Naomi and Esther. Becky shifted the siddur to her left hand and squeezed her right. She imagined her gaze boring a hole through the back of Miriam's head.

Chapter 10

Naomi

"M iriam, you're right. Just show up at the wedding," Naomi said. "This is all ridiculous. I bet Noah has no idea what's going on. He's the groom—it's his day, not his mother's. I'm sure he expects you to be there with the rest of your family."

"Excuse me, ladies," Esther interrupted. "We have more important things to discuss now. Naomi needs to find a date for the wedding."

Miriam stared at Naomi's face for a moment and tilted her neck. "You are so right, Esther. Naomi, when was the last time you had a date?"

The new subject pissed Naomi off. "It was 1986. Do you have a problem with that?"

"Yes, I do." Miriam removed her hat and raked her French manicured nails through her hair. "It's time for you to start dating. Jake's been gone for what? Three years? Four years? You're not getting any younger, Naomi. Well, at least you're thin now. You were much chubbier when you were married to Jake. Did you know this is the most difficult age to meet someone? The best ones are either married or starting to die off. You don't want to be an old woman living in one of those senior high rises, chasing men the minute they finish tossing dirt into their wife's grave."

"Miriam," Esther said and launched into a string of Hebrew curse words. "Naomi is beautiful and sweet. There are many nice men who would love to meet her. Actually, there is one sitting on the other side of the mehitza today."

"Who's over there?" Miriam asked, straining her chicken-neck to see over the top of the divider.

"That's enough both of you. Pick up your books and pay attention to the service," Naomi barked.

"Okay," Esther said, flipping through the pages. "I'll say prayers you find a man. And when I'm finished with that prayer, I'll pray for Becky to get over this stupid temper tantrum and invite Miriam, like she should have in the first place."

Ezra carried the Torah through the women's section. Once it passed, the kiddush ladies meandered into the kitchen. Naomi stood in the hallway for a moment to catch her breath. For some reason, she could not stop her heart from pounding against her rib cage.

"Okay, what's on the menu? And who's sponsoring today?" Becky asked, as she glided through the doorway.

"I am," Esther replied. "The kiddush is to welcome the guest my husband brought today. He's the number one candidate for the Dean of the English Department position. He's Jewish and originally from Pittsburgh."

Naomi's face flushed. She knew it was only a matter of moments before Becky demanded to know his name. Naomi waited for it to come and walked over to the coffee pot.

"Why didn't your husband apply for the job?" Miriam asked.

"He didn't want to apply. He likes teaching." Esther's tone and expression shot out annoyance.

"It's none of your damn business why he didn't apply," Becky shot back.

Relief flooded over Naomi. Becky looked too pissed off to bother asking about Lewis's guest. Naomi didn't want it to be the topic of conversation during lunch preparations. Let the shock occur naturally, when Aaron sat down at the lunch table.

"That's your problem, Miriam. You always ask obnoxious questions." Becky flicked a dollop of mayonnaise into a bowl of tuna fish. "Anyway, what part of Pittsburgh is this guy from and what's his name?"

"Well, he grew up in Squirrel Hill. His mother is ill, and his father passed away years ago. He wants to move back to help her. He's divorced. His son studies robotics at Carnegie Mellon."

"Yeah, yeah," Becky interrupted. "But what's this name? Maybe I know him."

"Aaron Brenner," Esther said, rolling the sound of the Rs.

Naomi watched Becky's eyes grow round, shock creep across her face, and the spoon fall from her hand.

"Aaron Brenner? As in novelist, movie producer, and former boyfriend of Naomi?"

"Yes," Esther said. "And I'm going to convince her to invite him to be her date for Noah's wedding."

Naomi concentrated on the boiled egg she was peeling. Hearing his name out loud in front of all of them made her want to cry—*stupid me—standing in front of a mirror primping. The only thing he probably remembers about me is my name.*

✡ ✡ ✡

Esther navigated the food cart through the kitchen door toward the double doors of the sanctuary. Only Laurie and Naomi remained in the kitchen.

"I've been thinking all week about this wedding fiasco, and I still can't see a way to fix it," Laurie said.

Naomi smiled, grateful for a distraction and a reason to stay in the kitchen.

"Have you had any grand epiphanies on the subject?" Laurie asked.

Naomi shook her head. "No, But Miriam told me that she's going without an invitation."

"Is that a good idea?"

"Maybe I should call Noah and ask him to send her one."

"I don't understand how this could happen. Didn't Noah and Maria create the guest list?" Laurie asked.

"My guess is they did," Naomi replied. "And Becky graciously offered to double check it before emailing it to the printer. Her finger hit the delete button before hitting the send button."

Laurie nodded and picked up two pitchers of water. "Grab the other two, Naomi," she said, as she left the kitchen.

Naomi didn't want to leave the kitchen. It had been twenty-some years since she wrote that letter, but suddenly, it didn't seem like such a long time. "Stop it," she said out loud then picked up the pitchers and walked into the sanctuary.

She recognized him from behind—something about his stance, and the way his hair curled above his shirt. He stood between Lewis and Becky. Based on the way Becky's hands flew in front of her face, it was obvious she was doing all the talking.

Naomi set the first pitcher in front of the rabbi and then walked toward the kid's table. As she placed the second pitcher in front of the rabbi's fourth child, she heard her name. Chills pricked up the skin on her arms. Her throat dried.

"Hello, Aaron," she said. He looked amazing. Still handsome, eyes as blue as the Caribbean water. His former silky black curls now contained a sprinkling of silver. His smile turned her knees to jelly. "How are you?" she asked.

"I'm great, and if we weren't in an orthodox synagogue, I'd give you a big hug. You look amazing."

He really did appear to be happy to see her. This made it even more awkward. It would have been easier if he didn't remember her at all. A blush heated her face. "You do, too." As she spoke the words, her tongue grew five times larger. "I was surprised to hear you're thinking about moving back. Pittsburgh seems a bit provincial for someone like you."

He cocked his head sideways. 'What do mean by 'someone like you'?"

First sentence and something stupid came out. "I'm sorry," she choked. "I mean, you're so successful. I've seen you on TV, the books, and the movie. You're a big shot now."

He laughed. His eyes matched the smile on his face. "Ah, Naomi," he said, squeezing her in a hug. "Synagogue or no synagogue."

She wrapped her arms around him and inhaled the earthy scent of his cologne. What really shocked her was the overwhelming desire to kiss his neck.

After releasing her, their eyes met. "For years," he said, "I wanted to pick up the phone and call you—just to say hello and to see if you were happy."

"Why didn't you?"

Now, it was his turn to blush. "Chicken. I didn't think you would want to talk to me. Then, I was afraid your husband would answer the phone and what would I say to him? 'Hello, I'm Aaron. Your wife dumped me for you'? I couldn't do it, so all the news about your life reached me via my mother. She heard things through what I call the Yenta Network."

Naomi smiled, but her mind jumped from thought to thought. She never imagined their break-up would be mentioned in the conversation today. In fact, in all the scenarios she anticipated, he barely remembered her, or the awful letter she wrote to him. And his mother reporting information to him? Had she just volunteered it, or did he actually ask about her?

The silence extended a heartbeat too long. It was Naomi's turn to speak.

"Same here, outside of the stuff in the newspapers, I would occasionally hear something about you through the 'Yenta Network.' After you released your last novel, I heard your NPR interview," she said.

"Aaron, Naomi," Miriam said, a bit too loud. "Come and eat, or all the food will be gone."

Aaron made a slight bend at the hips and swished his arm forward. "After you."

The table was packed with people already eating. At the end of the table, Becky saved her normal seat, but Naomi didn't know if she should sit with her friends or sit by Aaron.

"Aaron," Lewis said, standing and signaling. "I saved you a spot."

Aaron gave her an awkward shrug of the shoulders. His expression sent her back to another time, and she caught a glimpse of the young man she'd loved.

"Go, Aaron. We can catch up later," she said.

✡ ✡ ✡

People stayed longer than usual, excited to have someone famous sitting at the table. As the clock hands approached three, only the small group who knew Aaron

since childhood remained. Miriam monopolized the conversation, rehashing tales from high school, so Becky and
Naomi started bussing the table.

"Look at her—sitting and yakking like there's no work
to do here. I'm not putting her plate in the trashcan. She
can do it herself for once," Becky griped.

Naomi dumped a leftover bowl of egg salad into the
trash. "Enough, stop complaining about Miriam." She
looked at Becky. Maybe it was having Aaron in the
building, but suddenly, Naomi felt very sentimental.
"Come on, Becky. Me, you, and Miriam, we're closer
than family. I don't need to remind you of our history.
Hell, our childhoods completely intertwined. Your mother yelled at me. My mother fed Miriam, and Miriam's
mom did the alteration on every special outfit we ever
bought. Remember, your prom gown?"

Becky made a humpf noise.

"Fighting with Miriam is like fighting with your sister
or cousin—let it go. So what if she sent the Rebbetzin a
meal. It's over."

Becky stopped washing the bowls and the serving
utensils. "Do you think that's why I'm angry at her? You
seriously believe I'm not inviting her to the wedding because she's useless in a kitchen?"

"Yes," Naomi said, shrugging. "Am I wrong?"

Tears leaked from the corners of Becky's eyes and
rolled down her cheeks.

Naomi froze. Where was this coming from? "Becky,
I'm sorry. If it's not the baby fiasco, what is it?"

"Family, like family," Becky mumbled, slapping her
hands against a dry tea towel with the word 'meat,' printed on it."

"Please, could you explain to me what's going on?"
Naomi pleaded.

Rather than answering, Becky darted from the kitchen.

Naomi stood, hands-on hips, staring at the swinging kitchen door. Rather than following her, she stalled for a moment, filling a cup of water before walking back into the sanctuary, frustrated, by her inability to think of any other reason for this war.

Naomi scanned the lunch table. Becky wasn't sitting beside her husband, and her spot at the end of the table with their group of friends was empty. Laurie pointed out the window. Through frost-rimmed plate glass, Naomi watched the back of Becky's lowered head and mink coat move farther and farther away from the synagogue. Becky pulled a crumpled tissue from her coat pocket before climbing into the driver's seat.

"Naomi," Esther called.

Naomi joined the group surrounding Aaron.

"Aaron is staying in Pittsburgh for a while—to spend time with his mother." Ulterior motive saturated Esther's voice.

Naomi smiled and did a slight eye roll—enough to get her point across to Esther. If Naomi so much as uttered the word "really," it would be used to further Esther's busybody mission. In her matchmaking mind, getting the two of them in the same room accomplished the first step toward the achievement her long-term goal—Naomi's wedding.

"I may have to fly to New York for a few days," Aaron said, "but I plan to spend most of the summer here. My son enrolled in summer classes, and well, my mother is getting older."

"Wonderful," Esther said, clapping her hands. "You will come to our house for Shabbat next Friday and bring your mother and son," Esther said. "Naomi, won't it be fun having new people join us."

Nice play, Esther, Naomi silently conceded. *But, sitting together for a Shabbat dinner doesn't mean he wants to go to a wedding with me.* It was time to tell Esther about Aaron's ex-wife—a former fashion model.

"Hey, Mom. Sarah and I are walking back to our house. Are you coming?"

"Sure, let me get my hat from the kitchen," Naomi said.

She picked up the half empty Crown Royal bottle from the table and walked back to the kitchen. She put the whiskey into the refrigerator and walked to the wide marble window sill to retrieve her hat. When she turned around, Aaron stood in the doorway, watching her. When their gaze met, he dropped his chin and stuffed his hands into his pockets. Something he always did when he was nervous.

"I was wondering if you'd like to have dinner with me tonight? It would be really nice to catch up. I'm tired of being with people who just want to talk about declining student enrollment and the job outlook for graduates of the English department. Are you interested?"

She bit her bottom lip. This wasn't a date invitation—it couldn't be—just two old friends talking and eating. No big deal. "Sure, dinner would be great."

"I don't have your number. Rabbi Morty wouldn't be happy, catching me writing on Shabbat. So, I'll call Lewis later and get it. He can also give me directions to your house. Does eight o'clock sound good?"

"Sure," she replied.

"Great, I'll see you in a few hours." He did a little wave move with his hand before walking out the door.

During the walk home, Sarah and Ezra chatted about school and the wedding. Naomi was grateful for Sarah's presence because she didn't have to talk. She contemplated the bigger issues of the day. Like what the hell was eating at Becky? And Aaron—a forty-nine-year-old Jew-ish mother had no business getting all sweaty and nervous over an old flame. *Hell, this is exactly the reaction he caused me to have when I was eighteen, drooling the same way Ezra does over Sarah.*

When they got to the house, Sarah flopped onto the family room sofa; Ezra stood next to the TV, flipping through the list of movies; and Naomi walked around the kitchen, wiping away a few crumbs left over from breakfast. Then she broke two of her own rules. The first violation occurred when she unloaded the dishwasher, which was Ezra's job.

Next, she booted up her laptop. She avoided using the computer on Shabbat, but today, she wasn't in the mood for her novel and needed something to distract her thoughts from Aaron.

She scanned through a few celebrity gossip sites and read her horoscope, which was so generic she laughed. Out of guilt, she opened a real news site and skimmed the headlines. When the clock on the kitchen wall read five o'clock, she shut down the computer. Becky would be awake after her Shabbat snooze. Naomi picked up the phone and dialed.

"Hello."

Wonderful, no voicemail, Becky actually answered. "I'm so sorry. I didn't mean to make you cry."

"I know, Naomi."

"Please, tell me what's going on. Believe me, when I say this, Miriam has no idea why you're angry. If she knew what was bothering you, she could either apologize or explain herself."

"Too late for that and no apology will ever be enough," Becky said.

"This is so absurd. I don't have words for it."

"Naomi, I don't want to talk about this. Miriam and I are no longer friends, nor is there an icicle's chance in hell, we'll ever be friends again. If there was another orthodox shul in the neighborhood, I'd go there just to avoid seeing her face every week."

Stunned was the only word to describe Naomi's reaction to the poison Becky just dropped on her. "Becky, this is horrible. You can't mean any of it."

"Yes, I do, and don't ever bring it up again. Furthermore, she's not coming to my only son's wedding."

The phone went dead, but a few moments passed before Naomi removed it from her ear and set it on the kitchen countertop. She yanked open the sliding glass door, walked across the deck, and leaned against the cold wooden railing, unable to comprehend Becky's tirade.

Becky

As Becky hung up the phone, her heart raced inside her chest. Naomi needed to butt out. This didn't involve her.

"I heard you talking to Naomi." David walked into the kitchen. "It got a little loud."

"That's because Naomi refuses to listen."

"I don't think so, Beck. I heard what you said about Miriam." He wrapped his arms around his wife. "Are you ready to tell me what's going on inside your head? Hearing you talk like that about Miriam—harmless Miriam— is scaring the shit out of me."

Becky spun out of his arms. "Harmless, my ass."

He followed her across the kitchen and into the living room. "Will you stop? Look at me."

The last thing she wanted to do was talk or listen. There was nothing to say. Just thinking about it was a nightmare but saying the words out loud would kill her.

"Please, tell me what is going on. You and Miriam should be working together planning this wedding."

An angry fire ignited inside her entire body. "She's the reason this damn wedding is happening. She put the *ayin hara* on Noah the day he was born. It's all her friggin fault—all of it."

Before David could respond, Becky slammed her office door in his face. All of them needed to leave her alone—even David.

Chapter 11

Naomi

Aaron called at five forty-five. After a few seconds of small talk, he suggested they go to some place casual for dinner. "Wearing a suit to *shul*," he said, "was more than enough dress-up for one day."

After Naomi hung up the phone, her heart surprised her by doing a small jig.

She put on five outfits. Each turned out to be either old-fashioned, worn out, or made *her* look worn out.

When Laurie arrived to pick up Sarah, Naomi enlisted her help. Laurie yanked clothes from the closet, rejecting garment after garment. The smile she wore when she walked into the bedroom was replaced by a grimace usually reserved for invasive medical procedures. "I don't get you, Naomi. Sometimes, I think you're a fat person stuck inside a skinny person's body. Everything you own is either black, baggy, or both," Laurie said. "How am I supposed to deliver sexy from this stuff?"

"Hey, most of it fit when I bought it. Some of those pants were even tight—form fitting. I lost a few pounds after Jake left. And what's wrong with black? Isn't it the sophisticated color?"

Laurie rolled her eyes. "Here." She thrust a pair of

beige pants at Naomi, in the same manner the nurse at her doctor's office handed out paper gowns. "I hope you don't need suspenders to keep these things around your waist. They look huge."

Naomi pulled on the pants. Laurie nodded and then handed her a black silk blouse. "Maybe, turn around."

Naomi did a three hundred and sixty degree turn as Laurie studied her clothing. "Works," Laurie said. "Just throw on a chunky silver necklace, and you'll look great." She sat down on the bed as Naomi stripped off the outfit. "He's really handsome and funny, Naomi."

"I already know that," she said, pulling up her blue jeans. "And he's the ex-husband of a supermodel—Alicia Brenner."

"So what? Ex-husband, ex being the operative word."

Naomi headed for the stairs and Laurie trailed along behind her. "Well, from what I heard, you two were pretty serious when you were young, maybe this date will reignite something. You've been single long enough."

"Come on, let's have coffee. Aaron and I had something when we were children. Things are different now."

"Bullshit. If he loved you once, he can love you again. Besides, you always hear stories of long lost loves finding each other on the internet and getting married."

"Well, it won't be me and Aaron. After *shul*, I gazed into my crystal ball, and his future, tall, blond, trophy-wife waved back at me. So, can we change the subject to more pressing matters?" Naomi said, while pouring fresh coffee into a Happy Anniversary mug.

Laurie exhaled. "Actually, I can't think of anything more interesting than a handsome author asking you to dinner."

"Becky and Miriam."

"That's not interesting. It's stupid," Laurie shot back.

Naomi shook her head. "I'm not so sure anymore.

Becky let loose a tirade on me today, saying she'll never be Miriam's friend again. This is definitely not about the meal Miriam sent to Rabbi Morty's family. She made it clear it's something more serious."

"Well, what is it?"

Naomi shrugged. "She wouldn't tell me—hung up on me."

Inside, she struggled with the notion she was somehow betraying Becky by speaking with Lauri about this situation. But, the *shul* brought all of them together, Miriam, Becky, Laurie, and Esther. And truth be told, Naomi felt baffled, frustrated, and helpless and talking to Laurie didn't count as *lashon hara*.

Naomi didn't gossip. This was a case of two heads being better than one. "Becky's been hard-headed since we were kids. Whatever the reason is, she either believes I should know about it already, or it's so bad, she doesn't want me to know."

"Seriously, what could be so awful that she wouldn't tell you? Not telling me, I can understand, but you— you're like sisters."

Naomi shrugged. "I'll let her cool down for a few days and try again. Maybe I can convince her to meet for a drink after work. A couple of glasses of Shiraz may soften her or at least illicit some warm fuzzy feelings from our childhood adventures with Miriam."

"Well, it's probably not tied to the Miriam issue, but the only thing Becky wants from me is to convince Maria to convert. Maybe, I'll forget my rule do-not-intervene-with-wannabe-converts, this one time, and talk to the girl. It may not solve Becky's issue, but if it makes her happier, she may dig some forgiveness out of that stubborn heart of hers."

For a few moments, they silently sipped coffee, both absorbed in their own thoughts.

"Naomi," Laurie said. "Promise me you'll give Aaron a chance. I know you—you slammed the door shut after Jake left and pushed the furniture in front of it to block it from ever opening. Aaron has warm, honest eyes."

The sound of Ezra and Sarah trudging up the basement steps eliminated the need for Naomi to respond. Ezra burst through the door first. Sarah trailed behind him, giggling.

"What's so funny?" Naomi asked.

"Nothing, Mom. Just the movie," he replied.

Sarah covered her mouth to stop the laughter from erupting again.

Laurie and Naomi gave each other a look that said, "Do we really want to know what's going on here?" But, before either woman opened her mouth, the duo bolted toward the front door.

Laurie stood and pushed in her chair. It was nice to watch someone push it back into its proper spot under the table. After years of trying to teach Josh and Ezra, Naomi gave up.

Laurie and Sarah stood in the foyer, pulling on their boots and putting on their jackets. Before walking out the door, Laurie squeezed Naomi's hand. "Have a good time tonight. And I want all the details tomorrow."

✿ ✿ ✿

The grandfather clock in her foyer chimed 6:30, and the one on the oven read 6:33. An hour and a half to wait. It only took a few moments to put the mugs in the dishwasher, rinse out the coffee pot, and wipe off the table. The refrigerator contained a variety of leftovers—good, now she didn't have to cave in to Ezra's pleas for pizza money—"But Mom, there's nothing to eat in this house." She swore he couldn't find something to eat in a supermarket when he set his mind on pizza. Before closing the refrigerator door, she noticed the leftover bottle of wine inside the door rack. A half of glass couldn't hurt.

She set the wine glass on the dresser before walking into the bathroom—their disgustingly oversized master bathroom. After they bought the house, Jake insisted on knocking out the wall separating the bathroom from the smallest bedroom. Then, he decided the ceiling was too low. So he busted through to the attic and viola—the room had the intimacy of standing naked in a very fancy gymnasium. At least, he was considerate enough to design the room, so she could have her own vanity and chair. She always hated standing while putting on make-up.

The hot water felt wonderful, running down her back. The expensive lavender soap she saved for special occasions smelled divine. She lingered in the shower until her fingers began to prune. Then she stepped out, grabbed her robe from the hook, and wrapped her hair in a towel. The glass of wine called her name—the first gulp tasted pretty good and the second tasted even better.

After unfurling the towel, she combed out the knots and cursed herself for not bothering to color her hair. People always complimented her on her deep brown waves, but now the dark color just accentuated the gray. A collection of bottles, containing anti-wrinkle serum, firming moisturizer, a deep wrinkle filler, and SPF 30 hydrating foundation lined her vanity. Jake hated when she left any make-up or cream on the vanity. Since he moved out, she never put them in the drawer. But she didn't want to think about Jake, so she switched her attention to the image in the mirror. It looked its age, confirming her belief that cosmetic companies lied. But, in case they were telling the truth, she layered her face and neck with a little bit from each bottle, deciding that she

would probably look even older without it. The entire
process of getting ready took forty-five minutes. The
numbers shining from clock radio read 7:45. Nothing left
to do but sit and stress.

The doorbell rang at precisely 8:03 p.m. and the but-
terflies in her stomach took flight.

Miriam

Miriam plopped onto the sofa and shimmied up close
to her husband, Joe, who was flipping through the TV
channels—as usual. She pulled the remote control from
his hand and pushed the pause button. This got his attention.

"Joe, I've decided we should pay for Noah and Maria's honeymoon. I want to buy them a trip to Israel."

He looked at her, but didn't speak.

"We both know we have the money," she said.

"Sure, we have an extra five thousand dollars," he
said. "But—"

"Don't be cheap," Miriam interrupted. "The price of
the plane tickets is over two thousand dollars and a nice
hotel in Jerusalem doesn't come cheap, especially one
with a view of the old city. And, of course they'll need
money for meals. We don't want the poor things to spend
ten days eating falafel and *shawarma*."

"We don't?"

She patted his hand. "Of course not. I want them to be
able to enjoy the better restaurants in Jerusalem."

"Really?"

"Of course, where else, except maybe New York, can
you sit down to a lovely kosher meal in a first class dining room?"

"Squirrel Hill?"

"Drop the sarcasm. This is important. We'll give them a Visa gift card with five hundred dollars for food, and I think we should throw in an extra five hundred dollars for fun money."

Joe shook his head slowly. "Fun money?"

"Wait, I just realized something important. They'll need a rental car, exploring the country by bus is so...I don't know...uncomfortable and inconvenient."

Joe leaned forward elbows to knees and let out a groan.

"No," she said, shaking her head, "Forget the car. Israelis drive like crazy people. We can hire a tour guide and personal driver for them. Wouldn't it be great if the driver and the tour guide were the same person?"

"Marvelous." He clapped his hands together once and groaned—again.

"I calculate a ten-day trip would cost about ten thousand."

"Really? Ten thousand dollars," he said, leaning back into the sofa and crossing his arms in front of his chest.

"Why not? It's a good investment."

Joe laughed, not a happy laugh but more like a pained oh-great-my-wife-just-lost-her-mind type of laugh.

"Seriously," she said. "Maybe if they spend time in Israel, like we did, they'll fall in love with the place. And, maybe, just maybe, it will make Maria want to convert. Besides, it would be our small way of supporting the Israeli economy. "

"I'll write a check to an Israeli Foundation and tell them to deposit it into the Israeli economy, and I'll get a tax write-off."

"Funny," she replied.

"Becky didn't even invite you to the wedding. I know you love Noah, but this is extreme."

"No, Joe. It's not extreme. Extreme would be buying them an apartment in Jerusalem. This is just a little honeymoon, and it's what I want to do."

He shook his head and exhaled. She held her ground and remained silent until he broke the impasse.

"You two have been tighter than sisters since the day I met you. This hasn't always been so great for me, feeling like I had to please two wives. Right now, I know this rift is killing you, but she'll get over it. And I kind of like being married to just you."

Miriam pulled back. "No. She's not going to get over it—I feel it in my bones. I don't know why she's mad, but I know it's something serious," she said, clasping his hand between hers. "If there's a chance this will make her happy, it's worth every dime."

Joe shook his head.

Her eyes moistened. "Do you remember Rosh Hashanah when you and Simon kept everyone at the table laughing? That's what this is about—childhood and family."

He cocked his head, giving her an I-don't-understand-this-at-all look.

"Memories, Joe. It's all about memories. Your brother and sister confirm your history each time they say the words, 'remember when.' Brothers and sisters are connectors. They're the people who connect our past, present, and future."

His face softened as he reached for his wife's hand.

She sighed. "I could tell you stories about Elvis coming to our house every year to light the first Hanukkah candle, and there's no one in this world who could confirm if I'm lying or telling the truth."

Joe's face began to register understanding.

"After my parents died, I lost all connections to my childhood. The closest things I have are the memories I share with Becky and Naomi." Miriam stared at their clasped hands resting on her lap. "They really are the nearest thing I have to family, losing Becky is the equivalent of losing half of my family."

"Fine, I get it and I'm sorry. But does it really require me to spend thousands of dollars to keep you together?"

Her eyes drilled into his, pleading. "At this point, yes. Besides, Noah's never been to Israel."

Joe released her hand, reached for the remote, and aimed it at the cable box. "I'll think about it."

"Great, I'll book the trip tomorrow!" She jumped up from the sofa and headed toward the door.

"Wait, I said I'd think about it!"

Miriam trotted back to the sofa, leaned over, and kissed his cheek. "Think about it all you want. But while you're thinking, the flight ticket prices are going up."

He gave her a half-hearted sneer. Smiling, she wrapped her arms around him "I love you so much. Their honeymoon will be as amazing as ours. Watch TV now, I need to call Naomi."

Chapter 12

Naomi

Aaron looked distinguished, standing on her porch with snowflakes falling in the background. The entire scene reminded her of his last book. The descriptions he used in his novels actually turned Pittsburgh into fascinating place—a sign of true talent.

Naomi inhaled before opening the door. He stomped the snow from his shoes. "Gotta love this shitty Pittsburgh weather," he said, stepping into the foyer. "I now understand why all good Jews go to Miami. Viva la palm tree." He tilted his head and grinned—just like an awkward nineteen-year-old kid.

She smiled. "Come into the kitchen and don't bother taking off the shoes. I need to grab my bag and say good night to Ezra—not that he would even notice my absence."

"Nice house, Naomi," he said, walking toward the sliding glass door. "A yard, I miss having one. I'm sick of apartment living."

As he gazed through the glass, she yelled, "Goodnight" down the basement steps.

The words "See ya, Mom," blasted from the man cave. "How old is he?"

"Seventeen."

Aaron nodded, and his eyes sparkled in the soft light of the kitchen. He thrust his hands into the pockets of his coat. "I remember you at seventeen."

Her stomach completed a full somersault. Blood rushed to her face. Words—she needed words, but all she could muster was a stupid grin. The awkwardness that began in the synagogue continued. He moved next to her and placed his hand on the small of her back. A zing of electricity shot through a few neglected body parts.

He navigated her toward the front door, his hand lingering on her lower back. "Let's go find something to eat."

The conversation during the ride to the restaurant took on a neutral tone. He described the Pitt interview process, and like always, his depiction of people, down to the smallest detail, cracked her up.

He drove straight to a lovely restaurant on Mt. Washington. The weather must have deterred people from venturing out, because the crowd waiting to be seated was thin. The maître D ushered them to a white-linen-covered table with thickly padded chairs nestled into a corner where the two plate-glass windows joined—not the casual place she expected. They sipped Cabernet, enjoying the view of snow floating down onto the city.

"Naomi," he said, reaching across the table and grasping her hand. "You haven't changed."

A small lump rose into her throat as his hand lingered on top of hers. "Aaron, are you telling me that I looked middle-aged during college?"

His eyes lit up, and he leaned back into his chair, laughing. "You're nervous, and I can't believe you still crack jokes to hide it. Hey, you're not alone. I actually sang along with the songs on the car radio during the drive to your house. Now, you know that only happens when I'm really tense, or hungry. Today, it's definitely a combination."

She picked up the menu. "Fine, let's eat. It will stop you from singing and possibly put an end to the gymnastics meet inside my stomach."

They skipped the appetizers and went straight for the salads. "Today at the synagogue," Aaron said. "I overheard some talk about a drama occurring between Becky and Miriam over Noah's wedding. What's the story? It's been years since I've laughed over the stupidity of their wars. Entertain me."

She swallowed a forkful of lettuce. "I'm not sure if this one is funny. Actually, the situation is puzzling. Originally, I believed the feud began while we prepared the meal for the rabbi's last child's *brit milah*. You know Miriam can't boil water, and the only thing she likes to do in a kitchen is drink coffee and babble. Well, Becky got really angry and told her to 'either help or get out of the kitchen.'"

He set his fork down. "Yeah, I can picture the scene. Becky pointing her French manicured finger, and Miriam stomping out on her oversized feet."

"Aaron," she replied.

"We both know she has big feet. Continue the story." He flicked his wrist. The back of his hand told her to get to the point.

"As you know, I've been mediating their battles for thirty plus years. This afternoon, I tried to persuade Becky to send Miriam an invitation. I told her the brit luncheon fiasco wasn't worth ending a lifelong friendship." Naomi popped a fork full of salad into her mouth and tried to chew quickly. "My entire plea backfired. Becky let loose a tirade, implying I'm stupid if I believe she was upset over the luncheon incident. Then she informed me that hell would freeze over before they would ever be friends again."

The waiter silently cleared the salad plates, and before he walked away from the table, Aaron ordered two more Cabernets. "That's a good one," he said. "Reminds me of my daughter's behavior in elementary school. 'Daddy.'" He mimicked the voice of a little girl. "'I'm never ever going to invite Emily to my birthday party.' Emily being her best friend of the week." He grinned and then shifted his eyes from Naomi's face to the pink salmon on his plate and plunged in his fork.

"I missed that kind of drama—boys don't really care who comes to their birthday party as long as video games are involved. Right now, I'm truly perplexed," Naomi replied.

He picked up the fresh glass of wine, swirled it, and sipped. She gazed out the window. The moon broke through the clouds. The snowflakes continued their descent into the Monongahela River. New York was famous for its skyline, but viewing the Pittsburgh cityscape and rivers from above was spectacular.

"A mystery—I love a good mystery." Aaron interrupted the silence, which was lingering a bit too long. "Let's play detective. So, if this battle didn't begin over a luncheon, when did it commence? Did anything out of the ordinary occur in the days or weeks before the birth of this boy?"

She leaned back into the soft pad of the chair. Gosh, he was still sexy as hell. As he talked about Miriam and Becky, flashes of her fingers running through his curls sidetracked her.

"Naomi, any thoughts on this?"

Oops, she'd spaced out for a moment. Hopefully, he would write it off as a moment of memory mining. "Hard to say because Becky's dad died three months earlier. She was an emotional disaster—hypersensitive. Miriam organized the entire shiva and never left Becky's side. You know how much we all loved Mr. Greenburg. My parents flew in from Florida for the funeral. Maybe Miriam said something stupid during the funeral."

"Both of Miriam's parents are dead. Her father died about fifteen years after her mother," he said.

"Sounds about right, she died a little over a year before Noah's Bar Mitzvah, but how did you know that?"

His face tinged a bit pink. "Unfortunately, my mother tends to be the lead gossip connection in the Yenta Network. She has dirt on almost everyone who ever lived in Squirrel Hill for more than a month."

She laughed. "Hey, maybe listening to her stories is how you turned into such a fabulous writer."

He shook his head, appearing to be unhappy with her statement. "I remember something my mother said after Miriam's father, Al, passed away. It bothered me for years and thinking about it now is still unpleasant."

Naomi leaned forward. "You can't just dangle it and not tell me."

"Actually, I think the world would be okay if I dropped it, but I won't. I happened to be in Pittsburgh the week after his funeral because my mom had just been discharged from the hospital. I remember hearing her talking to someone on the telephone. She kept repeating 'no.' Then, I heard her say, and, believe me, I remember it verbatim. 'Can you believe Mildred sat in the first row between her husband, Sam, and her daughter, Becky, sobbing like she was the widow? The chutzpah, everyone in the room knew Mildred and Al started running around together a week after he buried his poor wife. Poor Sam such a nice man—shame on Mildred—that hussy.'"

Her throat constricted, and words failed to form sentences inside her head. "What?"

"I had a feeling you didn't know," he said, "but many people in the old neighborhood did. Becky's mom and Miriam's dad carried on an affair for years."

A chill rushed through her. She stared at him, but her mind's eye saw something else…

✡ ✡ ✡

Naomi rolled onto her stomach and peeked over the edge of the top bunk. Two congealed slices of pizza laying in a greasy box stared up at her. Yuck. She flopped onto her back and tossed her forearm over her eyes. It didn't stop the pounding inside her head.

Leftover alcohol molecules fuzzed her memory except for a vague recollection of Becky opening a third bottle of wine and Miriam ordering a pizza.

Naomi looked back down at the greasy box. Beside it sat an ashtray, heaping with menthol cigarette butts, and an overturned coffee mug beached in a wine puddle.

Miriam rolled out of the bottom bunk and staggered—one sock on, one sock off—across the shag carpet to the sole dormitory room window. "It stinks in here."

She whipped open the faded drapes and grabbed the old wooden window frame, groaning as she heaved it open.

Becky crushed her comforter around her head. "Shut the damn window. It's freakin' February."

"Keep the blanket on," Miriam said. "Cold is better than the stench." She took two steps and hinged over at the waist. "Why did you guys let me drink so much?"

"Because you're a fun drunk," Naomi said, propping her chin on her crossed forearms. "Last night was like the old days when we had sleepovers. Remember?"

Becky emerged from her padded cocoon, stretched her arms above her head, and moaned. "Yeah, but I don't recall us drinking wine in the old days."

Naomi grabbed the stuffed elephant lying at the foot of the bed and chucked it at Becky. "That's not what I mean. I mean the three of us, hanging out, talking, and laughing."

"Yeah, we had the best sleepovers," Miriam said.

"I wish I could live here," Naomi said. "High School stinks without you guys."

"Graduation is only a few months away." Becky ambled over to the closet. "Have you decided, Naomi? Will it be Pitt with us or Columbia with him?"

"I don't have a chance of getting into Columbia," Naomi replied. "I'll be one more Squirrel Hill girl moving down Forbes Avenue into the deluxe accommodations of the Pitt Towers."

She rolled and faced the wall. Just thinking about him in New York City and her stuck in Pittsburgh caused her heart to ache.

Becky grabbed the towel from the hook on the closet door and pulled her shower caddy off the top shelf. "Hangover or no hangover, the library reference desk calls." On her way out of the room, Becky stopped next to Naomi's bunk. She reached up and patted the top of Naomi's head. "Happy eighteenth birthday, Dumb-Dumb."

Miriam stumbled around looking for her glasses. To put an end to her frustration, Naomi jumped down and found them, hidden under the open lid of the pizza box.

"Thanks." Miriam took them from Naomi's hand as the phone rang.

"Hello," Miriam said. "Sure Mrs. Cohen, you can talk to Naomi."

"Yes, Mom," Naomi said.

"You and Miriam need to come home right now," her mom said.

Her mother's voice squeaked like it did when she was

crying. "Give us an hour to get dressed and eat. Then we'll catch the bus."

"No, you need to come home right now. Get a cab."

Naomi stared at the floor. "I don't have enough money for a cab."

She turned toward Miriam, who mouthed the words "What's wrong?"

Naomi shrugged. Maybe Miriam would help with the cab fare.

"I'll pay the driver when you get here and bring Becky home too."

"Why do I need to bring Becky home? Is something wrong?"

"Stop asking questions. Just get moving."

"Fine. We'll get a cab as soon as Becky gets out of the shower." Naomi hung up the phone.

"What's the matter?" Miriam asked.

"I don't know, but it sounded like my mom was crying. She wants all three of us home right now. I'll tell Becky to hurry up, while you get dressed."

The next morning, Naomi, Miriam, and Becky stood, surrounded by headstones engraved with the names of people who died before they were born. Rain drizzled from the heavy gray clouds, mixing with the tears streaming down Naomi's face. Becky and Naomi linked their arms through Miriam's. It reminded Naomi of the paper-ring chains they made every fall to decorate their *Sukkahs*.

Naomi gazed at her mother dressed in the same black suit she wore to her aunt Golda's funeral. It was an ugly suit. Naomi's mother and Becky's mother flanked Miriam's father, gripping his elbows. His body trembled, and tears reddened his eyes. It appeared that only the strength of the women held him up. She didn't want to look at him. He didn't look like himself. Miriam's dad was the funny dad. He teased all three of them mercilessly. Naomi loved it. Her family was much more serious. Today, he looked ready to crumble to the ground like one of the dead leaves disintegrating under the melting spots of snow. She turned away and watched her dad and Becky's father—suited, straight-backed, and red eyed, standing beside their wives.

The rabbi began chanting the ancient Jewish prayer for the dead—Kaddish, over the dirt-covered coffin belonging to Miriam's mother.

Naomi released Miriam's hand and swiped at the tear escaping from the corner of her eye. She scanned the people surrounding the grave and imagined that, from a distance, they all looked like dancers waiting for the music to begin.

✡ ✡ ✡

She pulled her mind from the memory and returned her gaze to Aaron's face. "After Miriam's mother died, my parents, Becky's parents, and Miriam's dad continued to get together for Shabbat dinners and summer cookouts."

"I remember a few Shabbat dinners at your house. That group was fun."

Naomi looked at a red wine spot staining the table cloth. "After a while, Miriam's dad fell out of the picture. I always attributed it to third-wheel syndrome. Do you think my parents knew?"

Aaron shrugged one shoulder.

"There's no way Becky and Miriam knew about this." Naomi shook her head. "Like I said, Miriam took care of Becky throughout the entire funeral and shiva. Impossible—neither knew." For a moment, she gazed at the broccoli lying on her plate, and then looked up. "No, my parents didn't know." The statement lacked confidence, because she was unable to convince herself that the words were true.

Aaron shifted his gaze to the window. The air moved in and out of her lungs, but barely. Her ribs crunched against the underside of her skin. He reached across the table and clasped her hand. "Naomi, I've missed talking to you. I never thought of you as just a girlfriend—you were my best friend for a long time. I wanted this evening to be light and fun. As impossible as it may seem right now, could we switch the conversation to a less difficult topic? Let's talk about our miserable divorces, instead. I'll complain about the exorbitant amount of alimony I have to pay, and you can whine about your cheap ex-son-of-a-bitch, and the mere pennies he gives you."

She pulled her hand away. "Aaron, I'm stunned. I don't think my brain can change subjects."

"So, Naomi, is there any chance of us having sex after dinner?"

Cabernet almost exploded from her mouth. "Aaron!" she said, and red drops dribbled from the corners of her mouth.

"Sorry," he said, not looking the least bit apologetic. "I needed something to make you laugh and that popped into my head." A self-satisfied grin spread across his face, and his eyes lit up. "Let's order a couple of unhealthy deserts and commiserate."

Her entrée was so-so, but the desert was amazing. They devoured a slice of raspberry swirl cheesecake and a peanut and chocolate confection that defied words. When the ramrod stiff waiter offered them a coffee refill, Aaron suggested one more glass of wine before ending the evening.

She didn't protest.

"You really haven't changed, Naomi, still a sarcastic wit with a sweet heart."

"I don't know about the sweet heart. The divorce left some jagged scars."

He sipped his wine, placed it back on the table, and reached for her hand. For a few moments, they sat quietly—this time it was warm, comfortable silence.

"So, how did you manage to let a beautiful fashion model wife walk out the door? From the pictures, I've seen, most men would crawl across a football field for the opportunity to touch her spiked heels."

"Wow, what a loaded statement." Aaron grasped the table and pushed back, elbows locked, feigning insulted. Then he released his grip and relaxed into his chair. "First of all, we both walked out the door, so don't try to make me sound shallow. I didn't marry a model. We met during my senior year at Columbia. She was a freshman majoring in film. The modeling stuff came later."

"Sorry, I didn't mean to imply—I just mean—she's so beautiful."

"So are you. If you had grown four more inches, you would have made a great model," he said, and the dim light of the room failed to dull his eyes.

"Flirt," she said, tilting her head to indicate she still expected him to answer the question.

"Our marriage ended with a cliché. We grew apart. When our youngest left for college, the apartment felt cold. Don't get me wrong, we ended on decent terms—good enough to meet for an occasional lunch. Right now, she's working day and night, trying to launch a new modeling agency."

"That sounds very exciting and glamorous."

"And very ambitious. Personally, I'm too tired for that kind of ambition. For years, with each book published, I did interviews, appearances, and book signings. Now,

I'm a tired introvert who wants to come home."

The conversation continued without a lull until Naomi noticed the snowflakes were beginning to resemble a junior blizzard. It was time to leave.

✡ ✡ ✡

Sunday morning began with a ringing telephone. And an excited Laurie asking for details.

"Laurie, we're not in high school."

"You might not be, but I am. Did he kiss you? And was it a real kiss or a good-to-see-you-old-buddy kiss?

Naomi flopped back on her pillow—laughing. When she finally stopped, she told Laurie it was a wonderful evening and the good night kiss was just fine.

"What the hell does just 'fine' mean?"

"I haven't had my coffee. I'll call you back when I have a hot cup in my hand."

"Forget that," Laurie replied. "Dan's bowling, and Sarah slept over at a friend's house. I'll be on your doorstep in fifteen minutes. Wait, if he's lying next to you in that big bed, kick him out."

"You're crazy."

"That's what Dan always tells me." The line went dead.

Outside, three inches of snow covered the sidewalk leading to her door. Time to fight with Ezra, who hated shoveling snow more than anything. She made the bed and gathered up the wrinkled outfit she wore for the date. Before shoving it down the laundry chute, she smelled the neckline of her shirt, hoping a bit of Aaron's deliciously masculine scent lingered from the brief moment their bodies pressed together during the kiss.

The kitchen held the remains of Ezra's night and, based on the number of plates in the sink, he didn't spend it alone. She walked down the steps to the basement and found exactly what she expected. Ezra and two friends crashed out on the worn sofa and the floor, exhausted from a tough night of video games. She switched off the light they had left on, and shut down the Xbox.

The smell of coffee engulfed the kitchen and she hummed while pouring it into her cup. The first few sips passed through her lips and over her tongue. The warmth reminded her of the good night kiss and the lusciousness of Aaron's lips on hers. She set the mug down on the counter next to the sink. *Was it really a friend kiss or...*

"Yuk," she said out loud, seeing the schmutz left over from last night's teenage eat-a-thon ingrained into the plates. She turned on the hot water and let it run over them. Gazing out the window above the sink, she smiled. The snow continued falling, but the sun's rays broke through the thinning clouds, replacing the gray sky of the day before.

She loaded the rinsed plates into the dishwasher, grabbed her mug from the countertop, and settled into her favorite spot at the table. It was time to push Aaron from her mind and focus on a way to approach Becky about the affair. This turned out to be futile. Mental movies of their parents drinking cocktails and barbecuing hamburgers on Miriam's parents' patio distracted her. She always viewed the little group as a happy extended family.

She shuddered off the image and shifted her attention beyond the glass door to a cardinal sitting in the tree behind her house. The bird appeared stark against the white of snow-covered tree branches. It reminded her of a Christmas card she once received from an acquaintance who didn't understand Jews don't celebrate Christmas. *Funny, what we believe people should know, but they don't.* It was a pretty card. The cardinal flew away, and the doorbell rang.

Naomi opened the door. Laurie stood on her front
porch, pink cheeked and grinning.

"Well?" she asked as a devilish glint sparked from her
eyes. "Sex? No sex?"

"Stop it!" Naomi playfully swatted her friend's arm. "I
told you, he kissed me good night. Don't get all excited.
It was a friendly kiss not a kiss-kiss."

"Aw..."

Naomi tried not to laugh, but the disappointment reg-
istering on Lauri's face cracked her up.

"Stop laughing," Laurie scolded. "This is serious. You
deserve a good roll between the sheets. Are you going to
see each other again?" She tugged off her left boot and
dropped it onto the small rug next to the door. It was supposed to be for Ezra's friend's wet shoes, but the boys
ignored it.

"You know we are. Esther's Shabbat dinner next
week. Remember, her grand attempt at matchmaking."

"I love that woman," Laurie replied as she hung her
coat in the hallway closet. "Pour me a cup of coffee and
tell me about your date."

"No."

Laurie followed Naomi into the kitchen and settled into Jake's old spot at the table. Naomi walked to the refrigerator and grabbed the small carton of half and half
from the shelf. She filled the cup and handed it to her
friend. "We have more important topics to discuss. Last
night, I may have discovered the source of the Becky-
Miriam mess." It pained Naomi to convey such intimate
information to Laurie, almost slanderous. But who else
could she trust with the information? Under normal circumstances, when she needed advice she called Becky or
Miriam or both. More than any time in her life, she needed advice. Because she didn't have any idea how to approach either woman with this information.

Laurie would keep the secret and only use the knowledge to help the situation. Spreading gossip wasn't her style. She was a natural born listener. Naomi inhaled and on her exhale, she launched into the story.

Laurie left Naomi's house at 10:30 a.m., declaring herself stumped. Together, they failed to generate one decent plan for mediating the mess. Naomi's date with Aaron became a mere footnote in the conversation.

Naomi tidied up the kitchen, walked through her living room and dining room, holding a dust rag but not doing much dusting. Ezra and his friends woke and invaded the kitchen. The three very tall teenage boys begged her to make pancakes. She relented without much of a fight and became pleasantly distracted, listening to them talk about school, girls, and video games. Then the phone rang.

"Don't you ever check your voicemail?" Excitement always made Miriam's voice squeakier. Today, not even an oil can would have helped.

"Sometimes."

"Well, I called you three times last night. We need to talk. I think I found the solution. I'll meet you at Panera in an hour—my treat."

Naomi hit the end call button and stared at the small screen. She scrolled through her contacts and hit the send button on the listing for "Mom."

Her mother answered after the third ring and launched into her usual interrogation regarding the well-being of Josh and Ezra. Naomi knew it was best to let mother do what she needed to do. Naomi referred to her mom's phone style as firecracker speech—open with a barrage of questions, barely listen to the answers, and eventually run out of things to ask. Sometimes it tried Naomi's patience, but there was no way to stop it.

Naomi answered the final question about the boys and

without missing an inhale, her mom launched into a dramatic description of the wonderful dinner she and her dad attended the evening before at some couple named Aronson's house.

"Mom, I need to ask you an important question. Please, tell me about the dinner another time."

"Okay, what's the question?" her mother asked, not the least bit sensitive to the graceful way Naomi just told her to shut up.

"I heard an awful story and you're the only person I know who may be capable of verifying the truth of it."

"Wow, honey, this sounds serious. Tell me." Her mom used the word "serious," but her tone rang excited, like she was about to become involved in a fun mystery.

"Is it true that Miriam's dad and Becky's mom had an affair after Miriam's mom died?"

Silence…Breathing…

"Mom?"

"Who told you this?"

"Not important."

"Yes, it's true. But it isn't a simple story."

"Of course it's simple. They either slept together or they didn't." Naomi clenched her fist and rolled her neck. Her mom's answer smacked her into the realization that mediating those two puffer fish was going to be deadly.

"I hate talking on this phone. I wish you were here. It would be easier," her mom said.

"Just talk."

"The three of us were best friends, just like you, Becky, and Miriam. You remember Agnes, Miriam's mother? She was an amazing seamstress—should have worked in Paris. But she wasn't a very warm person by nature. Always a bit distant, but I loved her anyway. Most people don't know this, but Miriam's parents were an arranged marriage.

"Arranged marriage, as in no choice?"

"I don't know the exact details of the arrangement, I just know the parents shook hands and Agnes and Al were married.

Naomi's mind drifted from her mother's words. An arranged marriage? Like the burka wearing women in Afghanistan? Arranged marriages only happened in third world countries or novels. They most certainly didn't happen to women like Miriam's mother. A woman who no one ever described as a cupcake. Agnes swatted her wooden spoon at any kid who cursed or, even worse, stepped a toe into her sewing room without an invitation.

"Al grew-up in the house next door to Agnes. He loved her from the time he was old enough to notice girls, which could explain why the parents made the match in the first place. Agnes didn't love Al. She was a dutiful wife and a good mother, but I don't believe she ever came to feel any real warmth toward him. And Hashem knows how hard he tried to earn her affection—fancy vacations, a beautiful house, and all the other trappings of success."

"Okay, I'll accept that she agreed to the arrangement, but why didn't she leave him? A lot of parents in the old neighborhood got divorced."

"The man Agnes loved died in Korea," her mom replied. "She was heartbroken when the news of his death arrived."

"Okay, I get the story. Now connect it to Becky's mom, please."

"This part is harder. Miriam's dad and Becky's dad went to high school together, played baseball together, and roomed together in college. If one of them was a girl, they would have married—inseparable"

"Then this affair must have killed Becky's father."

"That's the odd part of this story. Their friendship

caused the situation. After Miriam's mother died, Al spent his evenings with Becky's parents, Sam and Mildred. Sam and Al went from being two buddies to a threesome." Her mom chuckled. "Threesome, how appropriate is that word?"

"Not funny."

"Sorry. Anyway, during all the time they spent together, Mildred fell in love with Miriam's dad. She loved Sam and she loved Al. She cried to me about it all of the time, saying Agnes was so cold and Al deserved a little love. She tried to hide it from her husband, but you know how small Squirrel Hill is."

"Why did Sam stay with her?" Naomi asked?

"I can't answer that question. When Mildred killed herself, I feared what Sam would do—afraid he would go after Al. But she battled demons much more powerful than guilt over an affair."

Naomi heard the pain in her mother's voice.

"I'll never forget the day Becky found Mildred lying on the bathroom floor. Sam called me. I could barely understand a word he said, but I knew enough to drop what I was doing and run to their house. One of the worse days of my life. She was and always will be my best friend and I do know this, Sam loved Mildred until the day he died."

"I think Becky found out about the affair. She's refusing to invite Miriam to Noah's wedding."

Her mother moaned.

Naomi imagined her shaking her head and pursing her lips. "It's as if I'm in the middle of a fight between sisters. It's awful."

"Speaking of sisters, how's yours? Since the last baby, she never calls. Do you see her?"

"I try to call or stop by at least once a week. She's fine, just exhausted as usual. Mom, back to Miriam and Becky, please."

"Naomi, I don't know what to tell you. The situation caused everyone pain, but it happened a long time ago. It shouldn't have any bearing on Miriam and Becky's friendship."

Naomi hung-up the phone and walked to her china cabinet, wishing her mother's last statement was true, but she doubted it. The bottom drawer contained the bag of peanut M&Ms she kept hidden from herself. Only five left—bummer. It was time to meet Miriam.

✡ ✡ ✡

Miriam waved to her from a booth in the back of the restaurant. Naomi navigated through the aisle and around a few orange tray toting customers. She curled into the booth and set her bag down.

"Joe and I are going to send Noah and Maria on honeymoon to Israel!" Miriam blurted, twiddling her fingers like she always did when she was excited. "But I promised, my treat. What do you want to eat?"

"I'm not hungry. Just a cup of coffee."

"Let's celebrate and eat something gooey and calorie infested." Miriam pulled her wallet from her purse. "I'll be right back."

Naomi leaned forward and put her head down, resting it on her crossed forearms. *What the hell? This is getting worse. Yoga breathe.* She inhaled through her nose and exhaled slowly, straightening in her seat and rubbing her temples. Inside her purse, her phone vibrated. She looked at the screen, not a phone call, a text message. *I had a great time last night and have the afternoon free. Would you be interested in meeting me at the museum? Remember the Hall of Architecture?*

Naomi bit her bottom lip, unable to ignore the flash of embarrassment rushing through her. The last time they went to the museum together, a docent caught them making out in the back corner of the Hall of Architecture. The upset woman lectured them on the inappropriateness of public displays of affection and asked them to leave. Instead of leaving, Aaron pulled her by the arm into the Botany Hall, and they picked up where they left off.

What time? she typed back.

At 2:00. The clock on the cell phone read noon. *Would love to meet you. Having coffee with Miriam now. If I'm a few minutes late, forgive me,* she typed slowly on the phone that Ezra suggested donating to the Smithsonian.

Miriam set the tray on the table. "Who are you typing at?"

"Aaron, he asked me to meet him at the museum at two."

Miriam pushed the tray toward Naomi. "One coffee and a sesame bagel, cream cheese, and butter on the side. I didn't know which you would be in the mood for. There are two squirts of half and half in your coffee—just the way you like it. This little dalliance with Aaron is getting exciting." She said "getting exciting" in a sing-song voice.

"Thanks for the bagel." Naomi sipped the hot coffee. "This coffee is perfect. And, as for Aaron, no excitement, just friends catching up." After the words left her mouth, Naomi wondered if she was a hundred percent sure she was telling the truth. But now wasn't the time to contemplate that subject. She switched her attention back to the situation sitting across the table. "Why are you buying Noah a honeymoon and how will this solve the problem?"

Miriam launched into the same speech she gave Joe.

Naomi sat ramrod straight, listening and slowly rolling her coffee cup between her hands. "That is an incredibly generous offer. But I don't want to see you get hurt if it doesn't work. You know how stubborn Becky is."

Miriam leaned back into the vinyl pad of the booth. Her eyes began to tear. "You and Becky are my only family. I know you're not real family, but you're the closest thing I have. Someday, my kids will get married, and I won't have one family member to invite to the wedding—only your family and Becky's. Do you understand why this *balagan* is killing me?"

Naomi reached over and patted her friend's hand. "I know that's why this bullshit is killing you. It's killing me, too, but, I don't know how to help."

"If Becky would tell me what I did, I'd apologize. When I call her, she hangs up on me."

Naomi stared into her coffee cup, mentally wrestling with the information she held.

Tears dripped down her friend's face. Naomi knew that this was not the time to bring up the affair. She needed to speak with Becky first. "If you believe this honeymoon plan will soften Becky, do what you need to do. I'll pray it jars her out of this what-ever-it-is, but you have to prepare yourself for the possibility of it backfiring."

Miriam blew her nose on the rough brown napkin. "I could never hurt her like she's hurting me."

Naomi squeezed Miriam's hand a bit tighter. "I know." But the words brought back a long-buried memory...

✡ ✡ ✡

They loved hanging out in Miriam's bedroom. It was so pretty, walls painted pale pink, white furniture and a pink eyelet comforter covered her bed. "Becky, you know you're not allowed to use nail polish in Miriam's room," Naomi said.

Becky sat on the edge of the bed, nail polish remover

between her legs and a bottle of bright red nail polish resting on her thigh. "Don't worry, nothing is going to happen." As she turned her head to look at Naomi, the nail polish toppled off her leg. The red polish oozed from the bottle and onto the pristine fabric of the comforter.

"Oh, my gosh." Naomi watched as a blood-red liquid stain grew bigger by the second. "You're dead."

"Quick, hand me a towel." Becky's eyes filled with panic.

The towel just smeared the stain, making it worse. "When Miriam gets out of the bathroom, she'll see the stain. What am I going to say? She's going to kill me. Maybe I should wet the towel with nail polish remover."

Naomi shook her head. "That will smear it even more."

Becky stared at the red mark, no longer trying to remove it. Her head shot up when the bedroom door open. "Woo," she exhaled—Miriam, not her mother.

When she noticed the splotch, Miriam's eyes widened and she rushed to the bed. "What the heck, Becky?" she asked, gathering the stained part of her comforter into her hand.

"I'm so sorry, Miriam. I'll tell your mom, I did it. I snuck in the nail polish and tried to paint my nails while you were in the bathroom. You didn't know anything about it. If I tell her the truth, she can't be mad at you."

"Yes, she will. She'll be mad at both of us," Miriam replied, tears forming in the corner of her eyes. "Actually, she'll be furious at all three of us. Naomi, you should have stopped her."

"Me?" Naomi looked at Miriam as though she had left her brain in the bathroom. "No one can talk Becky out of anything."

The three girls sat silently, staring at the massive mess.

"It's reversible," Miriam practically shouted. "Let's flip it over, that way my mom won't notice it for a few days. Then, I'll say I did it, and you two won't get in trouble."

"Miriam, that's not fair. You weren't even in the room when it happened," Naomi said, walking over to the bed. Together, she and Miriam lifted the blanket, flipped it over, and remade it in her mother's approved fashion.

Miriam sat down on the floor. "You're my friends. Why should all three of us get in trouble? I'll be grounded no matter what, so I'll take all the blame."

✡ ✡ ✡

Naomi entered The Carnegie Museum of Natural History through the rear entrance. As she began her descent down the ramp that led to the lobby, she spotted Aaron at the bottom. He waved before she could. His smile could have melted the steel sculptures lining the giant foyer. His eyes made her long for the warm sand of the Caribbean. Such the opposite of Jake, his gray eyes smoldered, but lacked warmth—a deep, cold New England sea.

As much as she hated to admit it, there were nights she lay beside Jake, remembering what it felt like to be wrapped in Aaron's arms. Actually, what she fantasized about most was the way Aaron kissed her on the soft spot behind her ear. She raised her arm slightly over her head and waved back.

He greeted her with a huge hug and then stepped back to loop the string of the admission tag around the button of her blouse. She stifled a laugh, because this tiny touch aroused her more than Jake had in years.

"Art side first or natural history side?" he asked, while giving a slight tug to the tag to make sure it wouldn't come off.

"You pick."

"Art." He linked his fingers through hers and led her back to the ramp she just walked down.

They wandered through the galleries laughing like college students, making fun of the fat women splayed across the canvases of the old masters. In the abstract section, prompted by a large white canvas with blue drips, they told each other stories of their children's adventures in elementary school. When they reached an enormous sculpture comprised of giant paper clips, coat hangers, railroad ties, and pink ribbons, Aaron doubled over laughing.

Naomi looked at the artwork. "I don't get it."

"Of course you don't. There's nothing to get. I met this guy at a cocktail party once."

Again, he started laughing. This time Naomi joined in, not having any idea why she was laughing, other than watching him do it made her happy.

Aaron caught his breath. "He was dressed in a broccoli-green silk shirt, a kilt, and combat boots. He insisted everyone refer to him as R Squared. I was with my ex-wife. He tried to convince her to model for his next sculpture. Seeing this, I wish she'd done it. She would be a sculpture of shark teeth, money and slim fast cans."

"That's terrible, Aaron."

"You're right. She's not that bad, no shark teeth. Enough art, I want to see this new upgraded dinosaur exhibit."

Children and tired-looking parents pushing even smaller children in strollers packed the exhibit. Most of the adults looked like they needed a drink and a nap. Some of the kids squealed, bouncing around in excitement. Others screamed out of the sheer terror of seeing the large bones strung together like beads on a bracelet.

She and Aaron bolted toward the door, not even bothering to read the information on the bones.

"I forgot how crazy it gets here on a Sunday. Let's go to the Hall of Minerals and Gems."

They walked inside, and Naomi remembered how much she loved this exhibit. It was fairly empty, a few college students and an older couple. They meandered through, stopping to admire certain specimens or to concoct fantasy schemes of robbing the glass display cases. Naomi's heart floated, feeling lighter than it had in years.

In the back corner, Aaron stopped in front of a tall glass case. He reached behind her back and clasped his hand against her hip. Before she could ask what he was looking at, he pulled her around and kissed her—this time it wasn't friendly.

Naomi's knees weaken and her heart pounded, but most of all she felt her lips moving with his.

"Sorry," he said, thrusting his hands into the pockets of his jeans. "I really wanted to wait and do that in the Hall of Architecture, but I couldn't take another minute."

Naomi knew her face was still red. The blood didn't want to flow back down into her body. She couldn't speak, partly from embarrassment and partly from the overwhelming desire to kiss him again.

"It's okay. This was a nice place to do it." Gosh, she sounded so stupid.

"Maybe we could do it again when we get there?" he asked, looking down at his shoes.

"Maybe," she replied.

The rest of the afternoon blurred. When they reached their spot, he did kiss her again.

"After I got over being totally devastated and angry over our breakup, I realized that every time something exciting happened in my life, I wanted to tell you. Don't get me wrong, at one time I was completely in love with my ex-wife, but she never became a best friend like you."

Naomi didn't know how to respond. It was the same situation with her and Jake, but if she told him that, it wouldn't sound real—more like she was parroting him.

"We did have fun together." They walked in silence for a while, a very heavy silence. Naomi broke through. "Remember the first time we met? I volunteered to work on the school newspaper, and you, Mr. Big Shot Editor, wanted to interview me first. You were such a snob."

"Funny, I remember that day too, but my most prominent memory is that we were making out in the darkroom before the interview was even over."

Naomi slapped him in the arm. "You were supposed to forget that part. I didn't want you to think I always kissed people after the first introduction."

Aaron chuckled. "Hell, I didn't care. I was just glad you were kissing me."

After lunch, Aaron walked her to her car—more kissing. "I have to fly to New York in the morning. I'll be back in Pittsburgh on Thursday night."

"Does that mean you, your mom and son will make it to Esther's for dinner on Shabbat?"

"Mom, yes. Son, no. And I can't wait. I heard Esther works miracles with a chicken and an eggplant. If you don't have plans, may I book you for Saturday night?"

Naomi nodded.

✡ ✡ ✡

Miriam

Miriam's fingers breezed along the keyboard. The screen, in front of her, flashed departure times from New York to Tel Aviv. She had to coordinate the flights from Pittsburgh to New York because she didn't want them to suffer through a six-hour layover.

Joy bubbled through her. Her only regret was she

wouldn't be there to see Noah and Maria's face the first time they glimpsed Jerusalem sprawled out majestically over the mountain tops.

She booked them into the King David Hotel. The same hotel she and Joe stayed in during their honeymoon. The history and tradition of the King David would add ambiance to the adventure. As she typed her credit card number into the website, a sensation of peace replaced the stress that pounded in her head and untied the knot in her neck. Becky would forgive her, and life would return to normal. Once the hotel booking was completed, she began searching for a tour guide. It didn't take her long to realize that finding one that met her requirements wouldn't be as easy as she expected.

The tour guide needed to be educated in history. There was nothing worse than a tour guide who just repeated the standard speech and had no ability to answer the more complex questions that two educated young people like Noah and Maria would ask.

The guide would also be doubling as a driver, so the person needed to have an outstanding driver safety record. Finally, the guide needed to speak perfect English. She didn't want Maria to miss out on anything if the guide mixed Hebrew and English.

After searching for a half hour, she located a private guide from Tel Aviv whose credentials met her standards. She booked him for their entire trip.

The question of who to tell first, Noah or Becky lingered in her mind. She pondered the idea of asking Naomi for an opinion, but changed her mind.

Becky

Becky sat on the overstuffed sofa waiting for Maria to

step out of the dressing room to model another white
fluffy concoction of fabric. Becky didn't want to be anywhere near Maria in a white dress and watching the girl's
mother sob with joy made her want to puke. Hell, she
would rather be sitting in the dentist's chair having a root
canal without Novocain. How did she let Noah talk her
into this? "Bonding opportunity." *Screw bonding.*

Maria stepped out from behind the chintz curtain
swathed in a silk column dress that transformed her from
a young college graduate to a regal princess. Becky
couldn't help but gasp. It was impossible not to see what
Noah saw in this girl.

"Oh, oh, that is the dress," her mother, June, said,
clapping her hands and springing onto her toes like an
overexcited kindergartner. Both women turned their
heads toward Becky, their faces covered in anticipation.
Even Becky couldn't be a bitch.

"That dress is simply stunning." Before Becky could
say any more, her phone rang. The name Naomi flashed
on the screen.

"I'll be finished with work in a half hour. Let's meet
for a drink," Naomi said.

"I'm not at work. I'm in Shady Side with Maria and
her mother, buying dresses."

"Fine, I'll drive over to Walnut Street and meet you
after you're finished shopping or are you having dinner
with them?"

Becky held the phone tightly to her ear and mouthed
the word "emergency," while walking out of the dressing
room area.

She began speaking, once she was sure she was out of
their earshot. "Hell, no. I'm not spending a second more
than I have to with these women. This actually gives me
an excuse to ditch out early. See you soon." Becky hung
up the phone.

"As much as I hate to break this party up, that was my best friend. Something has come up, and she needs me. Buy that dress, Maria. And, June, I liked the silver-colored dress you tried on first the best. Toot-a loo." Becky grabbed her bag, put her shoes back on, and bolted out the front door. *A drink—Naomi has impeccable timing.*

Becky reached the agreed-upon bar, knowing that Naomi wouldn't arrive for another half hour. She ordered a glass of red wine, pulled out her phone, and checked her email. Client, client, she couldn't care less about their legal problems.

Part of her wanted to tell them to get a new lawyer and leave her the hell alone, but the money they shelled out for petty contract squabbles and custody agreements was helping to fund this ridiculous wedding.

Becky loved this bar. Leather upholstery covered the booths, and the entire bar smelled expensive. Naomi gracefully slid into the seat across from her and placed her purse next to her. Sometimes Becky wondered how Naomi managed to get through almost fifty years without realizing that she was gorgeous.

"Hey, friend, I heard some gossip this morning about you and Aaron—kissing in the museum." Becky made a clicking sound with her tongue and shook her head in false disapproval. "Is he still a good kisser?"

"You talked to Laurie."

"Yeah, some best friend you are," Becky said. "You should have called me first, because getting anything out of Laurie requires me to go into lawyer interrogation mode."

"I didn't call either of you. She picked up Sarah on Sunday evening and interrogated me for fifteen minutes. Besides, you have enough to think about."

"Well, I'm thinking about you and Aaron now, and

it's a nice diversion. Do you think you two will get together again?"

Naomi didn't reply, just shrugged.

"Come on, don't tell me there wasn't a spark. He's
still handsome, and those eyes could melt a statue."

Naomi blushed. "The kiss was nice. But don't turn into Esther and try to match us."

"Fine, I'll drop it. But you should feel guilty for deny-
ing me a bit of fun right now."

"I didn't call you to talk about Aaron."

Becky looked at Naomi and didn't like the serious expression covering her face. "Who died?"

"No one died, Becky. I think I know why you are angry at Miriam, and if I'm correct, it's not her fault."

Becky looked at her, eyebrows furled. "Say it."

"It's painful to think about it. Don't make me say it
out loud."

"What do you know, Naomi?"

"There was an affair. It started after Miriam's mom
died."

Becky wanted to scream, yell, or throw something at
the wall. Instead, tears streamed down her cheeks. Humiliation overwhelmed her.

"How did you find out? Or have you always known?"

"No, I just found out. It doesn't matter how, but my
mother confirmed it. She knew."

"I found out after our Hanukkah get-together. Remember, I promised to empty my parents' house?"

Naomi nodded.

"While emptying the closet, I found a shoe box. Inside
it, tied together with a ribbon, were small stack of envelopes. They were from him. When I read them, a rock
slammed into my chest. It's been crushing me ever
since."

"I understand that, but why are you taking this out on

Miriam? She had nothing to do with it. And I'm one hundred percent sure she knows nothing about it."

Becky slugged back a gulp of wine. "Bullshit, she's known for years. The bitch didn't want to tell me because she only has two friends—had two friends. Now she has one. What a fake, with her 'one big family,' crap."

"Stop." Naomi lifted her hands, palms facing Becky. "Please stop talking and listen to me. You cannot pin the sins of your parents on her."

Becky felt her blood turning to steam. "What the hell? Are you kidding? My mother is dead. Every time something important happens in my life—she's not there! For years I've struggled to figure out the reason she did it. Why she wanted to leave me and my father. That bitch's father is the reason she killed herself. She couldn't live with the guilt over the affair, but she wouldn't stop seeing him either. I read all about it in the letters. He was more important than me." She whipped her head around, searching for the waiter.

"No, that's not true. Depression killed your mother," Naomi shot back.

"Sure, depression over that asshole, who was supposed to be my father's best friend. Waiter." She snapped her fingers.

A perky blond boy approached the table. He glanced at Becky's face and stopped a few feet from the table. "Scotch, neat," she barked at him. "And Miriam knew about the affair."

Naomi shook her head. "I think you're wrong."

"Bullshit. She knew."

Naomi reached across the table and tried to clasp her hand. Becky pulled away, but Naomi's eyes continued to bore into her.

"Listen to me," Naomi said. "My mother said that the situation caused your mother terrible pain. She loved your father and he loved her. But she loved Miriam's father too. But my mother doesn't believe the affair had anything to do with her death. She told me your mother battled demons beyond an affair."

The waiter gingerly set the glass in front of Becky. She grabbed the heavy cup and downed the liquid in one gulp, slamming it back onto the table. "You're wrong. The affair killed her and Miriam knew all about it."

Naomi shook her head.

Becky clenched her teeth. "A year after her mother died, Miriam dragged me to Century Three Mall to help her pick out a dress to wear to the spring formal at Joe's fraternity. As we walked into Kaufmann's, her dad and my mom walked out. My mom was holding his arm, laughing."

Naomi gripped the stem of her wine glass tighter as Becky continued.

"Of course, Miriam ran over to them, squealing like a little kid. I remember her words. 'Daddy, I forgot you and Mrs. Greenburg were shopping today.' Miriam turned to me and said, 'They're buying your dad a surprise birthday present!'

"I looked at my mom and saw the embarrassment in her eyes. At the time, I attributed it to Miriam's loud, attention-grabbing behavior. But looking back, it was the expression of someone caught committing a crime."

Naomi shook her head. "Even if that's true, Miriam simply believed they were shopping for a gift. That's pretty harmless. Think about it, if David decided to buy you a piece of jewelry, don't you think he would take me or Miriam for a second opinion?"

"Stop making excuses. Miriam knew exactly what was happening on that day because she said nothing about my mom holding her dad's arm."

"Did you say anything to her about holding his arm?"

Becky reached into her purse, pulled out the wallet, and tossed a fifty-dollar bill onto the table. "Of course, you would side with her. But I don't give a damn what you think. My mother slit her wrists over that man. And I will never, ever believe Miriam didn't know about the affair." Becky turned and marched away from the table.

"Don't you dare walk out on me."

Becky heard the words Naomi shouted at her back, as she pushed open the glass door, but the words didn't stop her from rushing down Walnut Street toward the small parking lot at the end of the block. She didn't want to talk anymore, just go home and crawl into bed. Love two men—bullshit. An affair is an affair. That man stole her mother away from her father. His best friend seduced his wife and because of that…

Becky climbed into the car, slammed the door, and crumbled onto the steering wheel, letting the sobs wrack her body. *She's gone forever.*

Chapter 13

Naomi

Naomi tried to focus on the document she was typing, but her thoughts flipped flopped between kissing Aaron and Becky's irrational behavior. Between Monday and Friday, Aaron fantasies wrestled for brain space against the problem of how to tell Miriam about the affair. But in the end, rehearsing a speech to give Miriam won the match.

The best part about working for a Jewish organization was that, during the winter months when Shabbat came in early, the office closed at 3:00 p.m. Today, she walked out even earlier, at 2:00 p.m., and drove straight to Miriam's house.

Miriam answered her enormous oak front door wearing an expensive workout suit. Based on her perfectly applied make-up and fresh smell, Naomi guessed she hadn't been to the gym. "Are you leaving now?"

"No. Come on in. My personal trainer cancelled on me. We were supposed to meet at 2:00."

"Good, make me a cup of coffee," Naomi said, walking into the foyer and taking her shoes off before stepping on the beautiful marble floor.

Miriam turned and walked across the entrance that

was bigger than the average person's living room. "Anita, please make coffee for me and Naomi."

The words, "Hi, Naomi," shot out from the kitchen. Anita began cooking Shabbat dinners for Miriam about sixteen years ago. She also cleaned her house on Mondays and Wednesdays.

Each year, one month before Passover, she scrubbed the entire six bedroom monstrosity clean of *hametz*. A bread crumb didn't stand a chance against Anita.

Miriam and Naomi settled into overstuffed chairs in the room Miriam referred to as her parlor.

Anita delivered the coffee on a small silver tray. Then she placed a few chocolate-chip cookies, carefully arranged on a dainty china plate, on the end table.

"Are you here to tell me good news about you and Aaron?" Miriam asked, eyes wide with interest.

"No, I'm not."

Miriam tilted her head sideways and her smile melted away.

"Miriam, I came here to tell you something that I didn't think you would want to hear in a phone call. All week, I've struggled with how to tell you and, honestly, I don't know how to soften it, so I'm just going to say it, okay?"

Miriam leaned forward, elbows to knees, the coffee mug between her hands. "Okay, say it."

"Becky found some letters addressed to her mother when she was cleaning out a closet." Naomi inhaled. "They were from your father."

"My dad? Why would he send her mom letters?" A perplexed expression covered Miriam's face. She set the cup on the glass top of the coffee table and leaned back.

"Oh, gosh, this is so hard," Naomi said, shifting her eyes toward the ceiling and squeezing her head between her raised elbows. Inhaling through her nose, *Please, Hashem give me strength.* She exhaled.

"Well?" Miriam looked uncomfortable in a chair she bought purposely for its comfort factor.

Naomi sighed. "After your mom passed away, Becky's mother and your father had an affair." There she'd said it. The tension in her shoulders released—a bit.

"Excuse me?" Miriam paled. Tears began filling her eyes.

"From what I understand, it was a true love affair."

The words obviously sank in because Miriam let out a loud screech. Anita came running from the kitchen, and Naomi signaled for her to leave the room. Naomi quickly moved to her friend's side and wrapped her arms around Miriam's shaking body.

Finally, questions began pouring out of Miriam. Naomi answered the best she could, up until the final question. "Why is Becky mad at me? I didn't cause this to happen. I didn't even know about it."

The dreaded question, how was she supposed to respond? *She's making you the scapegoat because she's crushed by Noah marrying Maria, and she's directing her anger about that situation at you. But, most of all, she's still grieving over the loss of her mother.* Naomi knew this was not a territory she wanted to venture into, so she shrugged.

The women sat in silence as their coffee turned lukewarm until Miriam cleared her throat. "Since she won't talk to me at *shul* or take my calls, I'm going to write her a letter. A real letter, not an email she can delete. No one, not even Becky can resist opening a hand addressed envelope."

The women sat in silence for a long time. Naomi held Miriam's hand as she quietly sobbed. Eventually, Joe came home and took over the hand holding. Naomi kissed them both goodbye, escorted herself to the door, and tottered down the frozen uneven fieldstone path leading to her car. Her heart felt like rocks in her chest, heavier than it did when she knocked on the door. During the short drive down the hill, across Scrubgrass Road, and onto her street, she spaced out...

✡ ✡ ✡

"When I grow up, I'm going to have three children, a boy and two girls," Miriam said while changing the record on the new stereo she got for Hanukkah.

"Really?" Becky said. "And you can plan that in advance? Wonder if no guy wants to marry you?"

Naomi stopped leafing through the teen magazine she found lying on the top of Miriam's desk. "Of course, she'll get married. There's someone for everyone."

"Easy for you to say, Naomi, you're gorgeous. Every guy in school is in love with you," Becky said, flopping from her back to her stomach. "Even my brother thinks you're cute, and he's in college."

"Shut-up, Becky, Miriam's pretty and she already has a boyfriend—remember? You and I don't have one."

"I really like Joe," Miriam said as music from the sound track of Saturday Night Fever began filling the room. "Come on, Naomi," she continued, thrusting out her arms. "Dance with me."

Becky jumped from the bed. "No, dance with me. I need practice for the school dance."

The two girls swung around the room, trying to recreate the steps they saw in the movie. More than once, Miriam stopped and said, "No, no, like this." When the song ended, both were winded. Becky flopped back onto the bed, and Miriam crumbled to the floor.

"Having you two is like having sisters. That's why I

want three kids. I hate being an only child. You guys are my family," Miriam said.

"I agree," Naomi said, lifting her can of Diet Coke above her head. "Sisters."

"Sisters," the two other girls replied.

✡ ✡ ✡

Naomi slammed the car door, walked straight into the small basement pantry, and reached over her head to the top shelf. She grabbed the first bottle of wine she could wrap her hands around—chardonnay, the good stuff, left over from Jake's collection. She needed a drink. Upstairs she could hear Ezra bumping around in the kitchen.

"Where've you been, Mom? You're late."

"I stopped by Miriam's house. Do you have something to wear tonight?"

"Yeah, jeans and T-shirt, like I always wear to Mrs. Raz's house."

"Not tonight, you're not. There will be other guests. I'll let you wear the jeans, but at least put on a polo shirt. Preferably, one without a stain—please."

"Sure," he said, picking up a plate containing leftovers from the previous night—reheated spaghetti and meat-balls. He sat down at the kitchen table and began eating and texting. She picked up the almost overflowing wine glass and walked upstairs to the bedroom.

As Naomi pulled off her work clothes, she smiled at the thought of seeing Aaron and the memory of kissing him. Plus, she always liked his mom, a straight talking woman if there ever was one. Seeing her would just add to the evening.

But gloom returned when she stepped into the shower. Damn Becky's stubbornness. During the amount of time it took to shower, step out of the shower, towel the excess water from hair, and knot the robe around her waist, Naomi decided that tomorrow, after *shul*, she would walk to Becky's house and talk to her.

Naomi picked up the wine glass and took a long pull from its contents. She sat in her make-up chair, *God, please give me the wisdom to bring my friends back together.*

Esther's Shabbat dinner was a roaring success. Aaron kept them all in stitches, telling stories about the famous people he knew in New York. His mother updated them on all the Squirrel Hill gossip, and Esther's food, as always, was delectable. But, for Naomi, the best part of the evening was when Aaron and Ezra got into a deep discussion about computers. She knew Ezra was up on technology, but it never occurred to her that Aaron would be a computer geek. At the end of the evening, the two of them were sitting alone on the sofa going over the features of Aaron's new expensive cell phone. Naomi had to pull Ezra out the door.

"Hey, Mom," he asked as she started the car, "is Aaron the friend you went to dinner with last week?"

"Yep."

"He's a nice guy."

"Yep."

When Naomi entered the *shul* the next morning, she spotted Becky sitting cross-legged in her usual spot. Naomi didn't bother to grab a siddur or the reading glasses she always left on the bookshelf. She walked straight to Becky, clasped her hand, and pulled her into the lobby.

"She didn't know either," Naomi said.

Becky stuck out her hip and crossed her arms in front of her belly. "Yes, she did. She's a good liar."

"I mean it," Naomi said. "I saw her face—complete shock. There's nothing to hold against her. The damn affair had nothing to do with either of you. The people you should be mad at are dead. You're friends. Something that happened so many years ago has nothing to do with your friendship today."

The door opened and cold air blasted through the vestibule as Laurie's family walked inside. "Hi," she said, pulling her arms through the sleeves of her coat. Her husband, Dan, nodded and continued to the coat rack. He hung up his top coat, made a shivering movement with his hands, and stomped into the sanctuary, snow falling from the bottom of his pant legs.

"Another crappy, gray day," Laurie said. "Will this snow ever melt? What's up with you two?"

"Nothing," Becky shot back. "Absolutely nothing." She turned sharply and her heals clicked a hard staccato sound as she rushed through the double glass doors leading to the sanctuary.

"Don't ask," Naomi said, shrugging.

Laurie held the sanctuary door open for Naomi. "I didn't even get to compliment the new hat. Red—a good color for the present atmosphere around here."

As always, the kiddush ladies meandered into the kitchen after the rabbi's *Dvar Torah*. His sermon felt incredibly long today. They settled into their regular spots around the big stainless steel work table.

Naomi sliced bagels. Laurie mixed tuna. Poor Esther fished the herring from the disgusting jar and put it into styrofoam bowls. Miriam leaned quietly against the side counter top sipping her coffee. Halfway through the preparations, Becky walked into the kitchen.

"What can I do?" she asked.

"Egg salad—peel the eggs," Esther said.

"You know I hate eggs," Becky replied.

"Fine, cut the pineapple," Esther conceded and turned to Laurie. "When you finish with the tuna, could you do the eggs?"

"What's another stinky job? Sure, I'll do the eggs," Laurie replied, slopping a large dollop of mayo into the bowl.

Becky pulled the pineapple from the refrigerator and began slicing through the thick skin. After a few moments, Miriam slithered over to her and whispered into her ear.

"No," Becky shouted. "I don't want to talk to you. Leave me alone."

Miriam froze and her eyes widened. Everyone ceased moving and stared at Becky.

"Don't you all stand there looking at me. Chop, slice, I don't give a shit, but don't stare at me."

"Calm down, Becky." Naomi moved to her side and extended an arm around her waist. Becky slapped it away.

"Please, Becky," Miriam asked softly. "Talk to me." Her face was flushed with embarrassment. Her hands quivered.

Becky slammed the knife onto the steel table and stomped out. Everyone flinched at the sound of it smacking the table then flinched again when she slammed the door behind her.

"Well," Laurie said, planting her left hand on her hip. In her right hand, she wielded the mayo covered wooden spoon like a torch. "Someone has to go and talk to her."

All eyes shifted to Naomi. "Aghhh," she said, clasping her head. "Fine, just let me finish these last few bagels. I need a minute to think."

By the time Naomi reached the sanctuary, Becky was gone. Naomi peeked around the mechitza and spotted David, still in his seat. Outside the window, there was no sign of their big white Mercedes Benz. Naomi returned to her chair, took three steps back and three steps forward, and began praying the Amidah.

After the table set up was completed, Naomi walked the length of the pushed together banquet tables toward the spot where her friends congregated. Halfway down the length, Aaron pulled her into the seat next to him, which happened to be directly across the table from the rabbi. She felt awkward being out of her normal spot, but enjoyed the conversation. Except for one minor problem, controlling her constant desire to turn in her seat and look directly at Aaron. She didn't think Aaron would mind the adoring gaze, but it would cause the poor rabbi to be stuck staring at the side of her head.

"So, Aaron, do you think that you'll stay here in Pittsburgh?" Rabbi Morty asked.

Naomi felt her face heat-up. Midway through the rabbi's question, Aaron reached under the table, slid her skirt up a bit, and squeezed her knee. She hoped the rabbi attributed her blush to the spicy pepper *schrug* she dabbed on her bagel.

"If Pitt offers me the job, I think I will," Aaron replied, creeping his hand higher up her thigh.

This squeeze aroused more than a blush. Naomi rose from her chair, excused herself to remove plates from the table. Esther gathered the plates and bowls at the other end of the table. "I'll finish the disposable stuff," Esther said. "You take the leftovers into the kitchen."

Naomi grabbed the bottle of Crown Royal and the leftover herring and walked into the kitchen.

Inside, Laurie rinsed dishes and loaded them into the dishwasher. "Are you going to call Becky when you get home?" she asked, washing the large serving bowls.

"I have too," Naomi replied. "Not that I want to, but someone has to tell her she's acting like a bratty kid."

Laurie set the last wet bowl on the drying rack and wiped her hands on a paper towel. "Keep me posted, okay?"

They walked out of the kitchen and straight to the coat rack. While Naomi put on her coat, Aaron struck up a conversation with Ezra. When she walked toward them, she overheard Aaron. "I'll bring it with me when I pick up your mother tonight. Our dinner reservations are for seven o'clock. I'll come at six-thirty and show it to you. In fact, you can play with it while we're at dinner."

Ezra looked so excited. Whatever Aaron offered earned him major points with Ezra.

✡ ✡ ✡

Aaron knocked on the door at precisely six-thirty holding a small white pad that looked like a large iPod. He kissed her cheek. "Sorry, I'm not here to see you— yet. I'm here to see Ezra." He winked and smiled.

"Come in, please. Wait here for a moment while I get Ezra," Naomi said, playing along.

Within minutes, Aaron and Ezra sat side by side at the kitchen table playing with what turned out to be the newest and greatest iPad on the market. After forty-five minutes, when Naomi and Aaron left for dinner, Ezra failed to even look up.

Aaron drove down the hill to the end of the block. Suddenly, he swerved to the side of the street and put the car in park. Naomi didn't know what to think— something wrong with the car? Was he sliding on snow? Her question was answered when he reached over and pulled her close.

After the kiss was over, he put the car back into drive. "I waited all week to do that."

She just smiled.

Their reservations were at a little Mid-Eastern place in Mt. Lebanon. Naomi loved the food, but Aaron said it didn't come close to the food in Israel. She couldn't agree or disagree. She'd never been there, which shocked Aaron.

"You've never been to Israel? Every Jew has to go to Israel at least once."

She shook her head. "When I was married to Jake, all of our money went to medical school tuition. Once we did have the money, he didn't have the time. It's my dream to go there someday."

"How much vacation time do you have?" he asked.

Naomi sensed where this conversation was going. "I don't know, probably a lot. I rarely take a vacation day or use my sick time."

"Perfect, we're going to Israel in May. It's the best time of year to go—not too hot."

"Sure," she said, playing along. "And we can stay in the best suite at the King David Hotel and hire a private chauffeur to drive us all around the country. In fact, maybe we could schedule dinner with the prime minster."

Disappointment covered his face. "You think I'm joking."

Naomi smiled. "No, no," she continued. "Maybe dinner with the prime minister is a bit much."

Aaron set down his fork, reached over, and clasped her hands. His gaze pounded against hers. "If you are willing to accompany me, I would love to spend a large part of May with you in Israel."

Before she could say anything her phone buzzed—a text message. *Can I go bowling with the guys and sleep over Sam's house?*

"It's Ezra. Let me type back," she said, and quickly began texting. *Sure, call me when you wake-up in the morning and I'll come get you.*

"Is everything okay?" Aaron asked.

"He just wanted to know if it was okay for him to sleep at a friend's house."

Aaron grinned. "Nice that he asks."

The subject switched from Israel to what a great kid Ezra was. Naomi was grateful for the text message.

Dinner ended and they walked to the car, hand in hand. Naomi's heart pounded against her chest. She had to admit that her whole body felt alive.

They settled into the car and the conversation felt as comfortable as it did twenty plus years before. "Any updates on the Becky/Miriam situation?" Aaron asked.

Naomi leaned back into the leather seat and closed her eyes. "Disaster—complete mess, I don't know how to fix this one. I really believed that once Becky realized Miriam didn't know about the affair, she would get over it. Wrong, so wrong. She's dug those spiked heels even further into the ground."

"I wish I had some good advice. Miriam has always been a chatty sweetheart. But Becky," Aaron said, shaking his head. "Let's just say that history has proven that when she climbs onto her throne, heads always roll. Poor Miriam. It was always interesting watching the dynamics between you three."

Naomi turned to look at him. "Why, we were just three typical teenage girls."

"Not really. All three of you were very unique and brought something needed to the trio," Aaron said.

"Oh, really?"

"Yes," Aaron said, removing his eyes from the road to look at her.

"You need to explain this theory."

"Okay. Here goes—Becky was born with control issues and a need to be the center of attention. Miriam was
a born follower. Becky got the attention she craved having Miriam's adoring eyes always on her. Miriam felt
important being known as Becky's best friend,"

"So, all-wise oracle, what about me? How did I fit
in?" Naomi asked.

"That's an easy one," he said, reaching over and placing his hand on her thigh. "You were perfect."

A distracting zing of energy shot through her the moment he laid his hand on her. It was a momentary struggle
to remain focused on the conversation. "Seriously, tell
me, what was my role in the dynamics—tag along?"

Aaron became quiet and his eyes focused on the road.
"You were the voice of reason. Even though you were a
year younger, they both respected your opinion. I think
Becky envied your good looks. You made Miriam feel
important as a person, not just Becky's shadow. Both
loved acting the part of big sister, but no one outside of
you three ever saw you as the little sister—you were the
logical one."

Naomi gazed out the side window at the moon. Snowflakes quietly fluttered in the air. She never analyzed their
friendship. It always existed and she believed it always
would. Thinking about it now, there wasn't much to argue in his reasoning, except maybe Becky being jealous
of her good looks.

Aaron pulled the car into the driveway, put the car in
park, and turned off the engine. He leaned over and
kissed her. It brought back memories of long ago kisses
and feelings that, a month ago, she never expected to
have again. She loved kissing him.

He pulled his mouth away from hers and began inch-
ing his way up her neck, butterfly kiss after butterfly kiss.
She tingled—all over. As one hand stroked her hair, his

lips reached her ear. "Invite me in for coffee," he whispered low and seductive before resuming the kissing expedition and sliding his hand down the front of her body.

Naomi arched her neck. "I hope you like it black, I ran out of milk this morning."

Chapter 14

Naomi

Naomi woke first and ran her fingers through his curls, which stuck to his head. The result of sweat and sleep. Inside, she chuckled. All the times they made love when they were young, not once was it ever in a bed big enough to move around. She tried not to compare the experience with Jake—it was hard not to with Aaron sprawled across his former side of the bed. She stretched like a cat after a good nap, and then an arm wrapped around her waist and pulled her close. She loved his lips.

The phone rang at seven-thirty, Naomi wanted to ignore it, but feared it was Ezra needing a ride. But when she looked at the phone screen, Becky's name flashed up at her.

Naomi groaned, flopped onto her back, and threw her forearm over her eyes.

"Answer it, I'm not going anywhere," he said and began roaming around her stomach with his fingertips.

She didn't get a hello out of her mouth. Becky's words exploded into her ear. "You didn't answer the phone last night."

"It never rang," Naomi shot back.

"I called your house ten times and you didn't pick up and neither did Ezra," Becky said.

"I was out and so was he."

"Bullshit, you never go anywhere. You were ignoring me," Becky said.

"If I was ignoring you, why would I pick-up at this awful hour of the morning?"

"Noah called me last night. That bitch, I can't believe her. She's trying to buy an invitation to the wedding. And, even worse, she's trying to buy my son." Becky shouted the words into Naomi's ear. "I hate that woman."

"Stop it! You sound like a bratty child."

"Do you want to know what she did? Do you? She bought Noah and Maria a honeymoon trip to Israel! The chutzpah—and she told him that she didn't receive an invitation to the wedding. What a desperate ploy to get invited."

"Wait a minute—" Naomi tried to interject.

"Noah called me last night mad as hell—at me! As if I caused this mess. And get this, today, Noah and Maria are going to that conniving bitch's house to hand deliver an invitation. They want to thank Joe and Miriam for the trip." Becky said the last words in a snotty stuck-up sounding voice. "I want to spit on that woman,"

Naomi could hear Becky's heavy breathing through the phone and immediately thought of Becky's blood pressure. She rolled onto her side and leaned on her elbow. "No, Becky—you've got everything wrong. Miriam bought the honeymoon, hoping that Maria will fall in love with the country and Judaism. She hopes it will make her want to convert. Miriam thinks if Maria converts, you'll be happy."

"That's stupid, whether Maria converts or not doesn't change the fact that her father seduced my mother into a disgusting, humiliating affair that killed her."

"That's not true," Naomi replied.

"Yes, it is." Becky hung up.

Maybe it was the comfort of Aaron's arms. Or that she felt protected lying next to him. But, most likely, her frustration with the situation became overwhelming. Naomi wept into Aaron's shoulder.

"Escape from this, call in sick. Come to New York with me for a few days."

Her throat constricted. *Go to New York with him? What will I tell Ezra? And I can't lie to my boss.*

"I plan on keeping the New York apartment even if I accept the Pitt position. I want you to get used to the place. It will be our second home."

Naomi's heart began to pound. Second home? What was he saying? She lived alone with her son in Mt. Lebanon. She had one son in college. She was divorced—alone.

He sat up, his face radiating excitement, waiting for her answer. She excused herself and rushed to the bathroom. Sitting on the toilet, alone in the vacuous marble tiled room, she panicked and realized that the sex was a huge mistake. This was not what was supposed to happen—friends, old friends. That's all. She had to tell him no.

Aaron bought her story of a huge deadline at work. He was disappointed, but insisted they would find a better time. She kissed him goodbye just minutes before the Ezra pick-me-up text arrived. She scurried around the house, making sure there was no evidence left of the previous night's escapade. Ezra would die thinking his middle-aged mother had sex. She imagined him plugging his ears and shouting "gross." Maybe he was right. She was too old for this, romance was for young people.

After picking Ezra up from his friend's house, Naomi sat alone at her kitchen table, drinking coffee, watching more white flakes build up on her deck. Would it ever stop? The phone rang. She looked at the screen—her mother. She hit the silent button and let it go to voicemail. She wasn't in the mood for her mother.

Why did she agree to go out with him? she asked herself over and over. Catch-up, reminisce about some fun times, but that was it. Okay, they had sex—just like the old times. That's all. Like the kids say, friends with benefits. She walked to the counter, poured more coffee into the cup, and leaned against the black granite countertop. Two houses implied long term. A trip to Israel implied long term. He didn't mean it. Of course, he didn't. She shook her head. It was just a reaction to his divorce combined with a sentimental memory of childhood.

The coffee tasted bitter. She dumped into the sink. Her to-do list for the day was a mile long, but she sat back down at the table, thinking about her younger self. The Naomi Aaron remembered went away a long time ago.

She dropped her head down onto her crossed arms. His interest in worn out, boring her would last for a few months before his eyes zeroed in on all the young women strolling around the campus. She imagined a line of them with big eyes and perky boobs, fawning over him and his books. What man wouldn't choose a flower over an old cactus? This relationship couldn't go any further. If he called again, she would be unavailable.

She picked up her head and straightened her back. Unavailable, that's what she would be. It would be better for both of them. She rose from the chair, walked over to the bottom of the stairs, and pulled an Ezra move.

"Hey, Ezra," she yelled up the steps. "Let's go to the movies this afternoon. You pick."

She threw a load of whites in the washer and vacuumed the upstairs bedrooms. Then they drove to the theater at the South Hills Village. He chose an awful sci-fi horror fiasco, but the film did its job. She forgot all about Aaron, Becky, and Miriam.

"Let's get something to eat before we go home. I don't feel like cooking," she said, springing for a rare dinner in a restaurant.

She adored watching Ezra attack his food—such gusto, not one concern over fat or calories, just the pure joy of the smell, taste, and the texture in his mouth.

"I like Aaron. He's a nice guy. You knew him in high school?"

Naomi smiled. "Yes, we're very old friends. I met him when I was in eleventh grade."

"Was he your boyfriend?" Ezra asked, while slamming the palm of his hand against the bottom of the Heinz ketchup bottle.

"Yes, he was my boyfriend."

"Then you met dad," he said.

"That's right," she replied, wondering where this topic was leading.

"Dad's been gone a long time and next year, both Josh and I will be in college." He bit into a French fry.

She watched him chew. His stomach was bottomless.

He swallowed the French fry and popped another into his mouth. "Mom, maybe it's time for you to find a boyfriend."

She looked at his sweet face. "Don't talk with your mouth full." Then she shoveled a forkful of salad into her mouth. If it was only that simple.

Miriam

Miriam's doorbell rang at precisely three o'clock on Sunday afternoon. She glanced through the lead glass window to see exactly what she expected—two pink cheeked young people bundled in parkas and snow boots.

She answered the door, letting out her signature happy squeal, and wrapped her arms around Noah's insulated body.

"Hi, Aunt Miriam," Noah said. He planted a cold kiss on her cheek before pulling off his gloves. Maria stood at his side, smiling.

Miriam's husband, Joe, walked into the foyer and greeted the couple. "Noah, it's been weeks. You haven't been in *shul*."

"I know, Uncle Joe," Noah said, reaching out to hug him. "But my professors this semester seem to be competing to see who can dump the most homework on us. I promise to show up next week."

Miriam hushed Joe, reminding him that Noah and Maria needed to warm-up. She led them to the family room where the lit fireplace wiped away all their thoughts of snow.

Joe entered the room a few moments later holding an expensive bottle of wine in one hand and four glasses in the other. "Time for a toast."

They settled into their seats. Noah and Maria sat side by side, holding hands on the sofa. Joe relaxed in the recliner. His wine glass rested on the left side of a small table.

Miriam, sitting on the edge of a bentwood rocker, set her wine on the right side of the table. The smile on her face reflected the excitement she felt bubbling from her heart to her feet.

The foursome chatted about school and Maria's new job as a high school English teacher. Noah asked about their twin daughters, Jill and Leah, and their son, Nathan. But, it didn't take long for Miriam to switch the conversation to the wedding. Maria reached into her bag and pulled out a large envelope with Miriam's name embossed on the front.

"Mrs. Weiss, please—" Maria said.

"No, no, sweetheart," Miriam interrupted. "Call me Aunt Miriam like Noah does."

Maria nodded. "Aunt Miriam, Noah and I are so embarrassed and sorry about this situation. We couldn't image standing under the chupah without you being there."

Wow. They're going to have a wedding canopy, and Maria even pronounced the word right. She decided to push a little. "This isn't a Jewish wedding. You don't need a canopy. What made you two decide to have a chupah?"

Noah looked at Maria, who shrugged. "It's okay," she said a moment later. "You can tell her."

"Maria has been studying Judaism with a rabbi in Squirrel Hill. We haven't told anyone because she hasn't made a final decision. We thought it would be best to keep it to ourselves. That way, if she decides not to go through with it, my mom won't be devastated. And, if she chooses to convert, it will be a wonderful surprise."

Miriam clapped her hands together. "Then an Israel honeymoon is perfect. Maria, Jerusalem will make you fall in love with Israel and Judaism."

"If it were only that simple," Maria said.

Miriam popped off the chair and clapped her hands. "It is! Just wait and see."

"No, it's not," Joe said. "She's right. It's anything but simple. It's an enormous decision. Look at our history. If she converts, her children will be Jewish and at risk when the next madman comes into power."

Miriam turned her back to Noah and Maria and shot Joe a *shut-up* look.

"No, Miriam, I'm not going to be quiet." Joe shook his head at his wife before turning to face Maria. "In the long run, you have to live with yourself and your decision. If you convert, don't do it for Noah, Becky, or my wife—only for you. Otherwise, you'll end up resenting all of them. Study, learn, and see if the religion calls to you. If your heart draws you to the faith—convert. If you don't feel the attraction, remain Christian. You don't want to go to bed every night of your life with a lie sitting on your heart."

Miriam reached over and lightly smacked Joe's head.

Joe threw up his hands. "I'm finished. I'll leave this situation to the rabbis."

The sun began to set, signaling it was time for Noah and Maria to leave. The young couple pulled on their boots and parkas. "When you two come home from Israel, you'll come here for dinner, tell us all about the trip, and bring tons of pictures," Miriam said, while giving Noah a final squeeze.

She watched as they shuffled down the snowy path. The news caused her heart to pump joy. Everything was falling into place. The kids would have a great honeymoon, Maria would convert, and Becky would be happy again. Miriam waved one last time before they drove away.

Chapter 15

Naomi

Naomi pushed the shopping cart through the produce department of the Giant Eagle supermarket. Winter fruit and vegetables packed the refrigerated display case. She missed the peaches and watermelon of the summer.

While squeezing a head of iceberg lettuce, she heard a familiar voice, turned, and saw Esther, standing in front of a pile of grapefruit, complaining to a clueless-looking high school kid who had the misfortune of being assigned to replenish the display.

Naomi snuck up behind her, tossed her arm over Esther's shoulders, which felt like a pillow due to the regulation Siberian gulag puffy parka she insisted on wearing between Thanksgiving and Passover. Esther quickly turned, and her eyes lit with recognition.

Naomi chuckled. "Give the boy a break. He didn't grow them. He just stocks them."

"I know, but they are such *iksa* grapefruit." Esther rolled one in her hand and crinkled her nose. "I don't know why the US government doesn't allow people to bring in fruit from overseas. My daughter could mail us a case of real grapefruit—Israeli grapefruit."

"I'll email my congressman this evening," Naomi replied.

"So update me on Aaron. Is he coming to the wedding?" she asked.

"I didn't invite him. We were discussing grapefruit."

Esther put down the grapefruit. "What do you mean? You must invite him. He's perfect for you and will look so handsome in a tuxedo."

Naomi smiled at the image. He would look elegant in a tux. She shook her head. "What's wrong with this grapefruit?" She stuck it under Esther's nose.

"Stop it. That subject is over. The new subject is that sexy author."

"I don't think inviting him to the wedding is a good idea."

"Not a good idea? What are you talking about? He's falling in love with you again. I can tell by the way he looks at you."

"No." Naomi shook her head again. "He's not. Please, I don't want to talk about him right now."

"I don't care if you don't want to talk about him. I want to talk about him."

"Why?"

"He needs a wife and you need a husband. When you stand next to him—you match. Some couples clash—you know like spots and stripes. But, you two—match."

Naomi looked at her friend, lacking any logical way to argue Esther's statement.

"It doesn't matter anyway. Becky sent him his own invitation. He'll be there whether you like it or not. She agrees with me. You match." Esther picked up an orange. "These pathetic little balls are worse than the grapefruit. I might as well just buy that mushy fruit in a can."

Sometimes the Jewish community in Pittsburgh felt downright incestuous. Everyone knew everyone else, and therefore, had a right to an opinion. "Why were you and Becky discussing me and Aaron?"

"Look at these pathetic little baseballs they're trying to pass off as pomelos." Esther held up two of greenish-yellow pomelo impersonators. "Bowling balls. Pomelos should be the size of bowling balls."

"Esther, answer the question."

"Why wouldn't we discuss you and Aaron? You are the most exciting thing happening in this town. Besides, it spares me from listening to her complain about Miriam."

Naomi didn't respond. Esther climbed back on her fruit bandwagon as they walked into the next aisle. Naomi only half listened, wishing she had nothing more to worry about than fruit quality. Instead, she replayed Esther's words about Aaron needing a wife in her head. Even if she was right, and he did need a wife, why would he ever pick her? *I have nothing to offer him except a bitter attitude, an empty bank account, and a house that's falling apart.*

"You need to go to Israel to understand what I'm talking about." Esther pulled a box of crackers off the shelf and began turning it in her hand. "If it looks good, it doesn't have a kosher symbol. And why are there so many *hechshers* in this country? How many different symbols do we have to remember? Kosher is kosher."

Naomi smiled and nodded.

They continued trekking down the aisles. Esther chattered on about the lack of kosher products and the variety of hechshers. "You and Aaron should go to Israel on your honeymoon. Then you'll know what I'm talking about—delicious kosher food and ice cream."

"Stop it, please."

Esther stopped her cart and stuck out her hip. "No. I'm right. You're wrong. Aaron is your *bashert*. You just got

sidetracked by a pretty face when you were in college."
Esther chuckled. "That's funny. Prettier than Aaron is
damn hard to find."

Wife? Aaron's wife—impossible. She failed at being
Jake's wife. A man like Aaron needed a wife with brains,
class, and...well, everything else she lacked.

They pushed their carts to the checkout. Esther chose
the faster moving line. Naomi leaned against her cart as
Esther waved goodbye. Finally, it was her turn and the
slow-moving checkout girl decided to put a new roll of
paper into the cash register. Naomi pushed the loaded
shopping cart across the slippery parking lot. Between
dumping bags into the trunk, she pulled out her phone
and texted Ezra. *I'm five minutes away from home. Put on
your shoes. I need help unloading groceries.*

Ezra leaned against the wall of the garage, outfitted in
sweatpants and boots—of course, no coat. Coats, she recently learned, were not cool. He loaded bags up his arms
and carried them up to the kitchen. She followed behind,
holding the bags containing eggs and bread.

"Mom, if it doesn't snow, can I borrow the car on
Wednesday?"

Odd, pre-planning wasn't his style. He usually asked a
minute before he wanted to go somewhere. "Sure, where
are you going?"

He pulled the milk out of the ripped plastic bag.
"Squirrel Hill."

"What's happening in Squirrel Hill?"

"I'm having dinner with Dad." His back was to her as
he set the milk on the top shelf of the refrigerator. He
didn't turn around when he said the words.

"What?" she asked, not sure she heard him correctly
over the sound of the running refrigerator.

He closed the door and finally looked her in the eyes.
"Dad called today and asked me to have dinner with him

on Wednesday. He wants to talk to about the trip to Florida."

"If the weather is good, you can drive. If not, find out which restaurant, and I'll drop you off. I'll hang out with your aunt and her brood while you eat."

"Okay."

Becky

Becky sat on the chintz chair nestled into the corner of her bedroom, doing the same thing she did every day, rereading the yellowed letters. Each day and each read evoked a different emotion. Some days she cried. Other days she threw the letters in the trashcan, only to retrieve them an hour later. At this point, she'd memorized the words. They played like a loop tape in her head, wearing a rut into her brain she couldn't escape.

After Naomi told her about the affair in the bar, she came home and told David about the letters. His sympathy lasted for a few weeks, until he figured out that she spent most of her non-working time reading and rereading them. At the beginning of the week, he threatened to burn all the letters if she didn't stop. The next morning, before he woke up, she moved them to a better hiding spot. He caught her reading them when he arrived home from work today and told her to hand them over. She threatened to leave if he touched them.

To make matters worse, that bitch of an ex-best friend continued to pretend she knew nothing about the affair. And Naomi believed her—Naomi, who Becky thought would be at her side through fire.

If only Mt. Lebanon had another orthodox synagogue. She would pay double or even triple the membership dues, just so she would never have to look at Miriam again.

The doorbell chimed, pulling Becky from her reverie. "David, get the door."

The doorbell chimed again and no response from David. She carefully folded the letter she was holding and slipped it under the chair cushion. The bell chimed again.

"I'm coming," she shouted into the air.

She glanced through the glass side panel of the front door and saw Miriam bundled in a pink parka with a bouquet of flowers clenched in her pink leather glove. Before Becky could pull her face from the glass, she saw Miriam's face register her presence. Still, Becky didn't answer the door.

The bell continued chiming. "I saw you. Don't try to hide. Open the door."

Becky paced across her foyer and then back to the door. Finally, she opened it.

Miriam barged inside and stood shivering beside the open door. "There's nothing for me to apologize for—I didn't know either. And I wanted to tell you that I'm hurt too. But the affair had nothing to do with you or me. I miss you."

Becky looked hard at Miriam's face, the deep brown eyes that always reflected a childlike wonder and the high cheek bones she didn't deserve. The mere sight of the woman made her sick.

"I don't miss you. Get out of my house and leave me alone or I'm going to call the police."

"You don't mean that. Please. I know you're upset about the wedding and the letters. But Noah and Maria are going to Israel. I'm sure Maria will fall in love with the country and come home ready to convert."

"Bullshit. You think you can just throw money at them with a fancy trip, and it will solve everything." Becky reached for Miriam's arm and pushed her out of the house, slamming the door so hard the frosted glass window cracked.

Chapter 16

Naomi

On Wednesday morning, three more inches of snow fell. The weatherman called for freezing rain in the late afternoon. Naomi texted Ezra telling him to reschedule with his father. It wasn't safe for either of them to drive.

Her boss was on a business trip. He didn't leave much for her to do. When he called in at lunch time to check messages, she updated him on the local weather conditions. He told her to leave early.

By two o'clock, she was home standing in front of the freezer trying to decide what to cook for dinner. Ezra would be home at 3:30. She wanted to surprise him with an early dinner. She pulled out boneless chicken breasts, set them in water to defrost, and went upstairs to change out of her work clothes. As she pulled on her jeans, the doorbell rang—her stomach clenched.

As she walked down the steps, she figured it was probably someone trying to make a few extra bucks shoveling snow. When she opened the front door, shock reverberated through her. Jake stood outside, his hands thrust into his pockets as sleet drizzled down onto him.

She stood behind the storm door, like an idiot, just

staring. His gray eyes were downcast and lines radiated out from the outer corners. She was taken aback by how truly handsome he remained at fifty.

"Hi, Naomi." His tone was devoid of expression.

She didn't respond.

"The rain is really coming down, can I come in?"

Her stomach knotted, but her hand pushed down the small lever. "Why are you here? I told Ezra to reschedule. Didn't he text you?"

"I told him I would pick him up. I didn't know you would be home, but I saw your car in the driveway." He looked down and thrust his hands into his coat pockets.

"You can wait in your car."

He looked straight into her eyes. His reflected a sadness she wasn't used to seeing.

She sighed. "Well, don't just stand there dripping on the floor. Take your shoes off and have a seat in the kitchen."

"Thank you." He shuffled into the kitchen and sat in his old spot at the head of the table.

This action sent a shiver through her—Josh's word, *cooties*. She hustled over to the coffee maker. "Ezra will be home at three-thirty."

"The house looks good," he said.

"Really?" she said, hoping he could hear the sarcasm she intended. "It needs a ton of work—which costs money."

She wished the coffee would brew faster. She wanted to hand it to him and escape from the kitchen. It dripped slowly and steady—the caffeinated version of Chinese water torture. Finally, there was enough of the dark liquid in the pot to equal a full cup. She poured it into a mug and automatically scooped in a teaspoon of sugar and just enough milk to color it. Naomi refused to set it on the table in front of him. There was no way she wanted it to appear as if she were serving him. Instead, she thrust it toward him and waited for him to take it from her hands. "He comes in through the garage. You'll hear the door open." She turned and headed toward the steps.

"Wait, Naomi, please," he said softly.

"What?" she snapped back.

"Sit down a minute. I need to tell you something."

"Jake, I don't want to hear a damn thing from you, and I don't want to sit at the table with you."

"I know. And I don't blame you. But I'm begging, please give me one minute."

She inhaled, fighting the battle raging in her brain—sit and talk to him or throw the closest heavy object at his head. She poured herself a cup of coffee and sat down, at the far end of the table.

They sat in silence for a few moments. "I want to say I'm sorry for so many things. You were a wonderful wife, and I was a complete shit. I don't know what happened to me, but I didn't mean any of the awful things I said to you when I left the house. Most of them weren't even true."

He dropped his head. Naomi said nothing—surprised by the fact she felt nothing.

"I've been seeing a therapist for a year."

She set her mug on the table and leaned back into the chair. "So what?"

"I threw Brian out of the condo months ago."

Naomi stood up, walked to the sink, and dumped the coffee. "Whoopie, and I should give a shit?"

"There were never any other men. Just once, and it was during my freshman year of college. I was very drunk. I can't say I wasn't attracted to men while we were married, but I never acted until Brian. I was completely faithful to you."

"Then why did you lie?"

"I don't know."

"Tell your therapist you want your money back."

"I'm not gay—not completely, anyway. I've come to terms with being bisexual, but I prefer emotional relationships with women. If I had known this then, I would never have left."

Naomi reached forward and turned on the tap, just to hear the water run. Inside, she seethed.

"I loved you very much. I'm sorry for everything."

Something inside of her snapped. She reached forward and pulled the spray nozzle from the faucet, aimed, and pushed the button. He jumped from his seat, yelped, and held his hands up to block the water spraying his face. The anger that had been eating her alive sprayed out of that nozzle. She exploded with laughter as the cold water smacked his face.

"Stop! Stop!" he shouted, trying to cover his face.

But Naomi continued cracking up, crushing her finger against the button and watching him dodge the spray. The harder she pushed, the higher she felt. Elation washed away the rage she squashed since he left. Rage she never could express or even give herself permission to truly feel.

"Please, turn it off!"

She laughed as a puddle developed on the floor around him. Jake rushed to the drawer where he knew she kept her tea towels. She followed his steps with the sprayer, until the ringing phone made her drop the weapon.

"Hello," she said, barely able to suppress the laugh filling her chest.

"Hi, Naomi," Aaron's said.

"Aaron, how are you?" she asked, loud enough for Jake to hear. As he asked her to dinner, she wanted to stick her face through the phone and kiss him for his impeccable timing. "Dinner on Thursday and bring Ezra?

I'm definitely available, but I don't know what's on his schedule. Can I call you back tonight?"

Jake looked like a dork, standing in the middle of the kitchen, drying his soaked white shirt with a tea towel that read *Leftovers aren't poison.*

"Touché," he said, after she set down the phone.

Her insides calmed—a bit. "Sorry," she choked out between snickers.

"Fine. I deserved it. Anyway, I wanted you to know I regret everything and, moving forward, maybe you could find some forgiveness for me. And," he said, setting the towel on the counter, "maybe someday we could be friends."

"What? Friends—like going bowling?"

He smirked, almost a laugh. "Not exactly, maybe just acting civilized to each other at events like graduations and weddings."

She sat back down.

"Someday, we're going to share the same grandchildren," he said.

"I may be able to do civilized someday—but not today. Ezra needs a new suit and shoes. He's growing faster than I can afford. Civilized would include chipping in to dress your son. The amount of child support the judge gave me is pathetic. When he turns eighteen in two months, I'll lose that. You want to be civilized, help me feed and house your son."

Jake looked down.

"I'll take out the loans to pay for college, just like with Josh, but Ezra's going to need a computer, clothes, and books. You know how much I make."

"I'll pay back Josh's loans and set up accounts for both of them." He looked around the kitchen. "And, let me know how much you need for repairs for this place. I'll put a check in the mail next week."

"Thank you. It's about time you acted like a parent."

The sound of the garage door opening halted the discussion. Naomi tossed him the towel. "Wipe up the floor. I don't want to explain the puddle to Ezra."

He bent over and swabbed the ceramic tile. "Naomi, are you seeing someone?"

"Yes, yes, I am," she said, and hearing the words felt good.

Ezra burst through the kitchen door. "Dad? What are you doing here?" he asked and then noticed the soaked condition of his father's clothes. "You're all wet."

Jake looked at Naomi then back to Ezra and shrugged. "Caught in a downpour."

Ezra dumped his backpack on the floor next to the basement door and ran to the bathroom. She watched from the kitchen as Jake put on his shoes. When Ezra returned, they stood side by side in the doorway. They looked so much alike, but sadly, they didn't seem to have a clue as to how to act with each other.

Naomi watched through the window as they walked to Jake's car. Even their stride was the same, but Naomi knew that the insides of the two couldn't be any different. Ezra was already a grown-up.

After they left, she was filled with excess energy. Part of her wanted to call and tell Becky and Miriam about spraying Jake, but the other part didn't want to listen to either woman talk about the wedding or the affair. She decided to cook her chicken instead.

As she sat down to eat her dinner, she remembered Aaron called during the drama, and she agreed to have dinner with him. The thought of calling him back, chilled her energy. The chicken no longer tasted very good. She set her fork on the table. Every time she thought of him, her body tingled. She felt the silkiness of his hair on her fingertips, but it was an automatic reaction, not a rational one. Rational would be calling and canceling dinner. The right thing to do would be to tell him the truth—friendship was one thing, sleeping together was another. Her heart couldn't take anymore rejection and being with Aaron was the equivalent of being shot out of a cannon and flying straight at a brick wall. The flight was thrilling, but the wall devastating. Once his nostalgia wore off, she would be face to face with that wall. She picked up the phone.

Aaron answered on the first ring.

Just the sound of his voice caused a stirring between her legs. "Shit, stop that," she mumbled.

"What did you say?"

Oops, too loud. "Nothing, I was talking to the pilot light on my front gas burner. It likes to flicker." She exhaled and shook her head, swearing to never talk out loud to herself ever again.

"I can take a look at it the next time I'm in your kitchen."

An image of the two of them wrapped in each other's arms up against the counter top flashed through her head. "Thanks. I wanted to let you know Ezra's not available on Thursday, so it'll just be you and me. I can stay in Squirrel Hill after work and meet you someplace."

They agreed on a restaurant and Naomi hung up the phone. Yes, she was going to tell him how she felt, but doing it in person felt a bit more dignified.

Chapter 17

Becky

Only six days until the bridal shower and Becky didn't have a clue as to where it was being held— nor did she care. Maria's mother probably invited a roomful of nuns. The only thing this shower represented to Becky was the looming wedding. Three weeks until the end of her life. She might as well rip her clothes now.

The bed looked so tempting—a nap. So what if it was only eight a.m. She flopped backward, landing in the middle, and stared at the white ceiling. The white ceiling and trim complimented the deep tan walls. Their bedroom was her favorite room in the house, but today, it provided no comfort. She rolled onto her side and focused on the Irish lace curtains, draping the large window. They were evidence of a victory over David. He preferred blinds, claiming lace creeped him out, reminding him of his grandmother's house. She wasn't a nice old granny.

Becky slipped on her shoes and walked to the bathroom to check her make-up in the good light. She wasn't pretty like Naomi. Her hair wasn't curly or straight, just poufy in humidity. She always wondered what it would be like to be pretty for a day. Over the years, she mastered a style that was distinctive, but a flair for fashion couldn't compensate for her wide nose and heavy bone structure. She often wondered what David saw in her, but she was grateful every day that he saw something and loved her as much as he did. Today, she didn't care about being pretty or the fact that the face in the mirror looked old and defeated. She just wanted to get the day over with.

As she reached for the light switch, her gaze floated to the empty spot on the wall. She needed to have the wall painted to get rid of the faded outline of a picture frame.

Once she arrived at her office, she got caught up in her work—divorce after divorce. Some of them got ugly, like the husband who stole his kids and moved to Brazil—no extradition treaty with the United States. The poor wife almost ended up in a psych hospital. Then there was the couple who walked out hand and hand. They even scheduled a trip to celebrate their divorce. She always wondered why they were divorcing at all.

Becky always hoped the couples would work things out during the process. Today, she read the motion in her hand. The couple had been married for thirty-five years. You would think after that long, they would want to go the distance. What's left to fight about after thirty-five years?

Her mind drifted to Noah and Maria. She hoped it wouldn't take them that long to get divorced. Her phone rang.

"Becky, it's my week to do the kiddush shopping," Esther said. "I forgot that I'm scheduled to do an audit out of town on Wednesday and Thursday. Could you stop at Costco and pick up fruit and vegetables?"

Becky twiddled her pen. She didn't want to do anything that would benefit Miriam.

Miriam loved kiddush because she could sit and yak

for hours. But Becky had to go to Costco anyway.

"Becky? Are you there?"

"Sure, Esther, I'll do it."

"Thanks, when are you on the schedule next? I'll take your week."

The two women settled on the details and, within minutes, the conversation was over. Becky picked up the file she had been reading and tried to forget about the synagogue, Miriam, and everything else that the universe had thrown at her.

✡ ✡ ✡

On Thursday afternoon, the weather broke. The sun peeked through the remaining gray clouds. Becky hit the button on her key fob to open the trunk of her car, grabbing as many bags as she could, and headed into the synagogue.

Rabbi Morty's office door was open, so she glanced inside. He appeared engrossed in whatever he was typing on his laptop. But he must have heard the plastic bags slapping against her legs because he looked up. "Do you need help?"

"Not really, there are only two more bags."

He looked at her, but said nothing. She walked into the kitchen and dumped the bags onto the table. A few minutes after she returned with the last two bags, the Rabbi walked into the kitchen.

"I was wondering if I could talk to you for a minute?"

"Sure," she said, piling produce into the refrigerator.

"This business with you and Miriam. Is there any way I can help bring you two back together?"

"Rabbi, with all due respect, this situation is not your business."

"Becky, it became my business when Miriam showed

up in my office crying. She told me the whole story. You can't hold something your parents did against her. She didn't know about the affair either."

The kitchen wasn't very large, and there was only one way for her to escape the conversation. And he was blocking the door. Her heart ceased pumping blood and began pushing anger into her veins. Her head pounded— the spot directly behind her eyes. She stood her ground and stared him down. "She lied."

The rabbi shook his head. "I don't think so. Miriam's not a good actress. She wears every emotion on her face. I don't want to get involved, but the tension on the women's side of the mehitza is getting too thick. Please, consider sitting down and talking to her—for *shalom bayit*."

Becky's tenuous grip on self-control broke. She picked up the closest item she could get her hand on—a plastic serving bowl—and threw it against the wall. "No, no. It's all bullshit. She's sneaky and evil. She's the one who put the evil eye on Noah. She's the reason he's marrying that shiksa. Family, sure, we're just like a family— a back stabbing, lie to your face family. And you—you, I expected better from you. Her father seduced my mother. He and my father were best friends. Do you understand? My dad trusted him and loved him like a brother."

"Wait a minute." Morty positioned his hands protectively in front of his chest. "The people who had the affair are dead. You can't place blame on one or the other for starting it, any more than you could blame yourself for not stopping it."

"My mother is dead because of her father."

The rabbi shook his head, pure alarm registered on his face. She ignored it. Of course, Miriam's father started it. He probably played the poor widower card, taking advantage of her mother's caring nature. He had her under a spell. Just like the one Miriam put on Noah.

"Of course, you'll take her side," Becky spat out.

The rabbi sighed. "There're no sides to take. You're both on the same side, suffering over the sins of your parents."

"My mother didn't sin! And she wouldn't have killed herself if he didn't drag her into a disgusting affair," Becky shouted, but tinges of doubt flickered through her mind. "Move, I'm leaving."

He followed her out of the kitchen and into the vestibule. "Don't, please."

"Stay out of this, Morty. It's not your place." Becky smacked open the glass door and stormed to her car. *Damn him. Joe and Miriam's money has him brainwashed. Take away all the cash, and he would see her for what she really is.*

Becky pulled the car out of the parking lot and hit the gas pedal.

✡ ✡ ✡

Naomi

Naomi arrived at the restaurant first and ordered a glass of wine. She settled into the booth, nestling into the well-padded, leather upholstery. The jazz music, obviously chosen for its relaxing qualities, didn't work for her. Her stomach churned, even it didn't like the idea of saying what needed to be said.

He glided through the door. Naomi watched him cross the room. For a moment, the world felt surreal, as if she was an intruder in a Ralph Lauren commercial. Someone designed this restaurant, with its cherry wood paneling and lush oriental carpet, for sophisticated, handsome literary types—Aaron. The smile on his face as he approached lit up the room. Her whole body tingled with desire.

"Hi." He tossed his briefcase onto the seat before sliding into the opposite side of the booth. "Could you believe the sunshine today? It was glorious."

Naomi nodded in agreement.

He noticed her wine glass. "Good, I'm glad you didn't wait for me."

He extended his neck out beyond the edge of the booth, scouting the dining room for a waiter. He caught the attention of two young women leaning against the bar engrossed in a giggling fest with the bartender. The blonde one approached the table. A smile lingered on her face as Aaron placed his drink order. Moments later, she placed the single-malt scotch in front of him. She scratched the back of her neck and looked down at the floor. "Excuse me, I don't want to be rude, but my friends keep pushing me to ask."

Naomi studied the waitress's face, such a sweet smile and fine features. Josh flicked through her thoughts. She wondered if the girl was Jewish, but then remembered that Josh had a girlfriend.

"Are you Aaron Brenner, the writer?"

A slight tinge of embarrassment reddened his face. "That's me."

"My friend," she said, pointing to the other waitress, "just loves your books. She wanted me to ask you to autograph something for her."

Aaron looked around the table, picked up a damp cocktail napkin, and then put it down. The waitress tore a page from her ordering pad. He scrawled a quick message and signed his name. She thanked him and walked away, flashing it like a winning lottery ticket at the young woman now hovering in the doorway to the kitchen.

He sipped his drink. "That's embarrassing. It doesn't happen often, but I hate when it happens in front of people."

"Why? You write wonderful books. I'm surprised it doesn't happen more often."

"Enough, let's change the subject. I'm sorry Ezra couldn't come. Next time. Did anything on the menu look good?"

"All of it." Inside, she couldn't deny the comfort of sitting with him—lush and warm like the furniture in Miriam's family room. She wondered what it would have been like if she had stuck with him all those years ago.

"Naomi, do you still write?"

Did she hear him right? Was he asking if she still wrote? "Me—write? You're kidding, right?"

"No, you were a journalism major. Unless that changed after we broke up."

"No, my degree is in journalism." She twirled the stem of her wine glass and watched the liquid swirl, remembering the hours they spent sitting in the dark room of the school newspaper, dreaming of their future writing awards.

"I spend my days taking boring meeting minutes in shorthand and typing them up. The only writing I do is ghost writing magazine articles about fundraising that make my boss look good." She sipped the wine and couldn't believe the tears teasing her eyes. "I do get the honor of writing his president's report for the quarterly newsletter."

"You could freelance. Most magazines use freelance writers and some use only freelancers. You may not be able to quit your day job right away, but I know people who make a decent living doing it."

She shook her head and rubbed the edge of the linen napkin between her thumb and index finger. "No, my creativity supply dried up years ago."

"Bullshit." But before he could continue, the waitress arrived to take their order.

"How was New York?" Naomi asked, anxious to switch the subject.

"Great, but don't change the subject. I want you to write something. A short story, article, first chapter of a novel, press release, erotica." Her eyes widened. He smiled mischievously. "I knew that would get your attention."

More than anything, she wanted to lean forward and kiss him. Instead, she smiled back. "Erotica is the last thing I'm qualified to write." She smirked. "I couldn't even keep my husband. He left for a man."

"Stop it. I'm perfectly qualified to say this, you could write a best seller."

The waitress arrived with their entrees, saving her from having to respond. She placed the fish in front of Naomi and turned toward Aaron. "Mr. Brenner," she said. "Would you care for some fresh pepper or another drink?"

"No, thank you."

"If you need anything, please let me know."

She stood smiling at him, a few moments longer than appropriate before walking back to the bar.

"Looks like the waitress is enamored with you."

He popped a juicy chunk of steak into his mouth, shrugged, and did a slight eye roll. Aaron had no hang-ups about eating non-kosher meat, though he claimed to buy only kosher beef and chicken at home.

She shifted her gaze to the bland looking piece of tilapia lying on her plate and stabbed her fork into it. She had to tell him. This lusting like a teenager was completely inappropriate for a middle-age mother.

"You have until nine o'clock Sunday evening to get it into my inbox." He looked like a sexy professor of college girl's fantasies.

"Are you going to grade it?"

"Yes. And if I don't like it, you'll have to rewrite it."

Looking at him made her wish she could still write. Over the years, she tried a few times. No words flowed from her brain to fingers. After Josh, she still penned an occasional short story. The stories were okay—not *New Yorker* okay, but good enough to allow her to feel comfortable identifying herself as a writer.

The words went away after Ezra was born. Spending her days caring for two children and working a full-time job sucked the energy out of her. She remembered the day the words went away. It frightened her...

✡ ✡ ✡

Jake sat in his spot at the head of the table, munching on a bagel and shaking his head.

"I don't want to go out to dinner for my birthday, and I don't want a party," Naomi said. "What I want is an uninterrupted day to write. Take the kids to the zoo or somewhere for at least six hours."

She stared across the table at Jake. She wasn't giving in on this.

He shook his head. "That's ridiculous, spending your birthday alone. Birthdays are for celebrating, fun, parties, people." The look on his face said it all. Jake, a true party animal, had no comprehension of the joy she got from silence.

"You asked me what I wanted. I want to write something." She shook her head. "No, I need to write something."

"How about I take the kids out for a few hours in the morning and in the evening we can have dinner with Miriam and Joe and Becky and David. It will be fun. We'll pick someplace we haven't tried before."

Naomi put down the mug and crossed her arms in

front of her chest. "How about you take the kids for eight hours, and I write."

Jake reached over and clasped her hand. "Fine, you win—six uninterrupted hours. I'm not imaginative enough to keep those two boys occupied for eight hours." He shrugged, and his gray eyes sparkled. "You know that even six hours is going to make me drive to my mother for help."

After he and the kids left, the silence melted all the stress from her body. Naomi brewed a cup of tea and sat down in front of her computer.

The blank page glowed in front of her. All week she thought about ideas for a novel. Most of them, she dismissed. But one plot idea stuck in her head. She typed the first sentence and read it out loud. It sounded clunky. She rewrote it—not so clunky. Then her mind blanked, as if every one of her thoughts, dreams, and insights never existed. No more words came. She closed her eyes for a few moments and then hit the X in the upper right-hand corner of the document, closing it forever.

✡ ✡ ✡

There wasn't a thought inside her worth writing down. Now, she did have something to say. It was time to say it. "Aaron, we can't do this."

He looked at her. "Do what? Begin a writing class?"

She shook her head and tried to control the trembling in her hands. "This...I don't know what to call it." She dropped her chin to avoid eye contact. "When you asked me to dinner, I thought it was just two old friends catching up. I never imagined we'd end up in bed together."

He leaned forward into the table, grinning. "Nice surprise, right?"

"It was amazing, but wrong." She wished he had ugly

teeth. His smile triggered physical reactions that she didn't want.

She moved a chunk of fish around her plate. The garlic smell wafted into her nose. The tingling went away. The nausea returned.

The look on his face chilled her bones. For a brief moment, she debated whether to continue speaking. But it had to be said.

"We need to stay just friends. This romance won't work."

"Why do you say that? It's going fine now."

"I know. I love spending time with you, but…"

"But what, Naomi? Tell me?"

She inhaled, exhaled. *Just say it, Naomi.*

"I think about you all the time. You've ruined my ability to focus on anything—including my job. It's wrong. I feel like I'm eighteen all over, and I'm not. I'm almost fifty."

He locked eyes with her. "Where are you going with this?"

All the comfort and warmth she felt upon his arrival dissipated in an icy flash of his eyes. She uncrossed her legs and squirmed in her seat. "I'm just a walk down memory lane, Aaron. We'll go on like this for a few months. And then you'll realize that you can't bring back the old days. I'm not that girl anymore. You'll get bored with me, and beautiful young waitresses like her—" Naomi used her head to point at the blond waitress taking the order at the next table. "—will tempt you. I'll become the old woman you want to unload." She waited, heart pounding against her ribcage. *Please say something.*

"Did it ever occur to you that I've had girls like her coming on to me for years? I've taught as an adjunct professor for the last fifteen years at Columbia. I've had every type of female and male hit on me. They're not interesting. They're children."

They sat in silence, picking at their food.

"Naomi, I didn't move back just because of my mother."

She met his eyes, wondering where he was going with this.

"I heard about your divorce a few months after it happened." He sloshed the melting ice inside his cup. "Alisha and I were on a downhill slope by that time. Don't get me wrong, I tried everything to save our marriage, but it really was over. The moment she moved out, you were my first thought. I wanted to call you or something, but..." He shrugged. "I don't know, gutless I guess."

His face looked as if he wanted to say more, but silence lingered between them.

"When I heard about the Pitt job, it felt *bashert*. The universe was bringing me back to you."

His eyes never flickered from her face. Naomi was stunned. Never in a million lifetimes could she have imagined that he came back for her. She shifted her gaze from his eyes to her plate. "But, Aaron, I'm damaged. If we continue, you'll regret it."

"You are so wrong."

"No, I'm not. When Jake walked out, I was a mess. I don't think my heart could take another rejection."

His eyes widened and his face flushed. No sign of the earlier happiness remained. He pulled out his wallet and slammed his credit card on the table. The waitress picked it up within seconds.

He let out a quasi-laugh. "You're afraid of me dumping you and breaking your heart?"

Naomi remained silent.

"Now, that's a good one. I have a heart too. And this is the second time you've broken it."

✡ ✡ ✡

Miriam

Miriam sat in front of the monitor, shaking her head.
She didn't like what her horoscope said for that day.
"Trying to prove a point without evidence will fail miser-
ably." Again, she typed the word "horoscope" into the
search bar. Maybe, another astrology site would say
something more helpful.

Rabbi Morty was right. This situation was an unsolva-
ble catch-22. If she proved her father didn't start the affair, it would make Becky's mother the culprit. That idea
would make Becky nuts. If Miriam proved her father did
start the affair, Becky would hate her forever. "Time,"
Rabbi Morty had said, "will be the only solution."

He explained that Becky was projecting her anger and
frustration over Noah marrying a non-Jew onto Miriam.
He didn't believe the fight was over an old affair, and no
one believed Becky's mother's suicide was a result of
guilt over an affair. The affair just came to light at a perfect time. A place for Becky to transfer all her negative
emotions.

Miriam believed he was probably right, but she really
didn't care, because it didn't make a bit of difference.
Becky still wouldn't speak to her.

Naomi

On Friday morning, Naomi did something she'd never
done before. She called in sick, even though there was no
indication of rogue bacteria or virus inhabiting her body.
When Ezra hollered up the steps to tell her it was time to

leave, she yelled back, "Drive yourself to school, I don't feel well."

She heard his size eleven feet pound the stairs.

"Mom, are you sick?"

"Yeah, Ez, I feel awful, headache, stomach ache. Take the car. I'm not going into work today."

"Can I get you something?"

"No, just go to school."

Naomi got out of bed after he left and made a cup of coffee. After crying for a few minutes, she flicked on the television in the family room and watched *Last Chance Harvey*. Not a good choice.

In a moment of pure aching, she pulled out her old photo album. The one she always kept hidden from Jake. It contained happy pictures from her youth. She flipped through the pages of goofy pictures taken with Becky and Miriam to the pages dedicated to her romance with Aaron. As she ran her fingers over the smooth cellophane holding down the pictures, tears dripped down her cheeks. Maybe part of her never did stop loving him.

✡ ✡ ✡

Ezra arrived home from school and found her asleep on the sofa covered by the old afghan her grandmother crocheted for her before she left for college. Jake begged her to get rid of the ratty old thing for years, but Naomi clung to it.

"Mom, how do you feel?"

She stretched her legs out straight. "Okay, I want to sleep a bit more."

Ezra tucked the blanket around her feet and tiptoed out of the room. What felt like five minutes later, she heard him say, "Mom, it's time to get ready for dinner. We're supposed to be at the Raz's by seven."

It's Shabbat. She forgot and groaned, realizing she had

to get up, get dressed, and smile. "No, I can't make it. Take the car and go alone."

"I'm not going without you. I'll stay home and make you soup and tea."

"No, go. Esther will be expecting you. I just want to sleep."

✡ ✡ ✡

Ezra bounded into the house at nine thirty, yelling, "Mom, you've gotta see this. Look. Aaron was at Esther's house. He asked me to give this to you." He held a book. The cover design was beautiful—weeping willow trees lining an empty country road. He thrust it out to her. "Aaron was there. He's so cool. This is his new book. It'll be in the bookstores in two weeks. This is one of the first copies."

Ezra talked faster than she could listen as he handed her the book. She ran her hand over the jacket, enjoying the feeling of the smooth and cool paper against her palm.

"Open it, Mom. Open it."

She lifted it to her nose first, taking in the wonderful smell of a new book. "It's a lovely book." She slowly opened the front cover, surprised by an unwarranted sense of nervousness.

Ezra's eyes looked like they were ready to pop. "Speed it up."

"Calm down, it's just a book," she said and began reading the copyright page.

He bounced on his toes the same way he did when he was five years old. "No, it's not. Turn the page!"

She turned the page.

This book is dedicated to N and the long-held dream of a second chance.

Tears welled up in her eyes. He had to have written the dedication months ago, before they met at the *Shul*.

"Mom, you're 'N.' Aaron dedicated his new book to you! Can you believe it?"

She shook her head. Underneath the printed dedication, it was signed in his artistic scrawl.

Always, Aaron

Ezra grinned all over his himself. "Guess you have a boyfriend, Mom." He bounded out of the room, leaving her holding the book.

Chapter 18

Becky

Becky pulled a black dress from her closet and held it up. A blotch of something white marred the left shoulder. She didn't care. Spinning the hangar, she examined the back of the dress. The same dress she wore to her father's funeral. The back looked fine. She tossed it onto the bed. On a normal day, she would never wear black opaque stockings with a black dress, but today being wrapped in mourning colors felt right.

"Becky," she heard David shout. "You need to leave soon."

"I'm almost ready," she whispered in a voice much too low for him to hear.

She descended the stairs slowly. Each step caused the clamp on her heart to squeeze tighter. By the time she reached the bottom, her eyes floated in moisture. He gave her the once-over and shook his head. "That's just plain wrong."

"No, it's not. I just happen to like black—a lot."

"I'm not going to fight with you. The shower starts in a half-hour, and it's at least a twenty-minute drive."

Becky pulled her bag and coat from the closet. "I'm going."

She opened the door of the white sedan. With a flick of the wrist, she tossed her bag and the gold lettered invitation onto the passenger seat. After slithering into the driver's seat and adjusting her skirt, she grasped the steering wheel.

The tears started, again. As she stared at the back wall of the garage, it turned into an imaginary movie screen...

The flowers decorating the bimah looked stunning, exactly what she wanted. As she walked down the aisle, she felt smug over winning all the arguments with the florist. Stupid woman tried to sell her fall flowers. Noah's life was just beginning—his personal spring. Damn if she would drape the sanctuary in fall colors for her son, a young man with a bright future. She wanted colors that represented life—daisies, sunflowers, and lilies. This bar mitzvah would be an event people would remember forever.

Her son was becoming a Jewish man. He was already a mensch.

But, even as she gloated over Noah, she struggled to block out the thoughts of her mother—damn that woman. What would make her choose death over watching her grandson grow up?

✡ ✡ ✡

Becky heard someone pounding and looked up to see David waving his hands. She watched him mouth the words "Get going."

She turned the key and backed out of the driveway.

✡ ✡ ✡

Naomi

The restaurant party room wasn't very large, but the décor was beautiful and floral enough to make Laura Ashley smile in her grave. Naomi scanned the room, not to admire the leafy pattern of the wallpaper, but to locate something lost—Becky.

She glanced toward the door—still closed. Naomi took a gulp of her chardonnay and tried to fight off the tension seizing control of her brain and body. After another big swallow, she moved toward the buffet table where Esther and Laurie stood filling their plates.

Esther loaded Caesar salad onto her plate. "Isn't this room beautiful?"

"The food looks fabulous, too bad we can't eat most of it," Laurie said. "Aren't you going to eat something, Naomi?"

Once again, Naomi strained her neck to see the door. "She's not going to show up. If she's not here yet, she's not coming."

"Who, Miriam?" Laurie followed Naomi's lead and gazed toward the door.

"No." Naomi shook her head. "Miriam's not coming. She decided not to come because it would cause Maria too much stress. I'm talking about Becky. She's not coming."

"Poo poo, of course she's coming." Esther flicked her wrists as she always did when using her favorite all-purpose phrase, poo poo. "She's the mother of the *chatan*. The groom's mother must be here." Esther turned back to the buffet and bent over a bowl of pasta salad. After plunging the serving fork into the bowl, she flicked at something that could have been a small piece of bacon or a bizarre looking dried cranberry.

"Maybe she got lost. Did you try calling her?" Laurie

asked before popping a forkful of quiche into her mouth.

"Yes, I've called and texted," Naomi replied. "She's ignoring me. I even called David. He said she left the house almost an hour ago."

Both women stared at Naomi. "She would never do anything to hurt Noah," Laurie said, breaking the silence.

"I'll call her. She knows better than to ignore me," Esther said, pulling her phone from her purse.

The two women stood, watching as Esther held the phone to her ear. "Becky," Esther said.

Naomi and Laurie exhaled.

"You're late," Esther said. "Are you lost? Do you have a flat tire? If not, you better get here fast. This is wrong, and you know it."

The three stood in silence. Esther listened to the voice coming through the phone as Naomi and Laurie fidgeted.

"Bullshit. Get here or I'm going to come and find you. And I'll tell Noah what you did. Now, get into your car and think of a good excuse for being late. And you better walk through the door looking happy." Esther hit the end button on the phone.

"She's in a bar. She decided to stop for a drink."

"Do you think she'll come?" Laurie asked.

Esther looked at Laurie and twisted her mouth. "Of course she'll come. She's afraid of what I'll do if she doesn't. Trust me, she will stomp through that door within five minutes. Now, let's smile and be friendly." Esther returned to scooping food onto her plate. "I just love quiche, but what's a lunch without bagels?"

Becky

Becky pushed the end call button, shoved the phone

back into her bag, and raised her arm to signal to the bartender. The tired-looking, middle-aged bartender walked over to her.

Becky held out her empty rocks glass. "Give me another."

The bartender shifted on his feet. "Lady, it's none of my business, but since you're my only customer, I couldn't help overhearing. I gather you are supposed to be at bridal shower for your kid's future wife. Why are you sitting here?"

Becky sneered and shook her glass.

"You and I are old enough to know that when it's your kid—well, it's your kid. Don't mess up. It's easier to bite your tongue than it is to live without your kid."

"Excuse me, I don't recall asking for advice, just scotch."

"You're right, you didn't ask, but unfortunately, in my old age, I've developed a conscience. I don't want to go home tonight wishing I had said something. I'm paying dearly for my own mistakes. You need to get up and go to that shower, or I'll bore you with my story." The bartender shook his head. "Don't hurt your kid."

"Ah, shit," Becky replied, slamming down the glass and gathering up her purse. She looked at the bartender and his flat expression. "Fine, I'm going."

✡ ✡ ✡

Naomi

On Monday morning, Naomi stared at her computer monitor, thinking about the weekend. Fortunately, the shower was saved when Becky arrived breathless, claiming to have missed the exit off of Route 79. Maria's mother bought the story. Maria didn't, but she had the class to let it go.

On Naomi's desk sat a stenographer's pad covered with her shorthand notes. Some days she really regretted taking that shorthand class in high school. Back then, she thought it necessary skill for a journalist, who needed to take down information fast. Instead, it turned out to be the death of her career dreams. She didn't like transcribing notes, but opened a new Word document anyway.

The blank document made her think about Aaron and his challenge to write something—anything. She wondered. She wished she could. Instead, she pulled the steno book closer and began transcribing the boring meeting notes.

She finished a half-hour before lunch time and checked her cell phone. There was a text message. She opened it, expecting something from Ezra. Instead, she saw the name, Aaron.

Sorry, I shouldn't have walked out. If you just want friendship, I'll try to live with it.

Naomi bit into her bottom lip. What did she want? Why was he offering anything? She wasn't in his league. When they were young, they both had big dreams. He achieved his, and she gave up. Naomi inhaled and looked around the office. Maybe it was time for a change. Maybe, deep down, she still did have the ability to write something people would want to read. But she knew this wasn't the real reason she held back. It was time to stop lying to herself. When she was with him, the hole in her heart disappeared. She missed being in love, and she absolutely missed sex. It was impossible to think about Aaron without quivering with lust. Yes, the possibility of the relationship ending with a crash into a brick wall existed. But maybe, the bricks were fake, made from a spongy material like in the movies—a theatrical illusion. Maybe her fear was just an illusion.

She glanced down at her hands, gripping the phone in

her lap, and felt something new. Her fingers began hitting the buttons. *No, I'm sorry. I panicked. Can we pretend that dinner never happened? Will you forgive me if I write something and submit it on time, professor?*

She smiled to herself as she hit the send button. Maybe second chances existed.

Moments later the phone rang, not Aaron, but Miriam.

"Naomi, I bought the most stunning dress for the wedding. Please, stop by after work, I'm dying to show it to you. What are you wearing?"

Naomi rolled her eyes. Dresses were the last thing she wanted to think about today. She needed to focus on a story idea. "Sure, Miriam. I'll stop by on my way home, but I don't have much time."

"No problem. What are you wearing?"

"Miriam, I haven't even thought about it."

"Well, you better think about it. The wedding is two weeks away. I'll let you get back to work. See you soon. Tootles."

Ugh, Dresses cost money. She didn't want to think about money. She returned her phone to her bag.

✡ ✡ ✡

Naomi stopped at Miriam's house and confirmed that the dress was, in fact, stunning—seven hundred and forty-eight dollars' worth of stunning. The visit ended up lasting an extra hour due to Miriam's insistence that Naomi go closet shopping. Miriam had always been skinny and the post-divorce Naomi matched her, protruding bone to protruding bone. The only problem was the length. At five feet seven, Miriam towered over Naomi.

"Have it cut down. I don't care. I'm not going to wear it again," Miriam said, standing in her bra and underwear, examining the dress. "The color is perfect for you. Makes your eyes look...I don't know the word. Doey, that's the word. In that dress, you don't look as cold."

"Gee, thanks. You think I look cold." There were occasions when Naomi really detested Miriam's lack of brain-mouth filter.

Miriam pulled her jeans on and buttoned her blouse. "Yeah, now that I think about it, since Jake left, you wear too much black. It's not really your color. This dress is your color."

Naomi did a slow turn in front of the full length mirror and couldn't lie to herself. It was the most beautiful thing she had put on in years. The fabric felt sensual against her skin. A moment later, she shook her head. The cost of alterations exceeded her budget.

She let the dress slip to the floor. "I can't take it."

"Yes, you can." Miriam picked up the dress and hung it on the hanger. "And, you are." She pulled the plastic over the length and thrust it at Naomi. "Take it."

Naomi really wasn't in the mood to argue. She just wanted to go home and think about story ideas. "Fine."

Naomi drove the short distance, occasionally glancing at the expensive, slinky, salmon colored fabric draped over the passenger seat.

She exited the garage and stepped into Ezra's man cave. The elegant dress shrouded in clear plastic hung over her arm. As hard as she tried, she couldn't think of one decent explanation to give to Miriam when she showed up at the wedding dressed in something old and, of course, black.

The man cave looked like—the home of—cavemen. She glanced around the room and smiled. At last, the answer to the missing cereal bowls mystery. There must have been five of them littering the floor and ottoman, which served as a coffee table for teenage video game addicts. She set the dress over the arm of the sofa, began gathering the remains of the cereal festival and hummed.

Her thoughts kept returning to the dress. It had been so long since she wore something sexy. It was amazing how dramatically a simple dress could alter self-perception. Maybe, just this once, splurging for the alterations would be a good investment. She set the bowls on the ottoman, turned around, and headed back into the garage.

As Naomi slid into the driver's seat, her cell phone buzzed. A text from Aaron. *Does this mean sex is back on the table? :)*

She smiled and typed. *On the table, under the table, beside the table...*

She was still smiling when she walked into the tailor shop. She put on the dress and climbed onto the old milk crate her tailor, Tony, used as a platform. He pinned up the bottom four inches. "Naomi, this fabric is fantastic."

The words were difficult to understand. Tony's words often sounded like gibberish when his thick Italian accent combined with his habit of speaking with a mouthful of straight pins.

"This dress is so sexy, and the color is perfect for your skin tone. I would kiss you and try to take you home in this dress."

"Thanks, Tony," she replied, wondering what was it with her and gay men.

"Turn around."

She obeyed his instructions and caught a glimpse of herself in the full length mirror hanging on the wall. Her heart did a little leap.

Tony wasn't lying. The dress looked stunning. It clung around her middle and hip area, emphasizing her still flat stomach and draped over her breasts, giving them the appearance of being more voluptuous than the reality hiding under her padded bra.

Tony stood and began grabbing at the fabric under her

arms. "It is good in all of the right places. You can pick it up next Monday."

She handed him her Visa and surprised herself by not cringing. He made a few more comments about the luxury of the fabric. She smiled as she signed the credit card receipt. Before walking out the door she took another glance at the dress. The color, backlit by the sun shining through the plate glass reminded her of another dress...

✡ ✡ ✡

"Naomi," Miriam's mother said. "Stop moving or you're going to be wearing pins and not a dress."

Naomi forced her feet to stop moving as Mrs. Gold pinned the side of the dress.

"Naomi, if you would grow boobs, we wouldn't have to sit through this," Becky said.

"Hush, Becky," Mrs. Gold shot back. "Naomi looks beautiful in this dress." She patted Naomi's backside. "You don't need big breasts to be sexy. And, you have lovely shoulders."

"So, true, Mom," Miriam said, glancing down at her own underwhelming mountain range.

"I guess, you're right," Becky said. "For a junior to get asked to the prom by the most gorgeous guy in the entire school must say something for flat chests."

Naomi stood quietly as the blood rushed to her face. The strapless dress had a satin base with a lace overlay, but it was the satin ribbon angled across the hips that attracted her to the dress. For some reason, when she put it on, she felt taller.

"Yes, Aaron Brenner is a very handsome young man. And he's Jewish," Mrs. Gold said, shooting a stern look at Becky. "Turn around, Naomi. I need to pin the hem. This color is beautiful on you. Salmon brings out the gold in your eyes."

Becky accepted an invitation to the prom from a non-Jewish boy. Her mother tried to stop her, but stubborn Becky insisted that she was going.

In barely a moment, Mrs. Gold completed the hem. "Next," she said, turning to Becky.

Becky stood, lifting layers of tulle. Understatement was not her style.

✡ ✡ ✡

The ringing of the bells hanging over the tailor's door pulled Naomi back to reality. She had forgotten about Becky's rebellion-against-Judaism period. Times really do change.

✡ ✡ ✡

Becky

Becky stared at the Jewish calendar lying open on her desk. Passover fell early this year—only four weeks away.

Another square on the calendar, blackened with magic marker, screamed at her that the wedding was only two weeks away. She looked up when she heard her office door creak open.

Noah walked in and sat in the chair usually reserved for divorcing people. Still wearing his coat, he crossed his arms over his chest. "What the hell, Mom? Forty-five minutes late for the shower."

He looked so handsome, so grown up. Where did time go? Becky looked at his face. Who'd have imagined she and David could create such a beautiful creature?

"I want an answer."

"Noah, why don't you and Maria just live together for a while? Everyone does it now. It's no big deal. If it doesn't work out, you won't have to go through an ugly divorce."

Noah leaned back into his chair and shook his head. "Mom, listen to me. Maria and I don't believe in living together before marriage. Thanks to you for drilling that into my head since middle school."

Becky stared down at the mocking calendar. *He'll be enslaved to a shiksa two weeks before the Jewish celebration of freedom.*

"Look at me." He leaned forward and his eyes bore into her face. "I'm not snubbing my Jewish heritage. I was born a Jew and I will die a Jew. But I love Maria, and I don't want to live any life that doesn't include her."

"Fine," Becky murmured. "But your children won't be Jewish," she whispered.

The comment was loud enough for him to hear. "Mom, she's agreed to raise the children Jewish. They will go to the synagogue and suffer through Hebrew school like every other Jewish kid."

"Reform, Hebrew school."

"Hopefully, they will be accepted into a conservative Hebrew school. But if not, yes, our future children will attend a Reform program."

A vision of three beautiful children running through a meadow flipped a switch inside Becky's brain. "Stop it, Noah." She pounded the desk with her fist. "You know damn well that going to synagogue and Hebrew school doesn't make them *halachically* Jewish."

"They can be converted by an orthodox rabbi. That's not a big deal."

"Yes, it is! What if they decide they don't want to be Jewish?"

Becky buried her head into her arms and gave into her sobs. Noah rose from his chair. She glanced up, watching him hesitate for a moment—looking at the door and then back at her. He shook his head as he walked around the oversized desk and placed a hand on his mother's shoulder. "I'm not marrying her to hurt you. I'm marrying her so I won't hurt me."

Becky sat up and reached for the tissue box usually reserved for the dumped and deserted.

"Maria and I are not taking this lightly. We've discussed religion more times than I can count. Her religion isn't important to her. She's a lousy Catholic." Noah stroked his mother's back. "Mom, Maria promised me that she would even attend services with us."

"Then why doesn't she convert?" Becky asked, turning her head to look at his face.

He didn't answer, just turned and returned to the chair on the other side of the desk. Instead of sitting, he stood behind the winged back, his hands resting on the top. "Maybe she will someday, but it'll be her choice. I won't pressure her to do it."

"I wish I could be happy for you. If she was Jewish, I'd throw the most fabulous wedding this town has ever seen. But now you're having a wedding that I don't even want to attend. It's wrong."

He rolled his neck and inhaled. "I'm sorry you feel that way. I thought if you two spent some time together, you would see how wonderful she is."

"I'm not stupid. I saw that the first time you brought her home. This isn't personal. She's exactly what I would have picked for you, except Jewish."

"Mom, that's nice to hear." He released his grip on the chair. "Because she spends most of our time together crying about how much you hate her. Could you please tell her what you just told me?"

The air entering her lungs felt as if it would suffocate her, her chest felt tight, and her heart pounded against her ribs. She managed to nod, but even while doing it, she knew she could never repeat her words to Maria.

"And I need you to promise not to make a scene when you see Aunt Miriam at the wedding."

"She's not your aunt," Becky snapped.

"That's funny. For my entire life you referred to her as my aunt. Now, you're upset, so she isn't my aunt. As far as I'm concerned, she is and always will be. So, if you can't be nice to her, stay on the other side of the room. I think this battle between you two is stupid, but that's your business not mine."

"If you knew the reason, you wouldn't invite her."

"Tell me. What could possibly be so horrific that you cut off your lifelong best friend?"

"I can't tell you."

Noah stepped back from the chair and raised his hands above his shoulders, palms facing his mother. "Mom, all I'm asking is for you to control yourself for the next two weeks and let me get married in peace."

Becky, red-eyed and shaking, looked at him. A stranger. The person standing in front of her couldn't possibly be her son, because her son would never cause his mother this much pain.

Noah walked back around the desk and kissed her cheek. "I love you, but you have to get over this."

Becky sat frozen in her chair. She let the tears roll and wished for her own mother. Not the cheating version of her, but the loving woman who always made her feel safe.

Naomi

Naomi woke to sunshine streaming through the crack between the curtains. She rolled over and threw a hand across Aaron's back. He made a low guttural sound, rolled onto his side, and pulled her close.

"Aaron, it's morning. Ezra will be home in an hour. You have to leave."

He gave her his best wounded puppy look and began kissing her neck.

"I mean it. You have to go home."

He flopped onto his back. "I have a better idea. I'll get dressed and clean-up this room. You go downstairs and make pancakes. When Ezra walks in, it will look like I just came for breakfast."

Naomi started laughing and hit him with a pillow. She whipped the blankets off of him and started pushing him to the side of the bed. "He's young, not stupid. Get up."

Aaron finally gave in and got up. "I don't like being kicked out of bed after sex."

"Do you want me to kick you out before sex?"

"Do we have to play this game forever?" he asked, tugging his jeans over his hips. "Thirty years ago, we hid from our parents, now we hide from your son."

Naomi wrapped her arms around him and kissed his cheek. "Not forever—just until he goes to college in six and a half months."

He threw his head back and groaned. "Ezra really should be spending more weekends with his father."

Naomi rolled her eyes. "Get out and call me from the car."

As they walked down the steps, she couldn't fathom that she almost pushed him away. The weeks since had passed in a haze of happiness. Aaron accepted the position at Pitt. His official start date wasn't until May first, but he tried to spend as much time as he could in Pittsburgh. This proved difficult because of his new book on the market. But he made sure that at least one evening of every weekend was spent with her.

"This Friday, I'm hosting Shabbat dinner. It will be Esther and Lew and possibly Laurie and Dan. Do you think you'll be able to make it?"

"What, no Miriam or Becky?"

Naomi shook her head. "I need a night off. It's five days until the wedding. If I'm not working, I'm on the phone with one of them."

She kissed him goodbye, playfully smacked his backside, and pushed him out the door. Fifteen minutes later, Ezra pulled the car into the driveway. When he walked into the kitchen, she sat casually drinking coffee, engrossed in reading the newspaper on her laptop.

Becky

Before Becky glanced at the screen of her phone, she knew why it beeped. Another text message from Maria's mother. That woman was driving her insane over stupid things—issues with the caterer, the florist, and seating arrangements. Becky suggested a roomful of picnic tables and deli trays, but Maria's mother didn't think it was funny. Instead of replying to the text, she dialed Naomi—voicemail. She left a message asking her to meet for a glass of wine at their normal spot.

Becky arrived first and looked around the restaurant. Only a few people sat chatting at the bar, and most of the tables were empty. Unusual for 5:30 on a Wednesday for a place known for its after-work crowd. The hostess escorted her to a table for two against the wall in the back.

Becky watched Naomi approach the table and gave her a slight wave. Beautiful Naomi. Becky remembered the nights she wished she could look like her. But what Naomi had in physical beauty, she lacked in self-confidence. Becky shook her head. Kind, gentle, smart, and beautiful, if Naomi only could see it in herself.

"Why are you shaking your head?" Naomi asked as she slid into the chair.

"Was I? I didn't even realize it. I was thinking about you."

Naomi's eyes widened.

Becky leaned back into the soft leather upholstery, her eyes fixated on Naomi's face. "I wish you had more self-confidence. You should be writing, not typing for that creepy boss of yours."

Naomi ordered a cabernet. "Have you been talking to Aaron? He's been pushing me to start writing again."

"No. I haven't spoken with him since the last time he was at *shul*. But he's right."

"Becky, I just can't find any words, believe me, I've tried."

Becky locked a stern gaze directly into Naomi's eyes. "Try harder."

Naomi shook her head as the waiter set the wine glass in front of her. "I sit at my computer and stare at the screen. My mind's blank. Then I just feel disgusted with myself and walk away."

"Nothing's going to happen if you walk away." Becky leaned forward, crossing her forearms on the table. "Wait a minute, I just remembered something. You never wrote while sitting in front of your typewriter. You always said that you wrote your stories while you ran. Take up running again. The stories will come back."

Naomi cocked her head. "You're right. I forgot all about running and writing. I did write entire stories in my head and typed them up when I got back to the dorm."

"That settles it. When this wedding is over, I'm taking you to Dick's Sporting Goods and buying you a new pair of running shoes. Nikes will kick start your new career."

"Maybe I should start with walking shoes. It's been years since I ran. My knees aren't so great."

"Fine, you can walk and write."

They clinked glasses, both smiling.

Between sips of wine, they ordered appetizers. When David called, Becky told him that he was on his own for dinner.

The evening felt like a pre-life-crashing-disaster evening with Naomi, relaxing and easy. They talked about Aaron and gossiped a bit about Jake's sexual tastes. It was a relief to talk about something other than the damn wedding. But that changed as they walked out of the restaurant.

"The wedding is only days away. Are you ready?" Naomi asked.

Standing on Murray Avenue, Becky broke down and told her about Noah's visit to her office and how he made her promise to be nice to Maria. "And he made me promise not to make a scene over Miriam. I can't deliver on that promise." Becky shook her head and clenched her fists. "In fact, I can't deliver on either promise. That's it! I'm not going to the freaking wedding."

"Stop talking like that," Naomi said. "You're starting to sound crazy. Of course, you'll be at your son's wedding, and you can deliver on those two simple promises."

Steam shot through Becky's veins. "Why is it you don't understand? Miriam and Maria have crushed my world."

"Becky." Naomi placed her arm over her shoulder. "Nobody crushed your world. You're doing this to yourself. Please, think about what you're saying. Maria will be Noah's wife and your daughter-in-law. Can't you rake some kindness out of your heart?"

Becky hesitated for a few heartbeats and stared at the ground. "Fine, I'll tell Maria it's not personal, but I can-

not and will not stand in the same room as that evil son
stealer. It's either her or me, and he picked her."

Naomi removed her arm from the shoulder hug,
turned, and clamped both of Becky's shoulders. "Stop it!
Do you hear yourself? He's your son. Your only son!
Where are you getting this 'he picked her' shit? Listen to
me, I've had it with all of this bullshit. Noah loves you—
Miriam loves you. You're torturing them. They've done
nothing to hurt you. This insanity exists only in your
head. Do you hear me?" Sweat dampened Naomi's hair-
line and tears streamed down her cheeks, but she kept her
grip on Becky's shoulders.

"No, no," Becky said, shaking her head and clenching
her fists.

"Listen to me." Naomi locked gazes with her. "Maria
started studying Judaism in Squirrel Hill months ago.
They didn't want to tell you until she makes her final decision. The girl is really trying. And Noah has been meeting with Rabbi Morty for months. Noah isn't throwing
away his heritage. This can all work out if you just shut
up and play nice."

Becky froze in her spot. The sounds of the street faded
into the background. The only sound she heard was the
echo of Naomi's words in her mind. *Maria is studying to
convert? Noah's meeting with Morty?* "Why didn't anyone tell me?"

"Better to let you believe she's going to remain Catholic. Noah figures if Maria goes through with the conversion, you'll be elated. But if she decides against it, you
won't be devastated." Becky nodded. Naomi sighed. "Besides, it's their life. I'm not even supposed to know any
of this, but you know how fast gossip travels through our
small group."

"She's going to convert," Becky mumbled to herself.
The tension in her neck released and, for the first time in

months, the vise compressing her rib cage loosened. She felt lighter. She lunged forward, squeezing Naomi in a bear hug. "Thank you."

"You will not let on that you know about any of this. Do you hear me, Becky? Not a single word."

Becky fumbled with her car keys. A huge smile covered her face.

"I repeat—you will say nothing or do anything that would indicate you know she's studying with a rabbi." Naomi's face facial expression made it very clear that she was expecting a promise.

Becky nodded again. "I promise." She hugged Naomi, said good night, and then floated to her car, repeating to herself over and over, *She's converting. God does listen.*

The minute she sat down in the driver's seat, she pulled out her phone and dialed David.

Naomi

The smell of cilantro and rosemary chicken permeated Naomi's first floor. She and Ezra worked together. Well, actually, she worked, and he tried to talk her into letting him taste the chicken soup and the fish. She was attempting to recreate Esther's spicy fish recipe, which was proving difficult because Esther never measured. "Dump in a little hot paprika, add a half a palm full of cumin and some sweet paprika."

Naomi figured the trick was to find a balance between too spicy and not spicy enough, which was proving to be difficult with Ezra adding more hot paprika when he thought she wasn't paying attention.

"Ezra, I'll let you taste the fish, if you stop messing with it and start chopping vegetables for Israeli salad."

"Deal," he said before trotting over to the fridge. He reached in and grabbed tomatoes, cucumbers, green peppers, and scallions.

She watched him set up his chopping station and was overtaken by the urge to hug him.

"What was that for?" he asked when she finally loosened her grip.

She shrugged. "Just because."

They cooked and listened to Steely Dan music. It reminded her of the old days when she and Jake worked side by side to prepare Shabbat dinner. There were a lot of fun times. He was a good husband until the end. As much as she hated to admit it, she loved him even as he walked out the door. She shuddered off thoughts of Jake. "Put on something nice tonight. Sarah's coming."

Naomi watched Ezra's face redden. "Same to you. So is Aaron."

"You got me with that. But what's going on with you and Sarah?"

"What's going on with you and Aaron?"

Naomi smiled and shook her head. "I don't know."

"Well, I don't know what's going on with me and Sarah either."

"Ha ha, that means something is going on. Did she let you kiss her yet?"

Ezra clasped his head."Uggh. You drive me crazy. Let's change the subject."

"Why? That's no fun," Naomi said, enjoying watching him squirm.

"Fine, just to let you know, I told Dad that I'll go with him to visit Grandma over Passover. You already know that Josh is going."

She was surprised by her reaction—pleased, bordering on happy. Jake had stepped up since the kitchen sprayer incident. He kept his word and sent money for repairs, took Ezra shopping, and bought him school clothes, a suit, and a pair of expensive sneakers. And to her surprise, Josh called, excited about a big check he received from his dad. The memo line on the check read "spending money." Jake also asked for his loan information. He told Josh that he would pay them off.

Jake went back to being a father and arrived on time for visits. He even took Ezra to a hockey game. The one mistake he made was asking her to dinner. Naomi told him that it would take at least a decade before that would be a possibility.

"That's great, Ez," she said now, "but don't change the subject. I want to hear about Sarah."

Ezra continued chopping cucumbers. She stood behind him, smiling. Fortunately, the ringing phone replaced her need to wait for his answer.

"Naomi, I just opened my mail," Miriam choked out. "She photocopied the letters. I read a few."

"Calm, down. Those letters were written a long time ago."

"I'm not crying about those letters! It's the horrible one she included in the package. She said that if I show up for the wedding, she'll walk out. This is insanity."

Naomi held the phone to her ear and stared at the refrigerator. Miriam's voice was so loud Ezra heard it across the kitchen and stopped chopping.

"This is unreal." Naomi said the words, but her mind retreated to the scene, in front of the restaurant, when she said goodbye to Becky.

At that moment, she believed everything was moving in the right direction. Becky's anger level cooled, and she walked away with a smile on her face. Naomi really believed the happiness would spill over to the Miriam situation.

The sound of Miriam blowing her nose broke the silence on the line. Naomi didn't need to see her friend's tears. She felt them drip out of the phone.

"Miriam, listen to me. I know you're having Shabbat dinner at the rabbi's house tonight. Please, go wipe your face, fix your make-up, and forget about this until tomorrow. We can talk at the synagogue."

"Okay," she said. "But, Naomi, I've had enough of this. It's bullshit."

"You're right," In spite of the seriousness of the conversation, Naomi covered her mouth with her hand. Miriam never swore and hated when others did, so hearing her say "bullshit" sounded funny. "Try to enjoy the evening and tell everyone at the rabbi's house that I said *Shabbat Shalom*."

She set the phone on the countertop, looked at Ezra, and shook her head. "I'm really starting to believe Becky is going crazy. Not the slang kind of crazy. The inpatient kind of crazy."

"Maybe she should call Dad's therapist," he said.

They both cracked up.

✡ ✡ ✡

The group around the table agreed to not discuss the Becky/Miriam situation during dinner, but the ban broke down during dessert.

"Look," Esther said. "The way I see is simple. We sit her down and tell her to snap out of it. Just like those interventions they do on TV for alcoholics and drug addicts."

Aaron snickered and Esther shot him an arched eyebrow reprimand. "Sorry, Esther," he said. "But cornering Becky elicits the same reaction as cornering a wolverine."

"Fine," Esther said. "Do you have any ideas?"

"Break her knee caps?" Aaron suggested with a meek shrug and a smirk.

"That's what you would write in a novel? The main character has a huge problem and you would break her knees?" Esther asked.

"Actually, I don't create protagonists with stupid, self-imposed, irrational problems."

Everyone at the table stared at Esther—waiting.

"You're right," she finally replied.

The group let out a collective sigh of relief. Esther rarely—never—conceded an argument. Normally, she went in for the kill and left her opponent bloody and stunned.

"A fiction writer creates conflicts that a human being with a reasonable amount of intelligence and logic can overcome—that is, unless it's supposed to be a tragedy. But here, we really don't have a conflict, just a made up battlefield in her *mishegus* head." Aaron lifted his wine glass. "To the end of *mishegus*—craziness be gone."

"*L'chaim*," the group responded in unison.

"We'll crash into her office and tell her she's crazy." Aaron dramatically pretended to bust open the door. "Then give her a menu."

Everyone looked perplexed—a menu?

"Anti-depressants, anti-anxiety, or she could go old-school and just smoke a joint." As Aaron said this, rays of mischief emanated from his eyes. It didn't take long for the conversation to break down into college marijuana memories.

They lingered over dessert and coffee until the clock on the buffet read midnight. Laurie rose from the table. "Thank you for a lovely evening, but we need to find our daughter and head home."

Naomi opened the door to the basement and called down to Ezra and Sarah. Laurie's eyes widened when Ezra reached the top of the steps trying to wrestle his curls back into place. Sarah looked at her mom and dropped her eyes. Naomi fought hard to stifle a snicker.

Aaron lingered after the rest of the group filed out into the cold. "I'm sorry, but I won't make it to *shul* tomorrow. I have to take an early flight to New York. My agent wants me to make an appearance at another boring soiree."

She hugged him and kissed his cheek. "No problem. Just so you're back for the wedding on Thursday."

✡ ✡ ✡

Becky

Becky woke at 6:00 a.m. Outside the bedroom window, she could see the sun sitting low on the horizon, not shedding enough light to dispel the darkness. David continued his low snoring as she climbed out of bed and headed to the bathroom. Nausea gripped her stomach. Today was Noah's *aufruf*. The day he would be called to the *bimah* to read from the Torah as the chatan—the groom. She and the other ladies began cooking and preparing the kiddush luncheon on Wednesday. The double door refrigerator held enough food to feed an Israeli Army battalion.

It didn't escape her that under normal circumstances, she would be out of bed, bouncing with joy. Now, she focused on the bile rising into her throat. She flushed the toilet, washed her hands, and reached for the towel, hanging on the door hook. She stopped. On the second hook, hung the jeans she took off last night. She grabbed them and slithered them up under her nightgown.

As much as she wanted to believe what Naomi told her, she couldn't find any evidence to verify it was true.

Maria still looked as Catholic as ever and today, her entire Christian family would be sitting in the sanctuary for the service. What a nightmare—the bile bubbled up again—Maria's mother talking to Rabbi Morty.

Becky stepped inside her closet and grabbed the first sweater she saw, wondering when the cold winter would end.

A question had gnawed at her since the Rosh Hashanah engagement announcement and no matter how she wrestled with it, the answer eluded her—where did she go wrong? She and David made sure he attended synagogue every week. They sent him to expensive Jewish summer camps and, like all good Jewish parents, forced him to suffer through years of Hebrew school. Maybe they should have shuttled him to Squirrel Hill for a good Jewish day school education. In the beginning, her inability to answer the question angered her. Now, she felt crushed by a sense of utter failure.

She tiptoed out of the bedroom and down the steps. The kitchen looked spotless—depressing, because cleaning always relaxed her. She walked straight to the coffee maker. Today, the *shul* would be packed with Noah's friends, celebrating with *l'chaims* to the happy groom and bride. The final drop of coffee fell into her cup. It smelled good, and the cup felt warm in her hands. Her mother loved coffee. Not the fancy gourmet stuff like the kind Becky ordered online. Her mother only bought Eight O'Clock Coffee. As a small child, Becky loved grocery shopping with her mother, especially on the days she bought coffee. At the checkout, she felt her excitement grow because she knew what would happen after her mother finished paying. The cashier would dump the beans into the grinder and hold the bag under the spout. Even as a child, Becky adored the smell. Today, even the smallest whiff of the aroma reminded her of home and her mother. A woman, who like her son, Becky didn't really know.

She set the coffee on the table and sat down, after a few sips she realized that she didn't want to go to the *shul*. She didn't want to make small talk. And she, absolutely with every part of her soul, did not want to pretend to be happy. Why should she care about Noah? If he cared about her, he would cancel this marriage. *That's it.* She pushed the mug away. *I'm not going.*

She pulled a jacket from the closet, grabbed her keys, and headed for the garage.

She slithered into the driver's seat, reached up and pushed the button on the garage door opener, silently praying the sound wouldn't wake David. A moment later, she backed out of the driveway, put the car in drive, and pushed the gas pedal. When she arrived at the stop sign on Beverly Road, she relaxed. David couldn't see the stop sign from their front porch. She had made a clean get away.

She sat at the intersection a bit too long, contemplating left or right? Did it really matter? She kept her foot on the brake, reached under the seat, and found what she wanted. Tucked against the track that the seat moved along was a small green change purse. Inside was evidence of a bad habit she'd picked up in college and hid from the world. She pulled out the cigarette box and the lighter. Within seconds, she pulled the first drag of the cigarette into her lungs. Why couldn't cigarettes and twelve-year-old scotch be healthy? They were much better than exercise and those foul tasting juice concoctions Laurie tried to get her to drink—for her health—yuk.

There was more traffic on Banksville Road than she expected. Every Saturday morning of her life had been spent in a synagogue. She never even thought about what other people did on Saturdays. Based on the number of cars in the supermarket parking lot, they did a lot of grocery shopping. When the light in front of a little strip mall turned red, she eased to a stop and noticed a line inside the Starbucks. It looked no shorter today than it did on Mondays. The car radio was tuned to WESA, the local public radio station, but she wasn't in the mood for the jovial chatter of Car Talk. She shut it off and waited for the light to turn green.

The distance between her and the synagogue grew. She envisioned Naomi, Laurie and Esther trying to help the waitress get the kiddush ready. Let the congregation and the guests celebrate this farce. She would be miles away.

Becky flicked the cigarette butt out the window before she entered the Fort Pitt tunnel, which connected the South Hills of Pittsburgh to the city center. Pittsburgh, the city where you couldn't go anywhere without crossing a bridge or going through a tunnel. When she exited, the giant green signs presented her options. Drive straight into downtown? Take the right ramp toward Squirrel Hill? But the sign that grabbed her attention was the one that read Route 279 North. She veered into the left lane, out of the city and away from home.

This tree-lined road was beautiful in the summer—green and lush. Today, the scenery wasn't worth turning her head—dead trees, dead bushes, everything just looked dead. The tension in her neck started to creep into her head. Great, all she needed was a migraine. No, she refused to think about the pounding in the back of her head. Instead, she let her thoughts drift to Miriam who was probably sitting in the synagogue acting like she was the mother of the groom.

Becky pounded her hands against the steering wheel. *Damn, Miriam.* Of course, she would convince Naomi to take her side. Becky imagined the whining. "Naomi,

Becky's being mean to me—talk to her, pleeease."

She almost swerved off the road when she imagined Miriam, the son stealer, blowing her nose, honking louder than a Canadian goose, as Naomi consoled her.

How could Naomi be so stupid to fall for Miriam's poor-me-act? Miriam wore out that show when they were still in college.

"Shit," Becky said out loud, smacking the steering wheel again.

She drove far beyond the exits she was familiar with until a green sign on the right side of the road indicated an exit for a town called Zelienople. She had no idea where she was and where she was going, but she followed the exit sign, landing in a cute little town with an old-fashioned main street.

People walked along the sidewalk, moving in and out of the small shops. She parked, got out of the car, and put fifty cents into the parking meter.

A cold drizzle fell from the gray sky as she wandered along the quaint street, glancing into the store windows. A display in the window of an antique shop stopped her. Someone arranged the window around the theme of cups and glasses. Dainty china tea settings, Irish coffee mugs and German beer steins rested on a vintage sideboard covered with an Irish lace table cloth. But, it wasn't any of these cups that caught her eye. It was the large, silver challis resting on a small silver plate in the middle of the arrangement. It couldn't be.

She pulled open the door of the shop and walked straight to the chalice, twirling it to ascertain if it was a fancy wine glass or what she thought it might be. Etched into the base of the cup were four Stars of David. She smiled, her suspicions confirmed. A hand forged silver kiddush cup, most likely originating in Germany or Poland before the war. She turned it upside down, saw the price and did a little snicker. The owner of the shop obviously believed it was just an old cup.

Becky rolled it around in her hand…

✡ ✡ ✡

Her father lifted the large silver kiddush cup and began the chant. *"Baruch ata Adonai…"*

The cup overflowed, and the sweet grape concord wine dribbled over his hands onto his silver ringed white Shabbat plate. Each week, he spilled the wine onto his dinner plate and made an elaborate show of wiping the purple liquid with her mother's best linen napkin. It drove her mother crazy, but he was proud. "Hashem," he always told Becky, "fills our cup."

Each Friday night, he became the king, presiding over the people seated around their Shabbat table, chanting the same prayers week after week. Tonight she just wanted to scream "enough already." She hated sitting at the table through the gefitle fish course, the matzah ball soup, and finally, either brisket or chicken. It was always the same boring food, the same boring prayers, and the same boring conversation.

Ugh, she silently screamed inside her head. Every one of her non-Jewish friends and even a few of her Jewish ones were at the homecoming football game.

Her brother handed her the kiddush cup. As she raised it to her lips, she noticed her mother standing across from her, giving her what Becky dubbed the stop-now-or-you-will-be in-trouble look. She set the cup down and stomped toward the kitchen, passing her father in the doorway as he made his way back to his chair, having completed the ritual handwashing.

Her mother followed her into the kitchen and clenched Becky's shoulder. "Stop rolling your eyes and making faces. You know you're not allowed to go out on Friday night."

Becky lifted the ornate two handled cup and began pouring water over her hands. "I don't know why. It's the same thing every week. So what if I miss one night? It's not the end of the world."

"First, I let you go one Friday night," her mother said, "then you'll want another one. It will turn into two Friday nights and then three. Eventually, you'll forget the Sabbath. The Sabbath is a gift to the Jews from Hashem. When you lose the Sabbath, you throw away your gift—your heritage. Never, Becky, never put friends and the secular world in front of the Sabbath. When you lose your heritage, you have nothing."

✡ ✡ ✡

Becky picked up the small silver plate that went with the cup and walked over to the checkout counter. The pregnant lady manning the cash register gave her a cheerful smile. "I can't believe someone is actually buying this old thing."

"Really?" Becky replied. "I think it's beautiful."

"So did my mother. She used to buy for the shop. She brought this old cup home when I was still in high school."

Becky handed the woman her Visa card. "Well, your mom has good taste."

The young woman set the card in one of those old fashioned machines that pressed the imprint of the numbers onto a paper receipt. She handed it and a pen to Becky. "She had good taste," she said. "She died a few years after she found this cup. A year ago, my dad was cleaning out the house and brought it here."

"I'm sorry to hear that," Becky said, watching the

young woman carefully roll the cup in tissue paper.

"My mother said the cup reminded her of her grand-mother. She was Jewish."

Becky looked at the young woman. "Really, was it her mother's mother or her father's mother?"

She looked at Becky. "That's an odd question."

"I'm sorry. I didn't mean to be rude." Becky reached for the bag containing her new treasure. "It's not my business."

"Her mother's mother," the young woman said. "I don't know why I'm telling you this stuff."

Becky smiled and shrugged. "I'm glad you did. I'll think of your story when I look at my cup."

The silver sleigh bells hanging over the door tinkled when Becky walked out. It only took four generations for that family to totally lose its Judaism. Her mind switched to Maria and what Naomi told her. But studying to convert didn't guarantee anything.

Becky continued meandering up the street until there were no more store windows to peep into. She headed back to her car, climbed inside, and looked at her phone. One missed call. She didn't have to look. Her friends didn't even carry purses into the *shul*, let alone cell phones.

David must have borrowed a phone from Maria's father and snuck out between the end of the service and the beginning of kiddush to call her.

Before pulling out of the parking spot, she checked the time, two o'clock.

Who would believe that she bought a hand-forged kiddush cup in a town that probably never had a synagogue? Tears washed over eyes, clouding her vision. But who would believe her mother cheated on her father, and her only child was marrying a non-Jew? She swiped at her left eye and then the right. And who would believe

that dingbat of an ex-best friend had the guile to deceive
her for over thirty years?

Chapter 19

Naomi

Naomi's stress level increased with each second Becky's chair, in the third to the last row, remained empty. The rabbi was only minutes away from beginning the silent Amidah. Earlier, David walked in alone. She assumed Becky went straight to the kitchen to talk with the waitress. But giving instructions to the waitress shouldn't take long.

Naomi slid from her chair and walked to the kitchen. Inside, Margie bustled around the steel table, putting the finishing garnishes on bowls of tuna salad, egg salad, and plates of lox. "Have you seen Becky?" Naomi asked.

Margie moved to a bowl of Asian noodles and strategically inserted a few sprigs of parsley. "No. And I have a bunch of questions to ask her."

"I'm going out for the Amidah. If she doesn't come by the Torah reading, I'll do my best to answer them."

Naomi sensed the questioning gazes of her friends as she returned to her seat. She glanced at each of their faces, shaking her head. As the rabbi began the silent Amidah, she grabbed her siddur, took three steps back and three steps forward. Then she willed herself to forget Becky and focus on the words of the prayer.

When the repetition began, Esther tapped her on the shoulder. "Do you think she's upstairs hiding or crying?"

Naomi shook her head. "I don't know, but I sure hope she's somewhere in this building."

When Rabbi Morty stepped to the lectern to begin the sermon, Naomi glanced back at the still empty seat. Her heart went thud against her chest. Before she could turn forward, Maria caught her eye and gave her a long, pained look. All Naomi could do was shrug.

The rabbi continued to speak, but not a word of it registered in her brain. Where in the hell was Becky? When the sermon ended, she crept to the men's side of the mechitza and signaled to David.

"I don't know where she is. When I woke up, she was gone," he said, color draining from his face.

Naomi controlled her urge to hug him. The pain in his eyes defied description. "She'll be here. It's just like the shower. She'll come to her senses."

Naomi, along with Laurie, Esther, and Miriam entered the kitchen. Once inside, Naomi fielded Margie's questions, and the rest of the women began loading food onto the carts, even red-eyed Miriam.

Naomi exhaled through her nose—a long, sad release of the air choking her lungs. The next inhale filled them with oxygen that felt heavier than rocks. She placed her arm over Miriam's shoulder. "Stop, you look like a mourner at a funeral."

Miriam didn't respond.

Naomi couldn't find words of condolence for a dying friendship. Instead, she walked to the coffee urn and filled two Styrofoam cups and added the non-dairy creamer. She motioned with her head to Miriam. Miriam followed her into the Rabbi's office. Naomi closed the door. Before any words were said, Naomi wrapped her arms around Miriam and let her cry.

"She's not here because she knew I'd be here."

"No." Naomi shook her head. "That's not true. Stop crying."

"I can't. I've been crying since I read her letter. Do you believe she'd walk out of the wedding if I'm there?"

"No, I don't believe it. She isn't that crazy. She would never do that to Noah." Naomi shook her head, astounded that she would even need to answer such an absurd question.

"She's nuts. You know that." Miriam's hands trembled as she spoke. "Where is she? I don't recognize this person, living in her body. Do you? Our Becky would be here, doing what she does best—being a bossy control freak. This is just insanity." Naomi met Miriam's eyes in silent agreement. "I think about this situation twenty-four hours a day," Miriam continued. "There's no logic in being mad at me. How could she hold me accountable for something my dad and her mother did all those years ago?" Naomi shrugged. "If something I did really caused this fiasco, I would apologize." Miriam pulled her shoulders back and Naomi watched something in her eyes change. "I'm not going to the wedding."

Naomi's head shot up. "Noah will be devastated. Don't let her bully you."

"Noah needs his mother to be there more than he needs me. He knows how much I love him. My other son—but I just can't take the chance of her really walking out."

Naomi clasped her friend's hand. "That's a very noble decision, but my heart isn't agreeing with you. Maybe the excitement around the wedding will make her come to her senses."

"No, Naomi." Miriam dropped her friend's hand. "You'll take pictures and video the ceremony. I'll watch it on Friday morning."

An overwhelming feeling of love engulfed Naomi as she hugged Miriam. "You don't deserve this treatment."

✡ ✡ ✡

Naomi slipped out of the synagogue while David continued doing shots of *l'chaim* with the rabbi, Noah, and a few others. She walked straight to Becky's house and pounded on the front door—no answer. At the back door, she beat her fist against the wood until her hand ached. Becky wasn't inside. The noise would have annoyed her enough to open the door. But if she wasn't home, where in the hell was she?

Naomi walked home, stunned that Becky abandoned her family on such an important day. Poor David, he didn't bother lying when people bombarded him with, "Where's Becky?"

He just shrugged. "I don't know."

Naomi's heart ached for him.

For the rest of the afternoon she tried calling Becky's cell. It went straight to voicemail. In the early evening, she called David.

"She's home," he said. "But before I could say a word to her, she locked herself inside the office. I yell through the door, but she ignores me."

There was nothing for Naomi to say and, by Sunday morning, she lost all hope of talking to Becky.

She switched her attention to completing her own to-do-list. By six o'clock that evening she felt physically and mentally exhausted from worrying about her friend. She plopped down onto the sofa and booted up her laptop. Over the last few months, she'd acquired the habit of reading the *New York Times* society news.

Not that she found it interesting, but Aaron did publicity appearances for his book and pictures of him often showed up on the website. Her finger tapped on the downward scrolling arrow—reports on charity fundraising events and pictures of wealthy people smiling. No Aaron, she hit the down arrow one more time. At the very bottom of the page, tucked into the lowest part of the right-hand corner, Aaron and his ex-wife. His arm slung casually over her shoulders and both smiling widely. Naomi clicked on the photo to enlarge it. *Author, Aaron Brenner and ex-wife, super-model-turned-entrepreneur, Alisha Brenner, appeared arm-in-arm at the annual fund-raising event for The Arts and Letters Academy.*

Naomi's heart pounded against her chest as she reread the text below their beautiful smiling faces. *I'm such a jackass.* She exed out of the site. *That's why he's running to New York all the time.* She closed the laptop and stared out the window.

Ezra ambled into the room. "I'm bored."

"And that's my problem?" she shot back.

He plopped down onto the loveseat and swung his legs into a reclining position.

"Get your dirty shoes off the loveseat."

Ezra's eyes widened. "What's wrong with you? My feet are hanging over the end. They're not even touching anything."

"Get them off, because I said to get them off." Naomi rose from the chair and left the room.

"I'm assuming this means you don't want to go to the movies with me," he yelled.

"No, I'm not going anywhere." She walked into the guest bedroom/office and booted up the dusty desktop computer. Once the fancy opening sequence for Windows finished, she clicked on the icon for Microsoft Word. She didn't stare at the blank document, nor did she think about the keyboard. She knew exactly what she wanted to say.

Three hours later she wrote the words "The End." After running spell check, she saved the file, and then logged onto her email. She typed in Aaron's email address and wrote the words *First assignment*.

Dear Professor Brenner,
Attached is my assignment. It's long overdue. ~ Naomi.

She attached the file and immediately hit send. As she read the words, "message sent," she swiped her eyes with the back of her hands.

Chapter 20

Becky

T he morning sun shone through the lace curtains. Becky stared at the ceiling above her side of the bed, smelling the coffee David brewed in the kitchen. She rolled over and pulled the blanket over her head. No one was going to force her out of the bed.

"Becky," he shouted. "It's time to get up."

She heard his footsteps and, judging by the fading of the sound, he walked back into the kitchen. Good. At least he was leaving her alone. Her head hurt.

Her phone, lying on the night stand, began to vibrate. Her arm shot out from under the blanket that still engulfed her head. She looked at the screen. A text message from David that read, *Stop ignoring me. Get up or I will come upstairs and pull you out of bed.*

She exhaled deeply and put down the phone. The bed felt warm and safe. If she stayed in it, the whole wedding could be avoided. Less than eight hours ago, she and David hosted the rehearsal dinner, which insulted every cell in her body. Toasting with those *goyim*—ugh. Thank goodness for Naomi and Laurie. They filled her wine glass all night and graciously entertained Maria's family. Early in the evening, Becky tried to escape into the kitchen for a good cry, but the knife-wielding caterer didn't appreciate her presence and shooed her out the door. This didn't seem fair because they tolerated Esther, who spent most of the evening playing the role of *mashgiach*—keeping the kitchen kosher while supervising the professionals.

The steps were getting closer and they didn't sound happy. David clomped into the bedroom and grabbed the blanket. "Your son is getting married today. Get up."

"No."

He shook his head, sat down on the bed, and reached for her hand. "I know I'm not the most romantic of husbands. And I know I don't say 'I love you' very often."

Becky squeezed his hand.

"I'm saying it to you today, I love you and nothing could have stopped me from marrying you."

Becky reached for the tissue box on the night stand.

"But," David said, "if my mother acted like you on our wedding day, I would have told her to get the hell out and cut our ties forever."

Becky felt her eyes widen.

"Honey, that's how Noah feels about Maria. We raised a mensch. He's tolerating your behavior, but you have to stop pushing him."

Before Becky could respond, the doorbell rang. He dropped her hand. He knew she wasn't getting out of bed to answer the door.

"This conversation isn't over," David said, as he walked across the room.

Becky stared at the ceiling, trying to imagine never seeing Noah again. A wrench twisted her heart. She rolled out of bed.

She turned on the faucet and ran water over her tooth brush. The toothpaste was in the medicine cabinet. When she reached to open it, her stomach lurched. She didn't like the face staring back. The eyes reflected hardness. The hair sprouted gray roots and looked unkempt—witchy.

As she brushed her teeth, Becky couldn't shift her gaze away from her face. The rough image belonged to a bitter old woman. Her throat constricted.

When she left the bathroom, David stood in the middle of the bedroom, waiting for her. "You have a visitor."

"I'll be down in a few minutes. Is it Naomi?"

He shook his head. "Put on your robe, you don't need to dress." He left the room before she could ask any questions.

Other than Naomi, who would have the nerve to show up at her house at eight o'clock in the morning without an invitation? She cinched the belt of her robe tighter around her waist and followed him.

Becky saw the back of her head before her face. Maria sat on one of the tall stools, surrounding the island in the middle of the kitchen. Becky walked to the coffee pot, avoiding the young woman's gaze. "Where's Noah?"

"He's not here, Mrs. Rosen. I came alone—to talk to you. It's important and I need to say it before the wedding."

Becky sat on the stool across from her. No one could argue that Maria was a beautiful girl. Her light brown eyes reminded Becky of a character straight out of a Jane Austen novel. Maria's eyes radiated warmth, but Becky wouldn't fall prey to it.

"Mrs. Rosen, as you probably heard by now, I've been studying Judaism with the rabbi in Squirrel Hill for over a year now." Becky nodded and noticed the young woman's hands quivering. Maria lifted the mug to her lips and sipped. "Organized religion never attracted me. I stopped going to church when I was fifteen."

Becky watched her, wondering where the girl was going with this conversation.

"The first thing anyone who meets Noah realizes is Judaism and Jewish culture are a major part of his identity. Noah and I were just friends for over a year because he couldn't bring himself to date a non-Jew. During that year, I saw the joy he got from Shabbat and going to services."

"Must not be that important." Even as the words slipped out of her mouth, Becky regretted them.

Anger flared in Maria's eyes. "Mrs. Rosen, I'm trying to be respectful of you."

Becky stared into the half empty coffee mug. "I'm sorry. Please, continue."

"When we finally started dating, I felt it was important that I learn something about Judaism, so I enrolled in a Hebrew class. When the class finished, I began studying with the rabbi."

Maria stopped talking, obviously hoping Becky would react. She didn't. Maria sighed. "One of the things I admire most about him is his unwavering belief. The other is his connection to Jewish history."

Becky let out a little snort. "Well, at least he got that part right. It is his heritage." She leaned into the high back of the stool and closed her eyes. *I will not cry in front of this girl. I will not cry in front of this girl.*

"But I didn't want to insult him or the religion by agreeing to convert if I truly didn't believe it in my heart."

Becky sipped her coffee. Under normal circumstances, she would admire this girl's attitude, but in this situation, couldn't she just suck it up and convert? The silence grew uncomfortable.

"Mrs. Rosen, Noah and I both believe that an orthodox conversion is a true conversion."

Maria waited for some type of reaction. But Becky couldn't think of anything to say.

"Mrs. Rosen, I've made my decision."

Becky's eyes widened and her heart pounded against her ribcage.

Maria bit her lower lip, and Becky's stomach dropped. She could see the answer in Maria's eyes. It wasn't going to be the decision she wanted to hear. Maria was going to stay Catholic. Becky dropped her chin to her chest to hide the tears forming in her eyes.

"I'm going to move forward in the conversion process. I'm going to become a Jew."

For a few heartbeats, Becky sat, unable to look up, questioning her ears. When the news sank in, she looked up, but instead of seeing joy in Maria's eyes, she saw agony. She didn't understand why and didn't really care. Maria had spoken the words Becky dreamed of hearing.

"It's a miracle." Becky felt the muscles in her face pull into a smile. She sprang from her seat and walk toward Maria. "*Nes gadol*—it's a big miracle!"

"Wait." Maria motioned with her arms for Becky to sit down. "I have more to say."

Becky returned to her seat and started twisting the belt of her robe between her fingers. All the while, yelling *Hurry up* inside her head.

"I want you to know that I'm not converting to make you happy and not for Noah either. Throughout history being Jewish has proven to be dangerous. As much as you want our children to be Jewish, this was a huge decision for me. What happens if another madman rises? Maybe, it won't affect me or my children, but what about my grandchildren or great grandchildren. I didn't make a decision for just my soul, but for theirs too."

Becky nodded and continued twisting the belt. "That I do understand very well."

"I realize that I want to be a Jew and accept all of the laws. Noah's God is my God."

Becky sat smiling. All of Maria's words after "I'm going to become a Jew," sort of blended together in her ears. She inhaled deeply, enjoying a sensation of physical lightness, while controlling the urge to jump up and down. "Those are the words I've prayed for. All I ever wanted was to hear you say that you would convert. Honestly, I didn't care how you did it or what you felt. You could've faked everything for the rabbi, if it meant my grandchildren would be Jewish. This news is more than I prayed for—you'll be a real Jew."

Becky rose from the stool and began walking around the island. Again, Maria motioned her to back to the chair. "Wait, Mrs. Rosen, there's more."

Becky froze in her spot. She didn't want to sit down. She wanted to jump with joy. What else could there possibly be to say? The problem had been solved. Then it hit Becky, the wedding. Maria realized it wouldn't be a real wedding. "I think I know what you're going to say. Scheduling this civil wedding was a mistake. You want to wait until after the conversion to get married properly."

Maria shook her head. "No. That's not even close to what I want to say."

Becky sat back down.

"You decided not to like me before we met. But Noah thought that once you got to know me, you'd warm up to me. Obviously, that didn't happen. I've spent many nights crying and wondering why you hate me. I get the Jewish part, but your animosity seems to go beyond that. Your—I don't want to say hatred but serious dislike— even encompasses my family."

Becky poo-pooed her, flicking her wrists. "That's over now. You're going to be Jewish."

Maria fixed her gaze on Becky, a frozen stare. Becky

shuddered as a chill zapped through her. "I'm not okay with that," Maria said. "I'm the same person you disliked at Rosh Hashanah dinner. Jewish or Catholic, I'll still be me."

"I don't understand," Becky said.

"I'd never stand between you and Noah, but I don't want to come here and watch you put on an act, pretending you like me once I'm Jewish. We both love Noah, and to move forward, I think we need to be honest with each other, so I'm going to say it. You don't like me and I don't like you so much either."

Tears flooded Becky's eyes and streamed down her cheeks. She popped up from the stool and sprinted around the island. "You're wrong." She yanked Maria into her arms. "You're so wrong. From the very first day, I saw what Noah saw in you. You're exactly the woman I would have picked for him. I told all of my friends, I just wanted a Jewish Maria."

"What's all the yelling about in here?" David stood in the threshold of the kitchen but it didn't appear that he wanted to cross over it.

Becky ran into his arms. "She's converting! She's going to do it." She let go of him and turned back to Maria. "Get a bottle of champagne!"

"It's breakfast. This is wonderful news, but ladies, you both have a long day in front of you."

"We'll pour it in orange juice. Get it." Becky sat on the stool beside Maria, gripping the young woman's hands in her own. "I understand that you think I'm the wicked witch, but I swear to you, nothing I've ever said or done has been personal. You're wonderful. And your parents are very nice people. I promise I'll never be mean to you again. I love that you're going to be Jewish, but you're also a fabulous young woman."

David popped the champagne. Becky ran to the dining

room and returned carrying flutes. "Here we go," Her voice sounded shrill as she brandished the glasses.

David poured. Maria sat quietly. Becky babbled. "And after you convert, we're going to have a real wedding. I'll invite everyone in town."

Maria extended her arm and grasped the flute. "I'm having a real wedding in nine hours."

"Whatever," Becky replied, lifting her glass. "*L'chaim* to the marriage of Noah and Maria and to my future grandchildren." She gulped down the champagne and set it on the marble countertop. "I think, after you convert, we should begin calling you by your new Hebrew name. Maria doesn't work for nice Jewish mother."

✡ ✡ ✡

Naomi

Thursday morning—wedding day, Naomi smashed the pillow into her face. "Shit," she groaned, pulled herself out of bed, and began the mundane task of making her bed. She stopped mid-fold and growled at the undisturbed pillow on the side of the bed Aaron recently adopted. Hand on hip, she stared at the pillow, imaging what it would feel like to rip the feathers out and fling them around the room. She pounded it instead. Damn memory foam.

She moved in slow motion, dreading the day. By seven forty-five, she finished dressing, dumped her remaining coffee into a to-go cup, and set out for the bus stop, fifteen minutes behind schedule. Finally, the weather got the message that spring was approaching. The air held a chill, but the sun felt warm on her face, as she trotted down Beverly Road.

She planned to work until noon and then go to the nail

salon—a huge splurge, but her chewed up finger nails didn't match the dress Miriam gave her.

The bus arrived and Naomi ascended the steps. As she climbed, her phone vibrated in her bag. She pulled it out and tried to read Aaron's text while navigating her way through the standing-room only bus.

Love the story, I didn't expect the revenge theme, but it's good. I knew you still had it. I'm going to send it to my friend at Woman's Way magazine. See you in a few hours.

She hit the delete button and grabbed onto the bar over her head.

Miriam

Miriam sat in the family room, curled in her favorite chair and covered with a blanket. She gazed out the huge windows, watching a few squirrels running through the backyard. Normally, this was her favorite time of year, early spring—Passover. Each year, she held the second *Seder* at her house, stuffing her dining room with as many people as could fit.

For her, Passover embodied Judaism, and she loved sharing it. Most of her friends spent the first night with family, so she created the tradition of holding the second night to guarantee their attendance. Passover loomed three weeks away, and so far she only extended an invitation to Naomi.

The holiday without both of her best friends being together was unbearable.

The sound of footsteps pulled her from her reverie. "Miriam, I'm going to the office for a few hours. Does the wedding start at 6:30 or 7:00?" Joe asked.

"Hors d'oeuvres begin at 6:30 and the ceremony at 7:30."

"Shouldn't you be getting your hair done or your nails?"

Miriam raised her eyebrows.

"No, I didn't mean it that way." Joe chuckled and walked to his wife.

"You know I'm not going."

"Bullshit to that. You're going."

Miriam searched for the words to explain her reasoning. It was more than the fear of Becky making a scene. It was the memories, Noah's birth, his Bar Mitzvah, the time she sat in the hospital waiting room with Becky and Naomi while the doctor operated on Noah's almost exploded appendix. If she attended tonight, she would be there physically, but her soul and Becky's soul would be far apart. The thought of that distance created waves of nausea in her stomach.

The doorbell rang, and Joe left to answer it. Relief wafted through her. She didn't want to talk about the wedding. Maybe she would go alone to a movie tonight—a sad one where she wouldn't look like a nut for crying.

"Good morning, Mrs. Weiss." Maria glided through the doorway toward Miriam. The young woman approached her with opened her arms. Miriam rose from her chair, letting the blanket fall to the floor, and responded to the hug. Maria stepped out of the embrace and smiled as she sat on the love seat across from Miriam's overstuffed chair. "I just left Noah's parents' house. Before I drove back to Squirrel Hill, I wanted to stop by to make sure that you're coming tonight."

Miriam turned her head toward the window. The squirrels were gone.

"Mrs. Weiss, you are coming to our wedding, right?"

Miriam's eyes remained focused on the backyard, but she did manage to shake her head. If she spoke the words, she feared breaking down in front of this sweet young woman.

"Please, look at me. You have to come."

Miriam garnered the strength to look Maria in the eyes. "She said if I attend the wedding, she'll leave."

Maria shook her head. "Believe me, after what I just told her, she isn't going to leave the wedding. She's the happiest woman on the planet right now."

Miriam shot a questioning look at Maria, which elicited a small laugh from her. Not a happy laugh, but a you-are-not-going-to-believe-this laugh. "I told her that I'm converting."

Miriam clapped her hands together. "That's wonderful! Now Becky will be happy."

"Oh, she's happy. She'll be in such a great mood tonight. She'll forget why she's even mad at you. I bet she greets you with open arms." She eyed Miriam expectantly. "Really, Mrs. Weiss, I'm sure that nothing will happen at the wedding. I expect to see you there—on time. Don't try to slink in unseen. I expect you to be in the front row next to Mr. Weiss, Mrs. Feldman, Ezra, and Mr. Brenner."

Miriam's heart fluttered. Today was going to be wonderful—Noah marrying this beautiful girl and Becky ending her stupid feud.

"I will be there."

The two women said their goodbyes and Maria rushed to the car. Miriam dialed the nail salon, and then called her hairdresser and begged for an emergency appointment.

The night was going to be a dream.

✡ ✡ ✡

Becky

Becky eyed herself in the full-length mirror. Tammy, her hairdresser, had dyed the gray hair, put in a few extensions, and pulled her hair into a stylish up-do. Surprisingly, it didn't make her look old. As Becky precisely applied her make-up, she regretted not buying an evening gown. What was she thinking, buying a black evening suit? It looked so dire and dowdy. Her closet held four or five elegant gowns, but all of her friends were with her when she wore those dresses. Besides, it just felt wrong to wear a recycled dress to her son's wedding, but the suit didn't look chic. It looked frumpy.

She twisted around to get a look at the back of the jacket. Ridiculous. The outfit was appropriate for only thing—a funeral. The hell with it. She reached her hands behind her waist and pulled down the zipper. She was not going to appear at the wedding wearing this gothic rag. Whether she liked it or not, recycling was necessary. Maybe she could return the suit next week.

When she entered the kitchen, she watched David's eyes light up. "Now that's a party dress." He walked to her and scooped her into his arms. "You look beautiful."

Becky giggled. "You're wrinkling me."

He released the squeeze, sliding one arm down her back and clasping her hand with the other. Then he began swaying her side to side. Within moments, they glided around the kitchen dancing to an imaginary orchestra. "I'm so happy that the world righted itself, and I have my wife back," he whispered into her ear. "I missed her." He stepped back and twirled Becky under his arm.

She smiled as she moved back into his arms. "By the time we go to bed tonight, our baby will be a married man."

David smiled.

"I hope they wait until she converts to have babies."

He stopped and locked his knees. "Becky." He leaned back and raised his eyebrows into a stern expression. "Enough."

"What's so wrong with me wanting them to wait? If they do it before she's finished, the baby will also need to be converted—too complicated."

"Let's just enjoy the wedding." He twirled her one more time before releasing her hands.

"You're right. Let's celebrate." She twirled around and headed for the coat closet. "It's time to go."

Naomi

Naomi's phone rang at 3:30. She didn't need to look at the screen to know it was Aaron. He said he'd call at 3:30, and he was on time, as usual. She ignored the ring. It rang again, at 3:45. This time, she answered it.

"Hi," Aaron said. "I called a few minutes ago, but you were probably in the shower."

"Yes," she lied.

"Should I pick you and Ezra up at 6:00 or would you prefer to get there earlier?" he asked.

"No, why should you drive all the way out to Mt. Lebanon only to turn around and drive back downtown? I'll either drive or we'll ride with Miriam."

"What? I want to pick you up. I can't wait to see you."

Naomi could hear the disappointment in his voice. As much as she wanted to believe him, the picture she printed off the website showed otherwise. It now hung on the refrigerator door to remind her of the truth. "No, I'll see you at the wedding."

Miriam

Miriam wiggled into the slinky fabric of her new gown. It felt cool and soft against her skin. As she slipped on her pumps, she rehearsed the words she planned to say to Becky. First, she would wish Becky and David a huge mazel tov on the wonderful news of Maria's conversion. Then she would quickly shift the conversation by offering a sincere apology about the affair. She still had no idea why she was apologizing, but it didn't matter as long as Becky forgave her, and life returned to normal.

She lined her lips and filled them in with a deep mauve. As she began stroking on her mascara, the doorbell rang. She knew it would be Naomi and Ezra. Naomi called at four o'clock, asking for a ride. Miriam was grateful for the request.

Now she and Joe wouldn't be walking into the William Penn Hotel alone. It would be much less awkward to arrive as a group. She put the mascara wand back into the tube and shoved it into the drawer. "Joe," she yelled, "answer the door."

At the bottom of the stairs, Naomi and Ezra stood waiting. Miriam did a double take at Ezra. Standing next to his mother, dressed in a new black suit and white shirt, he looked exactly like his father, who Miriam secretly thought was the most handsome man on Earth.

"You look wonderful," Naomi said.

When Miriam reached the bottom of the steps, she hugged her friend. "You do too, and—" She turned to face Ezra. "—you look like a GQ model in that suit."

Ezra's face flushed. He thrust his hands into his pockets and stared down at the floor. His embarrassment didn't stop Miriam from gushing.

"You're so tall now. I bet the girls at school follow you everywhere."

"Ezra," Joe shouted from the kitchen. "I need some help."

Miriam and Naomi watched Ezra stride into the kitchen.

"Sounded like you needed saving from my wife." Joe said it loud enough for them to hear, as was the laughter that erupted from the kitchen seconds later.

Chapter 21

Naomi

Miriam abandoned Naomi as soon as they walked off the elevator. Naomi wasn't ready to socialize. She walked to the coat check, passed her ancient trench coat to the attendant, and stuffed the small chip bearing the pick-up number into her sequined handbag. She turned on her heel and scanned the room, hoping to see Esther or Laurie. Instead, she gasped. What was Jake doing here? It never occurred to her that either Noah or Becky would add him to the guest list. She headed toward the bar, wanting to avoid eye contact or speaking to him. As the bartender poured her wine, she felt a tap on her shoulder.

"You look stunning, Naomi," Jake said.

"So do you, Jake. I didn't expect to see you here."

"I still golf with David once in a while, and I occasionally see Noah and Maria in Squirrel Hill. A few Sundays ago, I ran into them on Murray Avenue, and we ended up having lunch together. Noah's a good kid."

"He is." Naomi felt awkward. "Well, I really would like to get a bite to eat before the service begins. Did you see Ezra yet?"

Jake scanned the room. "I see him." He turned in the

direction of Ezra, stopped, and turned back to face her. "Maybe I could have a dance later?"

Naomi rolled her eyes and walked away. What was wrong with that man?

Hors d'oeuvre tables outlined the perimeter of the ballroom. She didn't really want food. But she also didn't want what was standing beside the sushi table talking to Becky and David. Aaron turned his head slightly and caught her eye. She cursed her body for reacting, but he looked suave in his tuxedo. She turned and walked in the other direction.

Miriam

Miriam leaned against the wall and craned her head around the corner. She had ducked into the alcove when she saw Becky and David heading in her direction. She wanted to speak with Becky, but in her mental rehearsals, Naomi always stood next to her. Miriam needed to find Naomi before Becky spotted her.

Guests drinking champagne and nibbling hors d'oeuvres packed the hall. Why did Naomi have to be so short? Miriam leaned back against the wall and inhaled. Inside her head, the self-talk tried to convince her to stop acting like a little girl. There was no reason to feel this way. Noah and Maria personally invited her to the wedding.

"Miriam? Why are you leaning against the wall?" Joe stepped into the alcove. "I've been looking everywhere for you."

She leaned in and wrapped her arms around her husband. "I think this is a mistake. My stomach is telling me I should have stayed home."

Joe squeezed her tighter and then clasped her hand and led her out of the alcove and into the ballroom. As she watched all the happy people, her throat felt dry and her hands cold. Her intuition kicked into overdrive. This evening was not going to end well.

"Joe, Miriam," Esther walked toward them teetering on too-high heels. She clasped a glass of wine in one hand and a giant mushroom cap rested on a cocktail napkin in the other. "You have to taste these mushrooms. I must get the recipe. Why are you two standing alone against the wall? It's a party."

Miriam gripped Joe's elbow even tighter and mustered a weak smile. Esther didn't seem to notice.

"Did you see Golda Lipchitz's dress? Really, who wants to look at a seventy-two-year-old woman's boobies? I don't. Even if she does look good for her age, that dress is…" Esther shook her head and made a tsk-tsk sound. "Stupid. Come on Miriam, let Joe talk golf with Lewis and the other men. You have to taste the little meatballs. They're good, but I can't figure out what spice they used." Esther snatched Miriam's arm from Joe and pulled her toward the food.

Becky

In a room at the far end of the floor, Maria stood as her mother fiddled with her hair and Becky examined every fold and bead on her dress.

"Do you think the lipstick is too bright?" Maria's mother asked Becky.

"Absolutely not." Becky shook her head vigorously. "The lighting in the ballroom is so low, the bright lipstick will draw light to her face. "Maria, your make-up is perfect. Don't touch a thing. You look like the cover of a bridal magazine." She stepped back to take in Maria's whole body.

Maria looked radiant, but Becky wasn't sure if it was new bride radiance or her own joy, reflecting off the future Jewish Maria. A shiver zapped through her. The girl was perfect for her son. "I have to go and check on Noah." She gave Maria an air kiss and turned to her mother and kissed her. "Such a wonderful day."

As Becky made her way to Noah's dressing room, she crossed through the ballroom, greeting the guests with hugs and kisses. She thanked them for the *mazel tovs* and well wishes. When she ran into Laurie, Becky stopped to catch her breath.

"Everything is so beautiful and the food is delicious." Laurie wrapped Becky in a hug. "*Mazel tov.* I heard the news about Maria. I couldn't be happier for you. Everything is coming together beautifully."

Becky's heart filled with pride, except for the small spot that wished it was a real wedding, with a rabbi and a real chupah. She shook it off. "It is and once Maria finishes converting, we'll have a real Jewish wedding." She glanced around the room. "Well, maybe it will be a smaller more intimate Jewish wedding."

Laurie smiled. "One wedding at a time. Did you see Naomi and Miriam yet?"

Becky almost doubled over. Miriam?

Naomi

Naomi wandered through the crowd, hoping to avoid Aaron. It was hard enough being in the same building with him. But she knew she would have to face him at dinner. They were seated at the same table. She needed a few minutes alone to reign in her emotions.

She felt a tap on her shoulder and turned. Jake holding two glasses of wine. "Stop sneaking up behind me," she said.

"I didn't sneak. You just happened to have your back to me." He thrust out the hand holding the red wine. "Shiraz, your favorite."

"It changed. I'm a cabernet person now."

He shrugged. "I tried."

She gazed at his handsome face. Yeah, she could still see what she fell for all those years ago. Damn, she was so shallow. A sucker for a pretty face. She looked at the wine glass that was now in her hand. "Why would you bother trying?"

"I told you the day you almost drowned me in the kitchen. I want us to be friends."

"Jake, I told you then and I'm telling you again, I don't want to go bowling with you."

That statement cracked them both up. Jake raised his glass. "Here." He stopped talking for a brief moment and smiled—the kind of smile that used every facial muscle and originated in the heart. "To someday bowling with my ex-wife."

She sipped the wine. Maybe it was the atmosphere of the wedding or a slight resurgence of all the love she gave him over the years, but for that moment, she could envision a future where they could be…maybe not friends, but friendly.

As she considered what to say next, she felt fingers clamp the back of her arm.

"Hi, Jake," Laurie said over her shoulder and kept her fingers clenched around Naomi's arm. "I'm sure Naomi would love to play catch up with you, but now isn't the time. Hurry up, Naomi."

Naomi tried to tug her arm away. "Hey, you're going to leave a bruise."

"Then walk faster and I'll let go." Laurie did a quick head swivel. "See you later, Jake. You look great in that tux."

She yanked Naomi's arm again.

"Ouch, what the hell? That hurt. Let go of my arm." Naomi locked her knees and stopped—a rock in the middle of the room. "What's going on? Where are you pulling me to?"

Laurie's face flushed bright red—blotchy red. Everything about her expression radiated stress. "I made the mistake of telling Becky that Miriam is here."

"Of course, she's here. Noah and Maria invited her personally." Naomi jerked her arm away from Laurie's grip. "She knew Miriam would be here."

"Based on the look in her eyes when I said it, I don't think she believed Miriam would come."

"Where's Becky?" Naomi asked, turning to scan the room. "I don't see her."

"She went to check on Noah and the groomsmen. Hopefully, she's still in that room with them."

Naomi inhaled and exhaled. The other guests mingled and smiled while Naomi watched Laurie have a panic attack.

"Are you all right?" Laurie asked. "Why are you staring at me?"

Over Lauri's shoulder, Naomi spotted Aaron, talking to an older woman Naomi didn't recognize.

"Please keep moving. Remember, Miriam and Becky? We have to get there first," Laurie's eyes and voice pleaded.

Naomi disengaged her stare and scanned the room. Just being in a room like this made her feel special, graceful—not exactly taller, but not so short. Everything about the room screamed luxury—thick carpet, crystal chandeliers, and the music played by the jazz trio. She loved looking at the beautiful dresses and tuxedos that transformed the most ordinary of men into handsome ones. "No, I'm not chasing either of them. It's their problem." She felt resolute. It surprised her. "I'm too old and too tired to buffer their battles. Let them deal with each other for once. I'm hungry. Let's eat something before they take away this luscious food." She turned and walked toward the sushi table.

Laurie trotted along behind her. "Are you serious? You're going to quit now? This entire situation could explode at any minute."

Naomi picked up a plate and studied the sushi. "Their problem, not mine."

✡ ✡ ✡

Becky

Becky banged on the door of the room where Noah and his groomsmen waited for the ceremony to begin. She didn't bother to wait for someone to open the door. A few of his friends looked more nervous than Noah, who was deep in conversation with Naomi's son, Josh.

"Hey, Mom," Noah said. "Did you talk to Maria?"

"Yes, I did. She's fine. Stand-up, let me check your tux." Becky adjusted his tie and flicked a few pieces of dandruff from his jacket. "Turn around."

Noah followed her instructions, did a complete circle. When they were face to face, Becky gave him one last squeeze. "I love you."

There was so much she wanted to say to her son, but the rage inside her chest begged to get out. How dare that witch come to the wedding after her letter? Becky shot out of the room on a quest to find Naomi.

✡ ✡ ✡

Miriam

Esther babbled on about the food as she pulled Miriam into the party. Miriam scanned the packed room. Her gaze moved from friend to acquaintance. She and Becky shared everything, including the same social circle.

Miriam tried her best to smile while greeting people she hadn't spoken with in months and, in a few cases, years. Under better circumstances, she would have been thrilled to chat with all of them. Inside, she silently prayed that her heart wouldn't explode from her chest and nobody would notice the sweat dripping down the back of her neck.

"I'm not really hungry. You stay here and enjoy the food. I'm going to find Joe."

"No, you're not. You have that scared rabbit look in your eyes. You're going to run and hide. Well, you can't hide all night, so you better suck it up and let whatever is going to happen, happen."

If Esther meant for her words to be empowering, she missed the boat. The excitement Miriam felt while getting dressed disappeared. The hope that Maria's good news would set things right was naïve. Nothing had changed. She could feel it in her bones.

She and Becky were always emotionally in tuned with each other. She would dial Becky on the phone, and Becky would beep in on the call waiting. Or Becky would call to invite her to lunch at the exact moment she thought of dropping into Becky's office and surprising her for lunch. It was truly uncanny.

"After all, she's not going to make a scene and throw you out."

Esther's voice pulled Miriam's attention back to the party.

✡ ✡ ✡

Naomi

Aaron crept closer to Naomi, pretending to be interested in the people around him. She knew that she couldn't avoid him any longer. She excused herself from Laurie, and walked over to him.

"Hi."

"Hi," he said.

The silence lingered for a few moments. "You saw me and walked away. I thought I was your escort for the evening."

Naomi shrugged. She wanted to be angry with him, but couldn't when he stood so close.

"Is it because of that James Bond type who brought you the glass of wine? You both looked rather chummy laughing together."

Naomi didn't understand—James Bond type?

"Excuse me?" she said out loud to be polite. W*hat the hell is he talking about*?

"You looked very engrossed with the tall guy, who most women would probably describe as handsome. That is if you like that type. If I was a female, I would definitely prefer the shorter more cuddly type."

After he said that, it hit her. Aaron was talking about Jake. He was the only man she spoke with since she walked into the hotel. And he did hand her a drink. "Aaron, the man you saw me talking to was my ex-husband."

"That's your ex-husband? How tall is he?" Aaron asked and then shook his head. "He looked too happy to see you."

Naomi planted her hand on her hip. "He said I look stunning." Aaron avoided her gaze, shifting his weight from leg to leg, like he always did when he was nervous.

The moment was awkward, and she decided to enjoy it, sipping her wine, letting the tension linger for a few extra seconds. "Aaron, think about it. My ex-husband, remember why he left me?"

"You said he went both ways."

"This conversation is stupid, and why are you acting so jealous over my ex-husband?"

"You dumped me once for him."

"Well, after that lovely picture in the New York Times, I'm not sure you're even divorced from your wife. You two looked pretty comfortable at that what-ever-it-was event."

"The one from The Arts and Letters Academy fundraiser?" Aaron said, shaking his head. "I can't believe you saw that. I didn't even see Alisha until I walked outside. That's when the photographer told us to smile for the camera. She needs all the publicity she can get for the new agency. And, Naomi, I told you. We don't hate each other. We're trying to keep the relationship somewhere between civil and friendly."

She refused to allow the words inside her head to pass through her lips. They would sound completely inappropriate and juvenile. She bit her bottom lip and stared at the floor.

"Is this the reason you didn't want me to pick you and Ezra up this evening?"

She nodded.

Aaron reached out for her hand. "You look stunning and I don't want to waste a minute of this evening discussing Jake and Alisha—please."

She measured his words and tone against the look in his eyes. They matched. She clasped her fingers around his.

Aaron started walking away from the crowd.

"Where are we going?" Naomi asked. "I'm hungry

and every time I try to eat something, I get interrupted."

"This will just take a minute. Follow me."

They rounded the first corner and ended up in an empty hallway. Aaron didn't stop. He continued to move forward until they reached a door with an Exit sign hanging above. He pushed the door open and pulled her into the staircase. Before she could ask anything, he kissed her.

He pulled back first. "Never be jealous of my ex-wife." Naomi nodded. He pulled her close. "Send Ezra and Josh to their father's house tonight," he whispered while running his hand down her spine.

The kiss erased the jealousy. She leaned into his ear. "For a week." The next kiss sealed it for Naomi. Aaron was the man she wanted to grow old with.

They walked out of the stairway hand-in-hand, to find the hors d'oeuvres being whisked away and waiters ushering the guests into the Urban Room. The ceremony was about to begin.

✡ ✡ ✡

Miriam

Miriam smiled gratefully when she spotted Joe and Lewis gliding toward her and Esther. Esther kept urging her toward the ballroom, but she didn't want to go in without Joe or Naomi. But she lost sight of Naomi soon after they arrived.

When the men arrived at their side, Esther rambled, giddy with excitement. "There's nothing I love more than a wedding. Now that Maria is going to be Jewish, everything will be perfect. I wish one of my children would get married."

"Stop it, Esther," Lewis said, shaking his head. "You're being ridiculous. Let Eli finish graduate school and find a job first. And Anat is only twenty-one years old. I'm sure the commanders in the Israeli army love to give soldiers time off to get married."

"Poo-poo, Noah is only twenty three. What's wrong with being married in college?"

Lewis shook his head and twisted his mouth as if to say, "I give up."

Esther and Lewis switched languages and began speaking Hebrew. Within moments, the two were ten steps ahead of Miriam and Joe.

"Let's go, honey," Joe said.

Miriam shook her head. "No, this is wrong. It's a mistake, Joe. Let's go home."

He placed his hand on her lower back. "No, we came to see Noah get married and that is what we are going to do. Just wait, everything is going to be fine."

Five feet before the wide-open double doors of the ballroom, she froze. Becky stood inside, smiling and welcoming guests to the ceremony. She radiated happiness, but Miriam knew that with Becky, appearance could be deceiving. Miriam's stomach knotted. She swallowed hard. Then she tried to focus on the speech she rehearsed at least a hundred times. She took one last glance around the room, hoping to spot Naomi, who was nowhere in sight. Time to take the plunge. She gripped Joe's hand and moved forward.

Esther reached Becky first, giving Miriam the opportunity to avoid the situation entirely. "Joe," Miriam said. "Let's just shuffle around them unseen. Please."

Before he could answer, Esther moved forward, leaving Miriam face-to-face with Becky. Becky's nostrils flared and hate radiated from her eyes.

Suddenly, Miriam felt winded and her face hurt. She didn't see it coming, Becky's palm smacking her right cheek.

"You ignored my letter. Leave. You're only here to put the *ayin hara* on my son like your father did to my mother." Becky's voice oozed red.

Miriam stepped back, still holding her palm against her cheek. Joe maneuvered his body between his wife and Becky.

Esther rushed back to the scene. "Stop it! Stop it! This is ridiculous." She grabbed Becky's raised hand. "Don't you dare do that again. How could you make a scene at your son's wedding? That will bring the evil eye, not Miriam. She came because she loves Noah and you."

David rushed to his wife's side. "What's going on?" he said, directing the question at Miriam.

"She hit me," Miriam whispered.

Becky clasped David's hand. "Make her leave. I don't want her here." Her eyes burned fire at Miriam.

"Becky," Miriam choked out. "I didn't know about the affair, and even if I did, how could I have stopped it? Why are you blaming this on me?"

Becky turned sharply on her spiked heel and over her shoulder said, "David, get her out of here—right now!"

Joe wrapped his arms around his wife as she sobbed into his shoulder. He led her to one of the plush blue benches lining the hallway.

Miriam sniffled. "Please take me home."

David approached Joe and Miriam cautiously. "I'm so sorry, Miriam. Ever since she found those letters, she's been out of control. I've tried talking to her and threatened to shred them, but she keeps hiding them. She's convinced herself that the affair is what led her mom to kill herself, which is ridiculous. Only her mother knows why she did it."

"We know this isn't coming from you or Noah," Joe replied. "I think we should leave."

"I'm too embarrassed to walk into that room now.

Everyone will be talking about me," Miriam said through a sniffle. She looked up into David's eyes. "I've loved Noah since the day he was born. He's always been special to me."

"I know," he replied. "I wish she'd come to her senses. This isn't the woman I married."

Miriam saw the pain in David's eyes. Why couldn't the two people in the world who loved Becky the most, make her let go of this hate? Miriam stood up and gave David a quick squeeze. "*Mazel tov* on Noah's marriage. I wish him and Maria a lifetime of happiness. And I wish you and Becky much *nachas*—joy and pride from your future grandchildren." She stepped back and looked down at Joe, who sat frozen on the bench. "Let's go home."

Becky

Becky walked down the aisle to her seat in the front row. She didn't care who saw her slap Miriam. The woman deserved it. Becky folded into the linen draped chair and adjusted her dress. The letter had made her position very clear, and Miriam ignored it. The witch got what she deserved. Becky crossed her legs and lifted her chin. The slap served its purpose. Miriam wouldn't be in the room during the ceremony, and it eliminated any chance of seeing her during the reception.

David slid into the seat next to her just as the music started. The judge was already in position. All eyes turned toward the back of the room as the bridesmaids began their march down the aisle. "That was wrong, Becky. Just plain wrong," David whispered in her ear.

"Shush," she said, placing her index finger in front of her mouth. "It's starting."

✡ ✡ ✡

Naomi

Naomi and Aaron entered the room handed in hand. She felt so alive and in love. Just a few months ago, her life felt like a dark never-ending tunnel. She couldn't even dream of a light at the end, and even if she could, it wouldn't have involved a second chance with Aaron. She swore to herself that she would never again doubt the existence of miracles.

Naomi spotted Ezra's waving arm as soon as they entered the room. He motioned for them to sit in the seats he'd saved on his left side.

"Do we have to sit there?" Aaron asked, as Ezra's arm continued to flail in the air.

Naomi smiled and pulled at his hand. "Stop it. He's no big deal."

"That's your opinion," Aaron responded. "How tall is he?"

She shook her head and continued propelling him down the aisle. "Stop it," she said again.

They climbed over another couple who didn't bother to stand to let them pass. Aaron sat on Naomi's left and Ezra sat on her right. Next to Ezra was his father.

She reached out and very obviously clasped Aaron's hand. When she turned to see his face, he was smiling.

Naomi's hand remained locked in his throughout the entire ceremony, except for the few seconds, she needed to wipe the tears from her eyes. Noah was the first of her friend's children to get married.

All of their lives were changing—empty nest, marriages, relocation…

✡ ✡ ✡

"Mom," Josh yelled, stretching his tiny arms in the air.

"Let me answer the door before I pick you up, sweetie." Naomi waddled to the door. Josh toddled behind her, still begging to be picked-up. She was grateful to see Becky and Miriam, kids in tow, standing on her front porch.

Naomi pushed open the screen door. "Thanks for coming so fast."

"Do you really think it's time?" Becky asked.

"I'm not sure, but I've been getting these awful pains in my back just like I did with Josh."

Josh loved playing with Noah and Miriam's son, Nathan. When he saw the boys come through the door, he tried jumping, but his feet didn't leave the ground.

The three boys rushed down the basement steps heading toward the huge box of Legos in the part of the room Naomi and Jake designated as Josh's playroom. Miriam's twin girls found comfortable spots on the floor and disappeared into their books.

"You need to sit down," Miriam said.

"Do you think that's a good idea? I heard that walking can kick start labor," Becky said.

"I think you're right, but she's two weeks early," Miriam replied.

"Mommy." Josh reappeared at her feet and wrapped his arms around her leg. "Popsicles."

"Just a minute," Naomi said, wondering how he got back up the steps so fast.

Josh toddled back down to the playroom and within seconds, reappeared with Noah.

"Please, Aunt Naomi, can we have popsicles?" Noah begged.

Becky walked across the living room to the kitchen. "Sit down, Naomi. I'll get them."

Naomi sat down and sucked in her breath. "Aghhh,"

she groaned and began panting, blowing the air out through her mouth. "Yep, start timing the contractions. I think my water just broke. Help me up, Miriam, and then call Jake." She waddled to the powder room.

The plan was for Jake to meet her at the hospital. Naomi climbed into the passenger seat of Miriam's minivan. Becky stayed behind to take care of all the kids.

✡ ✡ ✡

"…you may kiss the bride."

The judge's booming voice pulled her back to the present. Yes, all of their lives were changing. She prayed the change holding her hand would last.

The happy couple walked down the aisle, smiling and waving. Maria glowed and Noah practically floated by, held up by the smile, covering his face.

A hotel employee trailed behind, directing the guests to move through the doors on the left side of the room, into the adjoining ballroom for the reception.

While standing in the aisle, waiting for the crowd to move forward, the awkward moment she wanted to avoid became inevitable.

"Aaron," she said. "I'd like to introduce you to Ezra's father, my ex-husband, Jake."

Aaron extended his hand. "So," Aaron said, a wicked twinkle lighting his eyes that made Naomi a bit nervous. "You're the guy Naomi dumped me for. Man, I spent a lot of years hating you."

Jake's eyes widened. Naomi elbowed Aaron in the side, but he just laughed. "I promised my twenty-one-year-old-self that if I ever met you, I'd say those words. Nothing personal, Jake. I just hate breaking promises."

Jake eyed Aaron's smiling face. Finally, he smiled back. "So you're the Aaron who inspired her to draw hearts all over her notebooks. She was writing Mrs. Aaron Brenner all over the cover of her notebook the day I met her."

"Yes, that may be true, but you won." In an attempt at pseudo gallantry, Aaron dipped forward and swooshed his arm across his body.

"Stop it, both of you. Let's be nice and go eat."

Awkwardness hung in the air and Naomi cursed the slow-moving crowd. Aaron must have read the stress on her face. He turned to Jake and patted Ezra on the back. "You raised a real mensch here."

Jake reached out and patted Ezra on the other shoulder, beaming with pride. "Thank you."

Ezra turned red and the crowd finally started moving.

Miriam

By the time Joe opened Miriam's car door, she felt as if her soul was releasing all the pain that it had been holding for the last months. The sobs racked her body and, once inside, she leaned forward, head against the dashboard, unable to form any words.

"Honey," Joe said, patting her gently on the back. "She's losing her mind. Becky's not right. She needs professional help. Nothing in this situation makes a bit of sense."

Miriam twisted her head to look in the sideview miror. Mascara streaked her face, and her eyes were already puffy and red. She returned her gaze to her lap.

"I never dreamed I'd say these words, but maybe your friendship is over."

She sat up straight and wiped her nose on the old Panera napkin she found stuffed in the glove box. "I know, but it feels like my sister just died. I don't know this person living in Becky's body."

Joe backed out of the parking space. He handed the pimply faced kid in the booth the parking ticket and a fifty-dollar bill. According to the parking receipt, they were at the wedding for only an hour and five minutes. The gate lifted. Joe turned left, the direction of home.

"I wish I could understand what she's thinking. We were college roommates when they had the affair. Maybe, I saw my dad once a month. She went home more than I did. Maybe she knew all these years and is feigning innocence."

The Parkway was empty. They were through the tunnel and on Banksville Road within minutes.

"I give up, Joe," Miriam said, swabbing the napkin over her still tearing eyes. "I'm tired of apologizing for something I didn't do. I'm through begging for friendship. To hell with her."

Joe patted her hand. "You're right, you did everything you could to save the relationship. Now, you have to let it go."

✡ ✡ ✡

Naomi

The minute Naomi walked into the ballroom, she was flanked by Laurie and Esther.

"We need to talk," Laurie said.

"Okay," Naomi said. "Let me set my purse on my seat. Then we can talk."

"No," Esther said, grabbing Naomi's elbow. "Now."

Naomi obediently followed them into the hallway outside the ballroom. "Becky smacked Miriam across the face and sent her home," Laurie said.

Naomi almost doubled over. Her mind went blank.

"It's true!" Esther said. "I didn't see the smack, but I heard it. She hit Miriam hard."

"I need to sit down."

Naomi shuffled toward the same bench that Joe and Miriam vacated forty-five minutes earlier. She leaned over, elbows to knees, clamping her head between her hands, feeling as if the wind was knocked out of her. She couldn't control the ache that now owned her body or the barrage of memories flashing through her mind.

Becky

A flood of well wishes and hugs from friends and family kicked off the reception. Becky wallowed in the attention. The ceremony was perfect. It was time for the fun to begin. Now she really understood the words, "nachas from your children." Noah brought so much joy to her life. Each Shabbat she gave thanks to Hashem for him.

Becky scanned the room, looking for Naomi, nowhere in sight. She walked to the head table and set her bag on her chair. Still no sign of Naomi, but she noticed Aaron heading her way holding two glasses of wine. "For me?" She took one from his hand, not waiting for his answer.

Aaron glanced around the room and shrugged. "Sure."

Becky took a big sip—cabernet. She was more of a Shiraz person, but at this point she was grateful for anything. Every time she'd held a wine glass during the hors d'oeurves, something distracted her, causing her to set the glass down and not remember where. "Where's Naomi?"

"I believe that she, Laurie, and Esther had simultaneous bladder issues."

"Okay, I'll check the bathroom." She slipped past him,

keeping her fingers locked on the stem of the glass. Halfway across the room, she spotted her three friends reentering the ballroom. They all looked so serious. As she approached, she noticed Naomi's red eyes. It looked like she had been crying. Becky hoped Jake hadn't said anything stupid to hurt her.

"What's wrong, Naomi?" Becky asked when the three women halted in front of her.

"What do you mean what's wrong with her?" Esther's words exploded from her mouth. "You, that's what's the matter."

Becky felt her nostrils flare and eyebrows furrow. "What are you talking about?"

"You smacked Miriam and sent her home. That's what I'm talking about," Esther said, as Laurie gently clasped her arm.

"Shush, this isn't the time or the place for this," Laurie whispered in Esther's ear.

Esther flicked her wrists at Laurie. "I will not shush," she said. "I heard the slap. She probably left a hand print on poor Miriam's face."

Becky's blood pressure climbed upward. "Poor Miriam! You have no idea what you're talking about, so please shut up right now."

"Your parents had an affair. So what. Let it go," Esther said.

"Please, stop fighting. The situation is bad enough," Naomi said.

"She's right. The situation is worse than I thought." Becky turned her back to them and walked away.

Naomi

The rest of the evening didn't matter. Naomi barely

ate her food and failed to find any energy to dance. Aaron insisted it was rude not to dance at a wedding. He pulled her onto the dance floor for a few slow songs.

"There's nothing you can do to help Miriam." He clasped her right hand and placed his left on her lower back. "The strain on your face is killing me."

"Sorry, I hate feeling helpless."

For a few moments they breezed across the almost empty dance floor. The younger crowd seemed to avoid the slower music. "Why do you feel any responsibility in this whole debacle? You're not their mother or their therapist. You're just a friend, an over-attentive, caring friend."

She pulled back and looked at him.

"That didn't come out right. What I meant was…"

"This better be good."

"You're an amazing friend. The kind of friend people dream of having, but you can't let their madness interfere with your life and happiness."

"It doesn't, really."

He gracefully pulled her close, spinning her around twice. "The mere fact that our current conversation is about them, rather than what I want to do to you when we get home, is proof enough that you're over involved."

"But—"

"No buts." He dipped her slightly. "You have to let the kids learn to fight their own battles."

They moved together so naturally and, for a few moments, they were alone in the room. But, half way through the song, the scenery changed.

Each time Aaron turned her, she ended up facing Becky.

When the dance ended Ezra met them at the table. "I haven't seen Aunt Miriam and Uncle Joe all night."

Earlier in the evening, Jake invited Josh and Ezra to

sleep at his house. She was grateful when both boys accepted the offer. Not just because she wanted to spend the night with Aaron, which was true, but because she needed silence.

To avoid answering Ezra's question, she picked up her bag and pretended to look inside for something, stalling, but the right words weren't hiding at the bottom of her clutch purse.

"How are you going to get home if we can't find them?" Ezra asked her and then looked over at Aaron.

"Don't worry, I'll make sure your mom gets home," Aaron replied.

"Okay." Ezra appeared relieved. He leaned over and kissed his mother's cheek. "Good night."

She watched his back as he headed out the door to meet up with his father. Now, it was time to locate Josh, who was in the middle of the mass of bodies partying on the dance floor.

When they found Josh, it didn't take long to figure out that he had done a few too many *L'chaims* with the scotch bottle.

"Good night, Mom." He took a staggering step toward her, kissed her cheek, and then turned to walk back to the dance floor.

Naomi clasped his shoulders. "No more dancing. Your father wants to leave—now."

Josh swayed, trying to keep his eyes focused on her face. "Why? The party isn't over yet."

Naomi gently turned him toward the door. "Go, your dad is waiting."

Aaron chuckled, watching the poor kid stagger across the room.

"Remember when you could drink that much and not need two days to recover from the hangover?" Naomi asked.

"Ah." He closed his eyes wistfully. "The good old days."

Naomi and Aaron searched out the newlyweds, finding them near the door, flocked by well-wishers. When it was their turn to offer mazel tovs, she hugged Noah and became teary eyed. Before walking away, she reached into her bag, pulled out a five-dollar bill, and stuck it in Noah's hand. "Take this, use it for *tzedakah* in Israel." She reached back into her bag, pulled out another five and placed it in Maria's hand. "When a Jew travels while carrying money for charity," Naomi said, "he or she becomes what is known as a mitzvah messenger. We believe that the person with this status receives extra protection for safe travel. So, this five dollars is for you to give to charity when you safely return home from your honeymoon."

Chapter 22

Naomi

Naomi woke, comfortably spooned against Aaron. She didn't want to move or think, just enjoy being in this wonderful man's arms. The sun was already shining through the windows. Last week, she wrestled with herself—take Friday off or work? A long, slow stroke up his arm confirmed that using one of her vacation days was a good decision.

He stirred, and she felt his lips on her neck—luxury, pure luxury. "Do we do something today or just stay in bed all day?" he asked between kisses.

Naomi gave a soft moan. "Bed, only bed." She rolled over to kiss his lips, which quickly escalated beyond the kiss.

Afterward, Naomi ran her finger along his jaw, enjoying the opportunity to stare uninterrupted in his eyes.

"Stay in bed?" he asked.

"Yes, coffee and breakfast in bed. You stay here and I'll be back."

"No." He slid his legs over the side of the bed. "We cook together. I make great omelets, but my coffee tastes like mud."

He stood and stretched, and she felt a stirring. *Wow,*

what a body for a man almost fifty. He pulled on the only pants he had—tuxedo pants. "No, you can't cook in those. I'll get you a pair of Ezra's sweat pants." She put her nightgown on and was about to leave the room when the phone rang.

She picked it up, but before she could say hello, a voice blasted her ear. "How freakin dare you."

It took Naomi a moment to figure out who owned the screaming voice. She extended the phone away from her ear and scrunched her face at Aaron. He mouthed the word "Becky," which made it pretty clear that he could hear her from across the room.

"You're supposed to be my best friend—like sisters— remember? I guess you don't remember because if you did, you wouldn't have told both of them."

As Naomi planned her words, the phone went dead in her ear. She stood in the doorway, still holding the phone to her ear for a couple of heartbeats.

"With all due respect," Aaron said, "I think she needs real help, not husband or friend help but the kind that sits in offices, holding clipboards."

As he spoke, Naomi walked back to the bed and sat down. The room went silent. Aaron shifted on his feet. She flung herself backward onto the bed, arms flapped open to her sides, staring at the ceiling.

He was right. How did you support a friend through a situation that didn't really exist? Naomi loved Becky like a sister. In fact, most of the time she felt closer to Becky than she did to her real sister. But how could a smart woman like Becky get stuck in such a bizarre obsession—stubbornness, pure pigheaded obstinacy. The same trait that made her such a good lawyer was pushing her into an abyss.

"All I want is to spend the day in bed with you, but may I request an hour, possibly two to take care of some unfinished business. You can stay in bed and read or play on your phone. That way, the bed will be warm when I come back." The thought of cooking breakfast with him made her giddy like a twenty-year-old college girl all over.

He sat down on the bed, reached over, and ran his finger slowly down the inside of her arm. The small act sent shivers from her head to her toes. "You're going to her house."

Naomi closed her eyes and nodded. He slowly drew his finger back up her inner arm.

"Let me come with you—moral support and all that other stuff your..." His voice trailed off for a moment. "...your significant-other-slash-possible-future-husband is supposed to provide."

Holy hell—what did he just say? Her brain froze. Did he just almost propose? She sat up, and he laid his arm across her shoulder.

"But if you need to do it alone, I understand."

When he spoke the word "alone," her brain snapped back on. Deal with Becky now, think about Aaron later. She kissed him deeply. "Alone."

He nodded.

"But if I'm not back, or you don't receive a text from me within two hours, come rescue me."

He kissed her. "I will pound on the door until she opens it."

"I wish I could get rid of the awful image replaying itself in my head," she said.

"What image," he asked.

"Becky charging at me, wielding a pair of sewing scissors."

"You really are a writer. Kiss me before you leave."

✡ ✡ ✡

Becky

From upstairs in the bathroom, Becky heard the doorbell ring. "David, answer the door," she shouted as loud as possible.

"I got it."

The melody of the bell made her so happy. After the horrible phone call with Naomi, she needed something good to happen. She knew Noah and Maria wouldn't leave for their honeymoon without stopping to say goodbye. She walked over to the top of the steps. "Is it Maria and Noah?" she called out to David, but didn't wait for his answer. "Tell them I'll be down in a few minutes."

Becky ran the brush through her hair with her left hand and attempted to apply lipstick with her right. Dumb idea, she missed the natural line of the left side of her lip. She yanked a tissue from the box and swiped at the mess, refusing to look like one of those old ladies Miriam dubbed pre-school dropouts because they thought coloring outside the line made their lips look fuller. She pulled on her jeans, shaking off the thought of Miriam, grabbed a clean top from the closet, and trotted down the steps.

Noah and Maria weren't waiting in the kitchen. Instead, she saw Naomi engrossed in a conversation with David.

"Why are you here?"

David jumped in before Naomi could respond. "She's here because she loves you and worries about you."

"I'm fine. You can go home now."

"No, you're not fine. You haven't been yourself since Rosh Hashanah. This obsessing over your mother's affair has to stop."

"I'm not obsessing. I'm just pissed off that you went behind my back and blabbed about my mother's business." Becky pointed her finger at Naomi. "Miriam's been a horrible gossip since we were kids, but I expected better from you. You betrayed me." Becky's face flushed with anger. Her hands quivered.

"I betrayed you by telling Esther and Laurie? They're your friends." Naomi emphasized each word. "Wonderful, caring friends who've spent the last months worrying about you and your bizarre behavior."

"What bizarre behavior? How would you act if that bitch deceived you for almost thirty years? Would you be all supportive of her if she cursed your son?"

"Give me break, Becky. Miriam has the heart of an innocent child. She's incapable of cursing anyone or anything."

"Bullshit. My son married a shiksa because she cursed him, and you know it's true."

"This bizarre behavior," Naomi shouted, throwing her arms into the air. "Miriam did not curse Noah. She did not hide the affair from you. The only crime she committed was caring enough to bend over backward to make you forgive her for something she didn't do. The woman paid thousands of dollars to send your son on a honeymoon to Israel. The Holy Land, Becky! The place every Jew dreams of seeing. She shelled out the money to make you happy. You dumb ass, she loves you."

"She just wanted to flash her money." Becky spat the words.

Naomi leaned forward and placed her forehead on the cold granite countertop.

"She knew about the affair." Becky shook her head. "She knew all along."

Naomi looked up at Becky. "So what if she did? It wouldn't have changed anything. She couldn't have stopped them."

Becky rolled her eyes, but said nothing.

"Becky, your mom had an affair. She loved two men

and it tortured her. And we'll never know what caused her to do what she did, but you have to forgive her and let her rest in peace. Your mom was a good woman."

"Of course she was. Miriam's slimeball father seduced her."

"You need professional help." Naomi stood and stepped toward Becky. "You need therapy or drugs. I'm telling you this as a lifelong friend who'd go into battle for you—the real you—the crazy, fun-loving, caring girl I grew up with. I don't know this irrational being inhabiting your head. Please, let me find a therapist to help you."

"Get out!" Becky stepped forward, closing the distance between her and Naomi. "Get out." She lunged one foot forward and shoved Naomi, sending her stumbling backward.

✡ ✡ ✡

Naomi

Naomi's eyes bulged as she tried to recover her balance and steady her legs, but her brain revved in overdrive. Insanity, this behavior was absolute insanity. Last night, Becky smacked Miriam. Today she shoved her. Naomi picked up her bag and walked out the front door, slamming it behind her.

The walk back to her house took five minutes. She returned to her kitchen exactly a half-hour after she walked out. Aaron stood at the stove wearing the tuxedo pants and an apron with a giant bleach spot on the front. Naomi walked over to kiss him and inhaled the aroma of frying potatoes. "Smells good." She planted a kiss on his cheek and then looked over at the coffee pot, empty. "I'll start some coffee."

"Good, I really need a cup. How did it go?"

"Not so good." She ran cool tap water into the glass pot. "She threw me out."

He stopped stirring the potatoes. "What?"

"She's so far gone, Aaron. She shoved me, like an angry child." Naomi poured the water into the canister and began measuring the coffee into the filter. "I don't know her anymore."

He lowered the flame under the potatoes, set down the wooden spoon, and hugged her. "Give her a few days to recover from the wedding. I'm sure once she relaxes, she'll wake up and see how badly she screwed up. She'll come around." He nuzzled his nose against her neck. "Becky can't live without her adoring fan, Miriam. And she could never survive without you."

✡ ✡ ✡

Naomi left Becky multiple voicemails and received no call backs. Finally, she called David.

"I don't know what to do either, Naomi. I work so hard to keep her distracted, but then I catch her reading those damn letters again. It's an obsession, and I don't know how to make her stop."

Naomi heard the pain in his voice. He sounded helpless. "I'll do anything to help bring her back to her senses. And so would Laurie and Esther, but she shut us out."

"She perked up for a few hours after Maria made the big announcement. I hoped with that stress removed, she'd get over this affair bullshit," he said.

"So did I."

"When we got home from the wedding, I went straight to bed. I don't know how long she stayed awake, but I know I was sound asleep and felt her shaking me. 'David, David, wake up. What if she changes her mind? What if she's lying and doesn't really want to convert?'"

Naomi inhaled and closed her eyes. "I don't know what to say."

"That's the problem, Naomi. Neither do I."

Chapter 23

Naomi

Naomi dropped Josh off at the bus station on her way to work on Monday morning. He missed two days of classes and faced a pile of work. She kissed him goodbye and told him to have a great time in Florida with his dad and grandmother. Just before he closed the door, she promised to drive out to Penn State with Ezra and Aaron soon.

Before she put the car into drive, she watched through the rearview mirror as he passed through the doors into the station. Sometimes, she looked at her sons and became so overwhelmed with love, words didn't do justice to the feeling. The love didn't come from her heart or her mind. It seeped from her soul into every molecule of her being.

She cruised slowly down Grant Street, getting stuck at each red light. No wonder Becky took the bus every day. She glanced ahead—The US Steel Building. *Why not one more try?*

It took her fifteen minutes to find a parking place, walk to the building, and push the elevator button. The elevator shot up to the fortieth floor so fast that her stomach fell. By the time the doors opened, she felt light headed. Between her dizziness and the stress of facing Becky, she walked straight to the sofa in the reception area.

"May I help you?" an older woman with an out of date haircut asked.

"I'm here to see Becky."

The woman turned to her computer and typed before asking, "Do you have an appointment?"

"No. Just tell her Naomi wants to see her."

As the woman dialed, Naomi glanced around the reception area. It had been years since she visited Becky's office. Her gaze rested, for a moment, on a beautiful oil painting hanging on the side wall. She, Becky, and Miriam spent weeks visiting galleries looking for the perfect piece of art. The shopping part was so much fun. They tried not to like anything, just for the chance to spend another day together at another gallery. In the end, Miriam chose this one and they agreed it was perfect for a law firm.

"Her office is the second door on the left. She isn't coming out to greet you." The woman flashed a smug smile, as if to say "You're not so important to barge in without an appointment."

Becky sat behind a huge desk surrounded by piles of paper that appeared to be piled on top of other piles.

"You might as well sit down, even though I know what your gonna say." Becky looked Naomi in the eye— almost defiantly.

"What can I say? You made a horrible scene at your only son's wedding. You smacked your best friend across the face and humiliated her. You shoved me out the door like a six-year-old brat on a playground. And based on the look on your face, there isn't any remorse floating around that brain of yours."

"It was her own damn fault. I told her not to come.

We're not going to talk about that bitch today. And you shouldn't have blabbed to Laurie and Esther. I'm sorry I shoved you."

"Thank you. That's step one. Now what about slapping Miriam?"

Becky leaned forward. "I said, we're not talking about her. Let's talk about the wedding. Wasn't it perfect? And have you ever seen a bride lovelier than Maria?"

"She looked stunning. Noah looked stunning and the whole wedding was stunning. Why did you slap Miriam?"

"Maybe we should have another, more intimate Jewish one after Maria finishes converting?"

"Why did you slap her?"

Becky dropped her forehead to her desk. "Stop, just stop."

"I understand where all this anger is coming from, but stop hanging it on her. Her pain is just as real as yours. The tangled web your parents were involved in did not include you or Miriam. Did it ever cross your mind that maybe instead of pushing her away, you should be leaning on each other. She loved your mother like her own."

"My mother missed Noah's bar mitzvah and his wedding."

"Do you understand how much pain she had to be in to do what she did? Whatever drove her to do it is something we'll never know. But my guess is it was something deeper, much deeper than loving two men."

When Becky lifted her head, Naomi saw tears. "My mother struggled with a lot of things. She always acted happy, but sometimes, when my dad wasn't home, I heard her crying in her room. One weekend, I was home from college. My dad went bowling on a Saturday night with Al. I heard her crying and knocked on the bedroom door. She actually let me come inside and lay down next to her on the bed. I hugged her. She kept crying and I asked why she was so sad. I'll never forget what she said. 'My family died and my babies died. I don't know why I lived.'"

"Maybe it was survivors' guilt that made her do it, but we'll never know. Could you at least meet Miriam for a cup of coffee? I'll come with you if you want."

Becky swiped at her eyes. "I'll think about it."

By the time Naomi walked out the door, Becky had composed herself and turned on her tough lawyer personality.

Miriam

Miriam held the ice pack against her black eye. It hurt but not as much as the pain of embarrassment.

She stayed in bed all day, with closed eyes, hoping the darkness would relieve the headache pounding against the back of her eyeballs.

But, instead of relief, all she got was a rerun of the wedding playing in her head. The humiliation was overwhelming. How was she ever going to walk into the synagogue again? Worse yet, the entire Jewish community of Pittsburgh was probably gossiping about her.

At 5:30, the doorbell chimed and she heard Anita invite Naomi inside. She didn't feel like getting out of bed. Instead, she texted Naomi to come to her bedroom.

Naomi was still dressed in her work clothes. "How are you feeling?"

Miriam shrugged in response. Naomi sat down on the bed and picked up her hand.

The tears broke through Miriam's control. "I'm so humiliated. It's all my fault that Noah's wedding was ruined by a scene. I should have stayed home."

"Stop it. The wedding wasn't ruined and very few people even knew it happened. I'm just sorry that she hurt you."

"Don't try to sugarcoat it. It was horrible. I bet Noah and Maria never speak to me again. First Becky and now them."

"They're going to come home and tell you all about the amazing honeymoon you bought for them. What Becky did to you was her issue, not yours or theirs."

"I've tried to make sense of the affair thing, and I'm mad at my father too, but I don't think Mrs. Greenburg killed herself because of him."

"I don't think so either."

"Naomi, do you think Becky will ever get over this and be my friend again?"

Naomi patted Miriam's hand and shrugged.

Naomi

Naomi pulled into her garage, grateful the day was ending. All she wanted was to slip on a pair of blue jeans and watch TV. The morning visit with Becky and the after work visit with Miriam sucked up all the brain energy she could spare. She didn't even feel like cooking, maybe a pizza would work. It sure would make Ezra happy.

She settled onto the sofa after calling the pizza place. Usually, Ezra hated to wait, so he would pick it up. But he wasn't home yet.

So, the forty-five minutes wait for delivery presented no problem. She turned on the computer and opened her personal email.

Spam, spam, and then one from *Women's Way Magazine*.

Dear Ms. Feldman,
We would like to publish your short story "Afternoon Revenge," in the August issue of Women's Way Magazine. *Attached is the release form. Please sign and return it to the address at the top.*
Sincerely,
Evelyn Rohm

Naomi read the words a second time before dialing Aaron.

"Celebration tonight. I'll pick you up at seven. Tell Ezra to put on pants that don't flash his underwear. We're going someplace fancy."

"But I ordered pizza."

"We'll eat it for breakfast."

✡ ✡ ✡

Promptly at seven, he arrived at the door. Ezra begged out of dinner, lumbering to his room to type an overdue English paper. "Leaving, Ez," Naomi yelled up the steps.

"Bye, Mom. Bye, Aaron."

Aaron drove to the restaurant where they had their first second-time-around date. He was excited about the story and the opportunity to say "I told you so." She was anxious to tell him about an idea she had brewing for a novel.

"Do it," Aaron said. "Just start writing. Let the story take you where it wants to go."

They toasted with champagne. "Naomi, I have something I need to say to you."

She looked at him. In her life, those words usually ended up bearing bad news. She closed her eyes and inhaled.

"Hey," he said. "What's with the look of terror on your face?"

"Those words don't usually lead to good news." She stared down at her half eaten salmon. It had lost all appeal, so she picked up her water goblet and swallowed hard.

"Tonight, whether it's good news or bad news is in your court." He leaned back into the chair. "I've been here in Pittsburgh for months now. In a few weeks, my job officially begins, but I already know that it's everything I wanted. I hope it will be the job I retire from someday."

She smiled.

"I have a great apartment in New York City but, in Pittsburgh, I'm just a fifty-year-old man living with his mother. We're annoying the hell out of each. I need my own place."

Her stomach rolled. This conversation was going somewhere.

"I want to live with you. I can't stand sneaking around for Ezra's benefit. And I don't want to wait until he goes to college in September."

She knew she was supposed to say something, but her heart, thumping against her chest, was so distracting.

"I like Mt. Lebanon and I want a house, but I don't want to live in Jake's house. I want us to buy our own house."

He stopped talking and waited. It was up to her to break the silence. She wanted to spend every moment with him. She wanted to roll over at night and feel his body next to hers. She wanted to kiss him as he left for work in the morning and wrap her arms around him when he came home. But Ezra and Josh. What kind of mother just sells her children's home and moves in with a man?

"I love you, Naomi. Let's start being a real couple."

Her head felt light, and it had nothing to do with the champagne. He said the words without hesitation. They flowed from his mouth as easily as hello. She never allowed herself the luxury of thinking about love, let alone saying the words out loud. But hearing him say it triggered her courage. "I love you, too."

He reached out and clasped her hand. "Where do we go from here? It's your call. We can live together or get married. Your choice."

"Married."

"How does next Wednesday sound to you?"

The entire discussion while driving home centered on a honeymoon trip to Israel, selling the house, and shopping for a new one. The whole conversation felt surreal. She was engaged.

As soon as Naomi walked through the front door, she called Ezra. He was thrilled when he heard they were getting married. Josh reacted similarly when they told him via Skype. That night, Ezra went to bed, and so did Aaron and Naomi.

Miriam

For days, Miriam walked around her house like a zombie. She lost her ability to think and didn't really want it to come back. Joe took her to dinner at her favorite restaurant and suggested they take a vacation after Passover. She didn't want to go anywhere or do anything.

On Thursday morning, unable to control the pain surging through her body, she dialed Becky.

No answer.

She couldn't find words to leave a message. She put down the phone and curled up on the sunroom chair, crying—until acceptance that her friend was gone forever sank into her soul.

Chapter 24

Naomi

Naomi reached her office late on Wednesday, due to a water main break on Banksville Road. She hated being late. She pulled out her bottom drawer to deposit her purse and heard her cell phone ring. The name on her screen read: Rabbi Morty. She'd called him the day before to tell him about her and Aaron's plan to marry.

"Hi, Rabbi," she said. "Thanks for calling me back."

"I'm not calling you back." His voice hitched. "You need to leave work and come to Becky's house as fast as you can. Just leave. There's been an accident."

"What kind of accident? Did Becky fall? Or David? Did something happen to David?"

"Just get here."

☆ ☆ ☆

Naomi heard the screams before she reached the front door. She ran inside and saw David on the couch slumped against Rabbi Morty—skin ashen white, as if all the blood had leached out of his face.

Both men sobbed. Becky's screams blasted from the kitchen.

Naomi ran down the hall to the kitchen, first spotting the *rebbetzin*, trying to talk calmly to Becky. Naomi and Becky spotted each other at the same time. Becky ran and threw herself into Naomi's arms. "She killed him! She killed him. That bitch killed my son!"

Naomi's knees buckled. Her throat constricted. "What's going on?"

"She killed them both. She sent them on that damn honeymoon. The driver wrecked the car. Noah and Maria are dead. My son is dead!"

Becky crumbled onto the floor. Naomi collapsed next to her. Becky screamed. Naomi sobbed. Time stopped.

Inside Naomi's head, her brain begged her to get a grip. Becky needed her to be strong. Naomi clenched Becky in her arms, using every bit of strength she could muster. She didn't know how he got there, but at some point Aaron was on the floor next to her. His arms clamped around her as she held Becky.

"Aaron, Noah's dead. Maria's dead. A car accident," Naomi said.

"I know, honey. I know." As he spoke, he rubbed her head, as if consoling a child.

They all heard it and looked up—Miriam's shrill voice ringing from the hallway. She ran into the kitchen. "Becky! Becky!"

Becky sprang up like a flaming arrow from a bow. "You killed my son! Get out. Get out." She ran to the drawer, pulled out a long knife, and headed toward Miriam. "I'm gonna kill you!"

Aaron exploded from the floor, grabbed Becky's waist, and struggled to restrain her.

Becky twisted and fought against Aaron's grip. "Let me go. Let me go. She deserves to die. Her father killed

my mother and she killed my son." She gripped the knife
and held it above her head. "I hate her! I hate her!"

"Drop it, Becky! Drop it now," Aaron shouted, pulling
at her arm, trying to reach the hand clamping the knife.

Naomi leapt from the floor to help Aaron. "Give me
the knife!"

She dove for Becky's arm as Aaron clamped his hand
around her elbow joint.

"I hate all of you!" Venom exploded from every pore
of Becky's body. She yanked her arm from Aaron's hand,
slicing his forearm wrapped around her rib cage.

Naomi froze and her eyes widened. Aaron kept his
arm clamped around Becky.

"If I can't kill her, let me die." Becky raised the knife
and plunged it into her own chest.

In the background, Naomi heard screaming.

"Call nine-one-one!" someone yelled.

Naomi rode to the hospital in the ambulance with
Becky, who was rushed straight into surgery.

✡ ✡ ✡

Aaron walked into the hospital an hour later. His shirt
sleeve was cut above his forearm and the bandage on his
arm appeared professionally applied. He sat down next to
her, leaned over, and pulled her into a hug with his good
arm. "How are you?"

She pulled back, lifted his arm, and looked quizzically
into his eyes. "Who bandaged you up?"

"Jake."

She cocked her head.

"At some point before everything blew up, the rabbi
had called Jake. He wanted sedatives for David and
Becky. The only person he could think of who could
write a prescription was Jake. Instead of calling it in to

the pharmacy, Jake came to the door with a medical bag. He saw the blood soaking through my sleeve and went to work sewing me up."

"Wow," was all she could say before resting her head on his shoulder and holding his hand.

They sat in silence. Both submerged in their own thoughts.

"What was happening back there when you left?" Naomi finally asked.

Aaron drew in a long breath. "The rebbetzin was on the love seat, holding Miriam, who kept repeating 'I didn't kill him.' It was heart wrenching. Jake gave David a Xanax. He was sobbing quietly on the sofa with Rabbi Morty sitting next to him. Jake was in the kitchen cleaning up the blood. I started to help him, but he told me to go and be with you."

Naomi blew her nose into a wet, worn tissue. "Miriam didn't kill Noah."

Aaron stroked her hand. "Of course, she didn't. It was an accident."

A few other people sat and paced inside in the surgical waiting area. A pink-coated volunteer sat behind a computer, giving out information as it became available. It was over two hours before she called Naomi to the desk. "The surgery is complete. The doctor will be here in a few minutes to speak with you."

Naomi nodded and returned to her seat. Moments later a surgeon—still clad in scrubs with a mask dangling around his neck—ushered her and Aaron into a small private room.

"The surgery went well," he said, pulling the door closed. "Luckily, she hit the wrong side of her chest. Her lung was punctured, and she slashed a vein, but the fact that you got her here so fast enabled us to stop the internal bleeding in time. She should make a full recovery."

Naomi exhaled. "Thank you."

"She'll be in recovery for a few hours and then moved to the ICU."

Naomi nodded.

"But," the doctor said, "she stabbed herself. When she's stable, she'll be sent to the psych ward for an evaluation and observation."

"Good!" Naomi blurted through tears. "She needs help."

"How long will she be in the ICU?" Aaron asked.

The doctor shrugged. "We'll have to see how she does. I don't like making those types of predictions. All looks good right now. We'll take it day by day."

Naomi and Aaron thanked the doctor and returned to the waiting room, not knowing where else to go.

"One of us needs to call Rabbi Morty," Aaron said.

"Could you do it, please? I don't feel like talking."

"Sure, but I need to go find a spot where I have a signal." He rose from the chair, leaned over, and kissed her forehead before walking out the door.

✡ ✡ ✡

Some days fly by and others last an eternity. For two interminable weeks, Naomi and Rabbi Morty worked with the United States Consulate in Israel and the local funeral home, making arrangement to have the bodies returned to Pittsburgh. During this period, Maria's parents holed up inside their own home, barely communicating with anyone.

Naomi used eight of her stockpiled vacation days shuttling between Becky's hospital room, checking in on David, and consoling the inconsolable Miriam. Naomi's heart felt like a dishrag twisted and squeezed until there was no water left to drip out. Thank goodness for Aaron and Ezra, who stepped up and took over the menial tasks of her life, cooking and laundry duties.

Becky's chest was healing nicely, but she remained a suicide risk and uncooperative with the medical staff. More than once, she screamed at Naomi to get out of the room.

Every afternoon Naomi took lunch to David, which he pushed around the plate before throwing it into the trash. "David, you have to eat something," she begged.

"Why?" he asked, looking at her through hollow, empty eyes.

Was there an answer to his question? He needed a reason to live, and at that moment, she struggled to find one for him. He refused to visit Becky, staunch in his belief that her craziness caused this tragedy. The only person he seemed to connect with was Miriam. She and Joe spent hours each evening with David, listening as he talked about Noah and the bright future he lost. Sometimes David pulled out the old family albums, and they all sobbed over the photos.

"The funeral is in two days," Naomi said, as she prepared a turkey sandwich. "Noah deserves to have you standing at his grave reciting The Graveside Kaddish. If you don't eat, you won't be able to do it."

He looked at her with a flash of understanding. "I must say Kaddish for my son."

She nodded. "Yes, and to do that, you must have all your strength."

✡ ✡ ✡

This morning, they were finally laying Noah to rest. Later in the day, Maria would be buried in a Catholic cemetery next to her grandparents. The weather felt their pain and reacted appropriately. Thick clouds blackened the sky. The rain didn't drizzle weakly from the sky. It shot down, hitting the mourners like knives thrown by an invisible knife thrower. Each drop sliced into her soul.

She stood hand-in-hand with Esther, Laurie, and Miriam, staring at the pile of dirt that was quickly becoming a mound of mud. The sound of rain water hammering against their umbrellas masked the sound of their sobs. Everyone watched as Noah's friends from law school took turns shoveling dirt into the grave. The young men and women wept at the sound of the earth hitting the coffin, containing the friend they would never laugh with again. Absent from the scene was Becky, who remained locked in the psych ward.

Naomi begged *Hashem* for strength, as she stepped forward and clasped the long handle of a shovel probably purchased at Lowe's that morning. Noah deserved a shovel of gold and platinum. She dug the blade into the heap of soil and lifted as much as she could. Before tossing it onto the simple wooden coffin, she whispered to herself, "Noah, you leave a hole in our world. I will always hold you close to my heart and love you."

The chunks of clay and mud flew through the rain and landed. She hoped to be able to do another shovelful, but her arms lacked the strength and her lungs felt tight. She stuck the shovel into the mud and picked up her umbrella. Esther pulled the shovel from the mound and took her turn.

Naomi returned to her spot with Laurie and Miriam and watched Esther toss shovelful after shovelful onto the box. Never did Naomi imagine that tiny-framed Esther had so much strength.

A half hour later, the rabbi declared the coffin completely covered. Naomi's heart thudded and her gaze shifted from the wet ground to David standing a few feet to her left, flanked by his brother and Becky's brother.

She prayed he'd be given the fortitude to survive this hor-rific moment and fought off the urge to run and embrace him. Jake, Lewis, Joe, and Aaron stood behind the three men, prepared to help if David crumbled.

"Kaddish," the rabbi announced in a voice loud enough to be heard over the sound of the pummeling rain.

They all lifted their heads when David choked out the ancient words—words every Jew knew echoed the past and put an end to a future.

Yis'ga'dal v'yis'kadash sh'may ra'bbo, b'olmo dee'vro chir'usay v'yamlich malchu'say, b'chayaychon uv'yomay'chon uv'chayay d'chol bais Yisroel, ba'agolo u'viz'man koriv; v'imru Omein...

The End

About the Author

Susan Sofayov is a Pittsburgh-based writer. She's married to a wonderful, but completely unsupportive husband who feels she should focus less on writing and more time on her "real job," running the family real estate management company. She has three out-of-the-nest children and an aging small white dog. Her debut novel *DEFECTIVE* chronicles a young woman's battle to live an ordinary life while struggling with undiagnosed bipolar 2 disorder.

She has a BA in English Literature and Political Science from the University of Pittsburgh and an MA in Teaching from Chatham University.

CPSIA information can be obtained
at www.ICGtesting.com
Printed in the USA
LVOW13s1713270218
568057LV00013B/666/P